ALL THE GOOD
IN EVIL

BOOKS BY JOE RICKER

Walkin' After Midnight
Some Awful Cunning
Porcelain Moths
All the Good in Evil
Still Monsters (*)

(*) Coming Soon

JOE RICKER

ALL THE GOOD IN EVIL

Down & Out Books
3959 Van Dyke Road, Suite 265
Lutz, FL 33558
DownAndOutBooks.com

Cover design by Zach McCain

ISBN: 1-64396-232-9
ISBN-13: 978-1-64396-232-0

PART I

ONE
Amos

An inch to the right and Amos Swain would have killed a man for the second time. A .38 hollow point would have shredded through the crest of skull just behind Bobby Sisk's ear, fragmenting, eliminating any chance for ballistics. Those fragments would have sliced through brain and severed nerve endings like ties to a relative who slept with your spouse. The main part of the bullet would have tumbled to an exit, maybe through the palate, blasting out the lower set of teeth. Bobby Sisk wouldn't have felt a thing—as merciful a death as any. Amos wanted him to feel something, so he put the bullet through the top part of Bobby's ear. Blood sprayed on the fading yellow curtains and the money Bobby had been counting. His head snapped away from the gunshot and he dropped to the floor, cupping his ear. Caleb, Amos's partner, swept the money off the table into a brown paper bag and they left him there, on the floor of his kitchen, howling like the wind of the winter night outside. Amos and Caleb slipped through the falling snow, their shoulders rolling into the shadows, and they were gone.

If his father had fallen an inch to the right, Amos wouldn't have been waiting for Bobby Sisk to notice that he and Caleb were standing behind him. Amos wouldn't have pulled the trigger and let a bullet blow out the tiny bones in Bobby's ear. He wouldn't have known that Bobby was a dealer or that he'd be counting a large amount of cash for his drop in the morning. He wouldn't have had to warn Bobby to stop peddling drugs at his bar. He wouldn't know the amount of tension it took to squeeze a trigger. He wouldn't know what spending three years in prison felt like. He wouldn't be a bouncer in his small Maine town just inland from the coast.

Tourists come into Maine after the sloping winter months, when the coastal air is sticky with salt, after the squeeze of winter has coiled into the mud along the edges of tidal rivers. They come north on I-95 from Boston and they hit Portsmouth and then the Piscataquis River Bridge. They pass the sign on the interstate telling them *this is the way life should be*, but they never see past that. They never get a chance to look close enough, and even if they tried, they wouldn't see past the veneer of *Vacationland*.

The streets and neighborhoods are stitched together with the weakening threads of the past that once made the place something more than just another dead New England mill town—more than the people who stayed because they had nowhere else to go. There are people trying to make it on three-hundred-dollar paychecks, but their jobs age them more than their cigarettes and drinking habits. Dealers sling stomped coke or whatever else they can fit in a baggy, and cabbage patch gangsters run neighborhoods thinking they're as hard as the empty threats they make. Echelons of single teenage moms push their babies in strollers over broken side-walks. The convenience stores pack with customers buying Megabucks tickets with their cashed welfare checks on the first and fifteenth, hoping for dreams that will never come true.

The mills are crumbling along the Mousam River and haven't been occupied in decades. The river continues to make its way through the dams and toward the ocean, heading out of town. Follow any street long enough and shabby, dilapidated houses and apartment buildings sneer with the contempt of a bitter, pain-riddled old man. Porches sag like weak shoulders ready to tear away, and inside, linoleum peels up at the edges of the floors waiting for the walls to buckle and let the place cave in. In the cemeteries, headstones lean toward the grave and break while the other rows wait patiently to follow.

Violence and crime and all fearful things get shuffled to the backs of newspapers and barbershops. To most people, Amos is just a bouncer, a washed-out criminal who couldn't make it through college, another flannel wearing, R-dropping townie. But, he knew every crack in every sidewalk and every rusted staple in the telephone poles. He connected himself to the whispers of desperate men in his attempt to break away from his town, from a place he, like everyone else, had gone back to because there was no other place to go. More than anything, Amos wanted to flee, but not to another town or another place. He didn't want to be someone else. Amos just wanted the freedom of solitude, the freedom to be alone. He wanted the freedom to move through his life without the snag from the fabric of his past.

TWO
Caleb

Caleb pushed a flat stream of smoke through his right nostril. From certain angles, it looked like he shot it from his ear, a clever trick that he used for entertainment even though he didn't remember that he did it to himself after he broke his nose with the fat end of a pool cue. Caleb leaned on the porch railing, flicking paint chips from the wood with his thumbnail, and finished his cigarette. The two-hour drive and cigarettes and coffee did little to help him wake up to make his collection in Lynn, Massachusetts. He looked down the street at the other houses. They were all just shitty enough to confuse with one another, like those portrait cut kit homes they build in places nobody should live, except these houses were rotting on their foundations. Boarded windows, broken vinyl siding and graffiti clung to them like bed sores. Trash twined into the rusted chain-link fences separating small yards while mounds of trash bags covered in snow were piled next to the steps—the houses that actually had steps leading up to the doors. Other houses sat like stacks of spine-mangled books, leaning or twisting with panes of broken glass covered with cardboard and plastic and the flapping of loose shingles or tarpaper on their roofs. The neighborhood had quieted for the day, but that would fade and the dregs would come out to shuffle along the streets with their noise.

Lynn, Lynn, the city of sin, Caleb muttered and rapped on the door.

The door opened wide enough for a sawed-off double barrel twelve gauge to fit through. A dull brown eye passed over the crack behind the gun. Caleb lifted his eyebrow and tilted his head to look in at the eye. The barrel retreated and the door opened.

Caleb looked down at the torn welcome mat. "Gotta collect, Crow." Nobody called Crow by his real name, and the racist connotations of *Crow*, which was short for Velcro, didn't seem to matter to him, except when he needed it as an excuse to accuse someone of being racist.

"Now?" Crow asked.

"I didn't drive two hours to have a fucking barbecue."

He sighed. "Come on."

Caleb entered the house, kicked through the pizza boxes and empty two-liter bottles of Coke. In the dim light, Caleb followed Crow's child-like stature through the hall. In the dark, his waddling movement made him look like a school kid struggling with a heavy backpack, and when they entered the light of the living room, Caleb could see the sag in his pants and the oversized stainless-steel revolver tucked into his waist band. The living room windows were covered with strips of blankets and towels. The air in the room smelled of dirt and motor oil. When Crow tossed the twelve gauge on the sofa in the living room, Caleb pulled his hand from the hole in his hoodie pocket and away from the pistol tucked into his belt.

"I figured you guys would at least give me another week."

"You already got another week. It's Moss's birthday soon. I'd like him to start a new year with nothing outstanding."

Crow pulled the screen off the right speaker of his stereo and pulled out four rolls of cash bound with rubber bands. "You guys got anything else lined up?"

"Construction's slow in the winter, and riskier, you know, with the snow, but we should have a couple things for you soon."

"Alright."

"How's the other business?"

"Same old, you know. Hard to find guys that won't roll if they get pinched. Plus, I got another crew trying to make moves and I don't have the posse to do shit. I was going to talk to you and Moss about that."

"Come up in a couple days and talk to Moss. I'm not counting this." Caleb held the rolls of money up. "You sure it's here?"

"Yeah, it's there."

"All twenty-five?"

"Twenty-five? The deal was twenty?"

"*Was* twenty. That was Wednesday, when you were supposed to meet me in Portsmouth."

"When I talked to you, you said, okay."

"Yeah. I did. But I didn't say there wouldn't be any points."

"This is fucking bullshit."

"So call the fucking NAACP."

Caleb heard lips smack behind him. He turned to the man half asleep in the recliner by a boarded window. Crow looked over, too, and jutted a thumb at him.

"My cousin," he said. "Motherfucker thinks it's a motel."

Caleb looked at the trash scattered around the room. "Definitely not a motel." Then he noticed the patches of pale skin on Crow's cousin's face. "What the fuck happened to his skin?"

"Vitiligo."

"Is that from sickle-cell or some shit?"

"Nah, man."

The man opened his eyes, worked them with his thumb and smacked his lips a few more times. "Yo, man. Shut up."

Caleb chuckled. "Is he talking to you or me?"

"Talking to you, bitch."

"Is that right?"

Caleb slipped his hands under his shirt and worked his fingers around the grip of his pistol. Crow pulled a beer can from the top of the speaker and tossed it at his cousin. It clanged on the

ALL THE GOOD IN EVIL

floor at his feet. "I'm doing business, man. Shut the fuck up."

The cousin had already fallen back to sleep. Crow snatched another roll of bills and tossed them to Caleb. He snapped the speaker cover back on. Caleb took another look around the room, crushed beer cans and empty potato chip bags. The cardboard box serving as a coffee table by the plastic-covered couch was littered with piles of marijuana stems and seeds. Butane lighters were strewn on windowsills and other flat surfaces. Empty Gatorade bottles and candy wrappers were piled in corners. Caleb took inventory—crack, meth, pot.

"You should really clean this fucking place up."

Crow sucked his teeth. "Man, don't be coming in here talking shit about my home."

Caleb ran his tongue over his teeth, annoyed with the sound Crow made. "I'll tell Moss you said happy birthday."

"Tell Moss to go fuck himself."

Caleb lifted an eyebrow.

"Just kidding, Jesus."

Caleb dropped the rolls into an inside jacket pocket. "See you 'round, Crow." He clung to the walls on his way out, keeping his focus on Crow and his cousin.

Sunlight broke over the narrow peaks of pines as Caleb drove up the interstate back toward Maine. A mile from the Lexington plaza, his ability to hold his stomach ceased and he pulled his car over the rumble strip into the break down lane. He opened his door and spun from his seat into the cold and an even colder blast of wind from a passing eighteen-wheeler. He slid along the edge of his car and retched into the dirty snow. Passing cars, rushing by in their early morning commutes, shook him inside his clothes. The gusts made his ears pop. He wiped his mouth on his sleeve and got back behind the wheel.

Caleb waited in his car for a while after he'd pulled into the plaza. He steadied his nerves and rested his head against the steering wheel. He dug his fingers into the back of his neck, pressing the muscle into his spine until his fingers went numb.

A silver Ford sedan pulled into the plaza and parked on the opposite side of the lot. The man driving climbed out and peered over his sunglasses at Caleb's car. He scanned the parking lot and adjusted the pistol on his hip. He sauntered over, rubbing out the bunching in his tailored blue suit. As he walked, he looked inside the vehicles he passed, especially those with a clear view of Caleb's car. Caleb lit a cigarette as the man approached the front of the car. He stood at Caleb's passenger door and tapped on the window.

"A bit fucking cold out here." The man said, and pointed down to the lock button.

Caleb leaned over and unlocked the door. The man got in. He pulled his suit tight around his back. Caleb looked down at the man's outstretched palm. He reached into his pocket and pulled out one of the rolls of bills he'd taken from Crow. He slapped it into the man's palm.

"Now," the man said, "tell me more about Amos Swain."

THREE
Amos

Amos stood on the cement platform at Wells Beach, sipping coffee and working his way through an early morning hangover. The only time he could turn his back to the world was there, staring into the pulse of waves moving back and forth. Tension surged through his spine when he had his back to people or a door, especially in bars or restaurants or other public places. He also hated standing in lines, and that had nothing to do with being impatient. His biggest fear was locked doors. They closed the walls in the room and he felt like an eggbeater was dribbling his heart against his ribs. Prison did all those things to him, and the most he could do for himself was to avoid those reminders. At the ocean, though, he could breathe with his back to the world.

Caleb leaned against the fence beside him rubbing his temples with his thumbs. The air felt soothing on Amos's face. It numbed the hangover. Down the beach, waves slammed against the jetty, sending a spray over the rocks. The wind heaved in gusts rocking the birds huddled in the water between the swells. The cloth of their suits was thin and Amos's skin was already burning from the cold. The smell of the ocean and wind and sand and the glitter of sunlight reminded Amos of his father, of the time they'd spent on the ocean. They reminded him of his father and the promises Amos made to make a better life for himself. The last time he saw his father was on his thirty-eight-foot Bristol. He was taking it out for one last run before Amos headed back to college. His father would have been proud of the suit, but not so proud of why he was wearing it.

Gulls careened to the sand and shuffled their wings between a retired couple who walked their golden retriever. The woman carried a plastic bag in her hand, waiting, with a condescending smirk on her face, for her dog to shit. When the couple looked up at them, Amos waved, as he did to most strangers at the beach, and they smiled. Caleb stared at him, shooting smoke from the corner of his mouth. Caleb pushed more of his weight against the chain-link fence and crossed one arm over the other. His eyes were red, moisture building in the corners from the wind. The stubble on his chin and around his thin lips was a few days grown. He flicked his cigarette out onto the sand. Amos rubbed two quarters together between his thumb and index finger inside his jacket pocket.

When Caleb leaned back, the wind loosed his tie and it fluttered over his shoulder. He rummaged his pockets for his cigarettes and his Zippo. Criss-crossing scars on the back of his hands stood out hard and red against the cold. He found his pack, exhaled smoke from the cigarette he'd just cast off, and lit another.

"Happy birthday," Caleb said.

"Thanks."

"I went to Crow's the other day. I figured I'd save you the trip to Lynn. I was going to tell you last night, but ah. Well, we were a little busy."

"No shit. It'll be a while before I hit Boston again." Amos took a sip of coffee. "Did he pay up?"

"I got it. Splits are under the seat."

"Why'd you have to go all the way to Lynn?"

"It wasn't a big deal. There are harder ways to make twenty grand."

"How'd he like you showing up at his place?"

"Same rambling and bitching he always does." Caleb grinned, and his dimples rose higher on his cheeks.

"Fuck him."

"How much closer does ten grand get you?"

"Close. Really fucking close."

"It's almost April and there's still snow on the ground."

"Keeps the tourists away."

The air smelled like ice as Amos forced it through his nose. Caleb scratched his chin then pulled the collar of his jacket tighter around his neck. He reached down and pushed a finger into his shoe.

"Why don't you wear boots?"

He righted himself. "I can't wear boots with this suit. These threads were nine hundred dollars."

"I didn't know JC Penny sold suits that expensive." Amos removed the lid from his coffee cup. The last few drops were cold, and the leftover sugar slid down the Styrofoam.

"What kind of suit are you wearing then, Versace?"

"Corbin." Amos pulled the flap of his jacket open so Caleb could see the tag stitched to the inside pocket. "Three hundred. Tailored."

Caleb leaned into the fence again.

Footsteps approached, and the man behind them cleared his throat before speaking. "Gentlemen, what a fine beach day."

They turned to face Detective Jones. He strolled up to them pulling at the wrists of his gloves. The wind toyed with his thinning blonde hair. His cheeks, raw from windburn, matched the misery of his chapped lips.

"Detective," Amos said, extending his hand. "It's been a while."

Jones slipped his hands into his pockets. "I figured you'd be here on your birthday."

Caleb turned and spat. Wind carried the saliva thirty yards.

"Holy shit, Dick. Did you see how far that hock went?" Caleb asked Jones.

"What can we do for you today, Detective?" Amos asked.

"There was a robbery the other night. Down in North Berwick. Some dealer got his ear blown off."

"That's a shame," Amos said. "Hope he has insurance."

"You don't know anything about that do you?"

"Nah. Caleb and I were at Logan's every night this week."

"There he is...Alibi Amos. Always quick with a lie, aren't you?"

"The truth comes naturally to me, Detective. Besides, isn't North Berwick out of your jurisdiction?"

"Just making the rounds for a friend." He stepped closer to Amos. He put his hands on Amos's shoulders. "You know the drill, Swain. Turn around."

"I suppose it still doesn't matter that I'm no longer on probation. Not to mention we're in Wells, which is also out of your jurisdiction."

"You must have learned all about that in college. No, wait. You didn't finish college because you went to prison. Maybe that's where you learned all about jurisdiction." Jones parted his lips into a tiny smile. "Turn the fuck around."

Amos opened his arms and turned to the ocean. Jones worked along his arms, down his ribs, around his belt, and then his legs. The retired couple looked up at Amos while their dog sniffed around the sand it had just shit on.

"Check his junk," Caleb said. "He keeps a bag of dope there."

Jones finished and pulled Amos around by his shoulder, gripping his suit and leaning closer to whisper in his ear. "Pretty nice suit for a bouncer."

"Appearances are everything."

"They sure are, aren't they?" Jones released the suit and worked the wrists of his gloves again.

"Nice suit, Dick," Caleb said.

"Piss off, Finny. You and your boyfriend have fun." Jones took a step back from them.

"Hey, Detective." Amos waved his finger over his lips.

"Chapstick."

Jones backed away toward his car. Caleb and Amos turned back toward the ocean.

"This guy knows your schedule better than I do," Caleb mumbled.

"You jealous?"

"No, just a little annoyed. How'd he get Sisk's name anyway?"

"Sisk has a big mouth, you know that."

Amos looked back toward Jones and then to Caleb. "Do you two shop together at JC Penny?"

"I did not buy this at JC fucking Penny."

Amos chuckled and stepped by him to throw his cup into the trash bin.

"It's not funny." He shook his head at the ocean.

They moved back to the car and leaned against the frame of the windshield.

"You think he's figured anything out?" Caleb asked.

"About as much as he ever has. I'm not worried about him."

Caleb unlocked the door of his car, a black '69 GTO he'd spent two years restoring, a job he'd taken up to avoid mourning the loss of his grandmother. He continued to mumble as he got in and stretched across the seat to unlock the passenger door.

Amos climbed into the car. The seats were already stiff and cold again. The metal of his pistol numbed the tips of his fingers when he pulled it from beneath the seat and tucked it into his belt.

Caleb tossed an envelope on Amos's lap. He thumbed through the bills.

"Where are we going, birthday boy?"

"We gotta go to Vassar's and give him his cut. Plus, Farrah's dog had puppies."

"Puppies, the ocean, if I didn't know better, I'd think you were a little, I don't know, dainty." Caleb tilted his forehead to Amos and raised his eyebrows.

"Is that why you wear such fine clothes, to impress me?"

Caleb shook his head and shifted the car into reverse. "Asshole."

FOUR
Ruth

Fire burned in the fireplace of the empty den. Ruth Archer looked down on the flames prodding the poker into the coals and feeling the men behind her stare at the slate gray business suit she wore. She was a woman deeply impacted by the death of her husband and the near estrangement of her son. The financial burden her husband left her after his death and the decline in real estate investments gave her a terse, rigid look, but she still carried a sly smile on her face. Her eyes were much like her son's, dark and piercing, which she used to glare at Richard and Avery after they'd walked in with a third man. Three was the sort of number that might make her feel intimidated, but Richard and Avery were a couple and the third was the only one who cared what was beneath her clothes. Richard introduced him as Seth. She could sense Seth's discomfort as he placed himself at a distance from the other two in an effort to assure her that he wasn't *one of them*. She left the poker in the coals and rested the handle against the rack with the other assortment of fireplace tools. She slipped her earrings out and placed them on the mantle, hand hewed from a nineteenth-century ship mast, and tied her graying hair into a ponytail.

"What's it going to be, Richard?" Ruth turned to face him and folded her arms over her chest.

17

"What you're asking is too much. We'll give you half that."

Ruth tilted her head. "This is the price it's been. I haven't changed anything. Let's take a walk around the place, shall we? Perhaps after you're reminded of its charm, you'll reconsider."

She turned to her right and entered the foyer. Her heels clicked in the empty hallway. She checked the long window by the door, taking note that her real estate sign in the front lawn was a bit crooked and snow had covered the last three digits of her number. She let the thin drapes that she'd parted drift back into place and started up the hardwood stairs to the bedrooms. The men followed.

Richard followed closest behind her and shifted from one side of the staircase to the other. He tapped his knuckles up the balusters, letting a deep, hollow thump cadence his ascent. He'd bought himself new clothes, Ruth noticed, a fitted suit much like the ones her son wore when he wasn't clad in hoodies and jeans and Converses or Timberlands. Richard was pretty and in a way that was soft, but not as soft as his partner Avery with the similar, gel-drenched hair. She could smell the product. He wore a suit as well. Also new, and also tailored, but Avery served as an accessory to Richard, much like a celebrity's toy dog with a ten-thousand-dollar collar. Ruth flicked an itch from the corner of her eye.

"You'll notice that the floors are hardwood, maple, actually. The owners had them done after they put the house on the market and moved out. We're not talking barely stepped on. Absolutely pristine. This is just one of the many qualities. So, you can see, gentlemen, that negotiating a lower price is just not feasible." She stood at the top of the staircase waiting for the men to finish climbing.

Seth had pulled his suit from another man's closet, a friend or uncle, Ruth thought. The sleeves were creased from being smothered by whatever else had hung adjacent to it. He was a few days beyond attractive stubble and his cologne irritated her, something cheap that came in one of those Christmas gift packages retail stores stocked their shelves with for easy, less thoughtful gifts. He wore his sunglasses inside, which was another element of his attire that she detested. He was hungover, trying to protect his eyes, and the cologne didn't cover the stench of the alcohol on his breath as much as he'd hoped. She led the men into the master bedroom.

"As you can see, the master bedroom is quite spacious. It offers you plenty of room to move around."

Richard adjusted his hair in the door-length mirrors of the closet. "We have enough room to move where we are now. The price needs to come down."

Ruth bit her lip. "I'm disappointed. Maybe you need more convincing. Let's go see how much heat the fireplace is generating."

Seth hung behind Avery and seemed anxious to speak, to say something clever to impress Richard. She studied him. He wanted their respect but would never have it. They wouldn't protect him, and they'd ridicule him. Every trio needed that. He was the younger brother or cousin or nephew—the straggler dragged down a path by two he could never keep up with.

The men followed her downstairs. She moved to the mantle and put on the canvas work gloves resting on the small pile of logs. "The place really is a steal," she said, picking up a log two inches in diameter.

The men leaned against the counter. "I told you our price," Richard said. "That's what it's going to be."

Ruth smiled. "You." She pointed to Seth. "How old are you? Come here."

"I'm twenty-two." He squared his shoulders and walked to her.

When he stood close, Ruth patted his cheek with her gloved hand. "Still a baby," she said. "The fireplace, gentleman, is my favorite feature. I enjoy the smell of wood. This is a stone fireplace. Hand built by the owner. This is a work of art."

Ruth turned from the third man and held the tip of the log

near the flame. She slipped her feet from her heels.

"And this, gentleman," Ruth pushed the ball of her foot into the floor to square her footing and swung the log, bashing Seth in the center of his face. The pop of his nose snapping echoed in the empty room. Ruth dropped the log and swung the poker from the burning logs, the tip glowing orange—a soft glow that would melt flesh. She rolled Seth to the side with her foot and held the tip of the poker over his face. "Is not a fucking negotiation. The price stands."

FIVE
Amos

On the other side of town, heading north, the sidewalks slowly disappeared. The shoulder of 109 got wider until it touched patches of woods and fields. There were no mills or convenience stores or kids hustling on the corners, only mailboxes posted at the ends of driveways that led to houses barely visible from the road. It took them nearly an hour to get to Vassar's from the beach. In the yard between the trees he'd left standing, black smoke rose like pillars from scattered heaps of burning items—a pile of dresses, a melting television atop a stack of brush, blackened brass handles in a mass of charred wood that had been a dresser, and a small mound of shoes and belts and some picture frames. The snow around them had receded revealing dirt and stones.

The exposed Typar wrapping on Vassar's house had faded. Caleb and Amos gave each other confused looks before getting out of the car. There were no steps leading up to the sliding glass door that they entered three feet above the ground. Vassar stood shirtless in front of the open woodstove. A red, fiery tongue lashed inside it beneath thick black smoke. The triceps of his left arm flexed into an inverted V and he held a white puppy by the scruff of its neck. The house smelled of burning hair and week-old garbage. Vassar glared over his shoulder.

"It's the only one left," he said, and toed the cardboard box at his feet. "You want it?" He held the puppy out.

Amos nodded while the faint, hovering yelps quickly died. Vassar flung the puppy as he turned toward them. Its paws and ears fanned out as it spun through the air and Amos caught it, barely. There was a black spot on its left shoulder—a mutt, like its mother. Vassar kicked the door of the woodstove closed and walked over to the counter. The floor was unfinished—plywood, grooved and splintered by the dirt tracked in. Amos scooted his ass onto the picnic table Vassar had in the kitchen. It was the farthest place to sit from the woodstove.

Vassar picked up the freshly lit cigarette from a plastic ashtray, the edges serrated by Farrah's dog during an afternoon of gnawing. "You guys hungry? I was about to grill a couple steaks." He blew smoke at the ceiling.

"I'm good," Amos said, holding his hand up.

"Me too," Caleb answered, and he stepped outside.

"That's one way to get rid of 'im." Amos massaged the puppy's ear.

"I told that bitch anything she left at my house I was gonna burn."

"I was talking about Caleb. I take it you and Farrah split up again."

"This time it's for good. Goddamn skank."

On Vassar's right arm, just below the shoulder, was a small scar where one night, while he, Caleb, and Amos drank after one of his fights with Farrah, he cut off the tattoo of her name. His coke habit had picked up consistently over the past six months and except for his arms, his body had gone soft, the clumpy consistency of wet leaves pushed tight in a trash bag.

Amos pulled Vassar's money from his jacket. "Here's your cut." He tossed it across the clutter of blood-soiled napkins, dirty silverware, and a tan work boot with the tongue ripped out.

Vassar slipped the money into his pocket and turned to retrieve a cutting board from the counter. He pushed the board onto the table and shaved dust off the white chunk resting in the middle. In the dish rack behind him, the barrel of a stainless .357 revolver poked out behind a plate. The kitchen, like every other room in the house, was walled with rough pine boards. Vassar had driven every nail in the house to build it. He snorted the line he'd cut and looked up at Amos.

"What's wrong with Cal?"

"He's a vegetarian. You got anything else lined up?"

Vassar laughed. "I got two things. A roofing job in Ogunquit and some interior job at the Port. There's a lot of cedar and a shit load of copper and stainless going there." He wrote the addresses on the back of an electric bill envelope and handed it to Amos. "What'll that get you?"

"I don't know but I'm sure I can get you at least ten percent on the metal. Five on the other stuff."

He took a drag from his cigarette. "You want a line?"

"No thanks. I gotta bounce."

"C'mon. It's your birthday."

"How do you know it's my birthday?"

"Everyone knows." He leaned over and made a white line disappear. Flakes of cocaine spotted his moustache. "Sure you don't want one?" He held out a rolled-up dollar bill.

"Nah. I really have to go. Where do you get that shit anyway?"

"You wouldn't believe me if I told you."

He cut another line as Amos stepped out with the dying whimpers of puppies pulsing in his head. The lifeless branches of the trees above clawed through the smoke until the wind swept over the hill and through the driveway blowing it sideways and into their eyes before they climbed in the car.

"What was that?" Caleb asked.

The puppy nosed Amos's chin. "I think it was his way of telling Farrah to fuck off."

"That's one hell of a way to do it. What are you going to do with a puppy?"

"Stop at my mother's."

"Serious?" Caleb's left eyebrow rose. "That's not going to piss her off."

At the end of the driveway, the puppy pissed on the seat. Caleb threatened to pitch it out the window.

SIX
Ruth

Ruth stopped on her way out to her car to brush the snow from the real estate sign posted in front of the house where two men were probably still struggling to scoop their friend from the floor. She slipped her leather briefcase into the trunk, got in her car, and drove away. A piece of bark had clung to her foot, and she rubbed it away on the floorboard carpet. At a strip mall off Route 1 in Wells, she parked at the far end of the parking lot from a grocery store and a Reny's.

She opened her trunk and pulled the box of Grape Nuts from her briefcase, which she had packed with Richard's cash, and slipped it into a plastic Shop N Save bag. She left the bag in the trunk, closed it, and walked toward the entrance, digging for the grocery list in her purse.

Ruth had made her way through the produce section and was reaching for the handle of the dairy cooler when she noticed the spot of blood just below her right eye. It was dry and flaked away as dust when she scratched it with her fingernail. She thought about the boy, which was all she could think of him as. A twinge of guilt peeped into the light of her thoughts, but she quickly shadowed it with hopes that he'd change his course in life, perhaps to something he was more suited to, like pumping gas or bagging groceries. Eventually, probably sooner than later,

25

they'd all get pinched and if he went to prison, he'd have wished he'd only had to suffer a broken nose. It was only pain and that was as much mercy as he'd ever get, and the most Ruth could show. She grabbed a gallon of milk and continued, crossing items off her list.

At the checkout line, a man in a blue flannel shirt and orange beanie met her at the same time.

"Go ahead," she told him, looking down at the one item in his hand, a box of Grape Nuts.

"Oh, that's okay," he answered. "I'm not in a hurry."

Ruth winked and stacked her groceries on the conveyer, where they were scanned and bagged. Ruth paid and made her way out of the store.

The man in flannel caught up with her in the parking lot. "Why don't you let me help you with those?"

Ruth popped the trunk and Tommy dropped his bag containing the Grape Nuts in the left side. He began pulling her bags from the cart and placing them in the compartment. The two of them dropped their casual dialogue and lowered their voices.

"How'd it go?" he asked.

"Wannabe cowboys," she answered.

"They try to cut the price?"

"They tried."

"Which one did you hurt?"

"The young one. They brought a third."

Tommy shook his head. "Ruthless Ruth strikes again."

"I hate it when you say that."

"I hate you taking on new clients. It's risky. You need to start bringing someone with you."

"Who, Tommy, my son?"

Tommy stopped moving her bags. "It wouldn't be that bad, would it?"

"Amos is on his own path. I don't want him on mine. I certainly don't fucking want him to know what his mother does."

"Moss is on your path, Ruth. He's right behind you kicking

back your competition, just like I did for your husband."

"And it can stay that way. It's bad enough he found his way into this mess on his own. I'm not kidding, Tommy. You made that promise to me."

Tommy held his hands up. "I know, I know. I was just saying."

"Well, don't. Keep my son in the bar where you can keep an eye on him."

"What about Caleb?"

"What about him?"

"Bringing him with you."

"I'm sure that Amos's best friend is an easy way to keep this a secret. I am a woman, but I don't need a bodyguard."

Tommy finished loading her groceries and took the bag of Grape Nuts on the right. "You have a good day, ma'am."

"Thank you, so much." Ruth reached into her purse. "Here, take this for your trouble."

"Oh, it's no trouble."

"Please, I insist."

Tommy shut the trunk and held his hand out, the severed pinky twitched when she dropped the quarter into his palm.

"Don't spend that all in one place, okay."

Tommy shook his head and Ruth let a soft laugh roll off her tongue.

SEVEN
Amos

When Amos's father's construction business took off, he built a modest house for his wife at the end of Ezekiel Avenue. Amos was in junior high and his parents were smitten with his academic achievements, planning out his future before he'd even considered his options. Amos's acceptance to Bowdoin charmed them with an exuberant pride that they shared with their friends, who all seemed to fade back toward a social comfort of becoming oblivious strangers when he went to prison. The two-story split-level custom house stood at the end of the cul-de-sac, the driveway lined with birches and lilacs. Glass tables and intricate cast-iron furniture sat in the corners of the rooms inside. Anywhere Amos stood in the house he could look around and know the hundreds of ways he didn't fit in among the pretentious display of feng shui bullshit. Over the years, expensive candlesticks and other shit on the glass shelves on the dining room back wall replaced pictures of his father. Amos's mother tried to eliminate any memory of him associated with the house, except the house itself.

The last thing Amos's father gave his mother was his sister Seneca—precocious, darling, and standing a few feet from the door when he and Caleb walked in. She squeezed her favorite doll between her elbow and ribs and held a painting outstretched across her torso—a winged mermaid. The details of it, shadowing in the faces and beneath the wings, the articulation of each feather, made it difficult to accept that an eight-year-old had done it.

"Hello, Uncle Caleb. Amos, I painted this for your birthday." She took a step forward and extended her arms, pushing the painting away from her. Amos took it by the top corners and knelt. Caleb squirmed to keep the puppy concealed in his jacket. Seneca stepped behind Amos while he looked over the painting. Her fingertips worked beneath the collar of his jacket, behind his ears, and along the edges of his eyebrows.

"You did this?" Amos asked over his shoulder.

She nodded and drew her hands back. Her fingers patrolled nervously through her blonde curls.

"I don't know. It looks pretty good to me. Are you sure you didn't sneak this out of the museum?"

"Nope. I made it." He looked up at Caleb who stared down at him mouthing, *What the fuck?*

Seneca's eyes grew wide and she pointed a finger at Caleb. "You said a bad word, Uncle Caleb. You said fu—"

"Ey." Amos cut her off before she could hear the word escape her mouth and become addicted to the sound of it like most children did. "Let's not say that."

"How about when I'm a teenager?"

"We'll see."

"Uncle Caleb, what do you have in your handsome jacket?"

Amos looked up at Caleb again and motioned his head toward Seneca. He pulled the puppy from the inside of his jacket and held it out with one hand like a piss-soaked rag. She took the puppy in her arms and it sniffed her nose. Her squeal rolled into a giggle and she turned her head away. "His nose is cold," she said, and sat on the floor.

"Where's your mother?" Amos asked.

She was still giggling. The puppy pushed his nose against her face and kicked its hind legs. "She went to get groceries."

29

Caleb moved to the sink and washed his hands. Small soap bubbles flew and landed on the petals of the yellow irises on both sides of the sink. The sun funneled a cone against the kitchen floor where Seneca sat with the puppy.

"You remember the rules when you're home alone, right?"

"Yes."

"What are they?"

"Don't unlock the door for anyone. Tell them I don't know the code for the security alarm. And, if you mess with me, my badass brother will cut your balls off."

Caleb threw his head back and cackled and clapped his soap gloved hands together. Amos stood and placed the painting on the kitchen table.

"When did that last part become a rule?"

"I made it one."

"Who said I was a badass?"

"Some boy at school." She answered quickly, turning her head from side to side away from the puppy's nose.

Amos knelt in front of her again and took the puppy, tucking it under one arm. He palmed her shoulder and had a hard time not laughing himself. "Look, Sen, tell that boy I'm not a badass," He paused to look at Caleb then back into Seneca's eyes. His cell phone vibrated in his pocket. "I'm the boogey man." Her eyes flew wide again, and her head moved back. Then she rolled them and threw her arms out, palms up.

"Puppy," she demanded. The puppy went back to nosing and licking her face and kicking. Amos shook his head and stood to answer the phone.

Caleb sat on the floor next to Seneca while he spoke. He tugged on the puppy's ears until it yelped, and Seneca whined for him to stop.

"Who was that?" Caleb asked after Amos hung up.

"Tommy. He says there's a couple roaches at the bar. He wants us to come down and take care of it."

"Finally, some action. Fucking dealers. How hard is it to

hand someone a baggy?"

"Uncle Caleb said, fuck," Seneca whispered to the puppy, massaging its ears.

"Uncle Caleb's going to get soap in his mouth." Amos kissed Seneca on the cheek. "Be good. I love you."

EIGHT
Ruth

Ruth strolled into the house to find Seneca on the kitchen floor holding one end of a hand rag and a small white puppy tugging on the other end. She let the weight of the grocery bags pull on her shoulders, the handles stretching between her thin, hooked fingers.

"*Gividdame*," Seneca whined.

Ruth put the groceries on the table. "Seneca, honey, you can't pull that hard. It's just a puppy. Its teeth can't take that." She knelt beside her daughter and ran her hand over the puppy's head. It released the towel and bobbed, lifting its paws from the floor. A shrill bark followed, and Ruth squinted with its sound.

"Mommy, I named it Ariel." Seneca smiled and the brightness of her blue eyes filled Ruth with a rush of quiet delight that she hid with a blink.

"That's a pretty name. Did your brother come by earlier?"

"Yes, and Uncle Caleb."

"And how is Uncle Caleb?"

"He's funny."

"Yes, he is. What do you want to do for supper?"

"Can we have pancakes?"

Ruth stood, smiling. "No, Seneca. We can't have pancakes for supper."

"But it's Amos's birthday."

"Yes, honey, I know, but Amos is celebrating his birthday with Uncle Caleb."

"Where?"

"Down at Logan's."

"Why does Amos and Uncle Caleb hang out in that shithole?"

"Seneca."

"What, Mommy?"

"Language."

"But I only said *shit*. That's not even that bad of a swear word."

"Do I have to go through this with you every day about your language? Speaking of which, do you have your progress report from school?"

Seneca circled the corners of the room with her eyes. "No."

"Don't you lie to me, young lady. Where is it?"

Seneca snapped her arm at the dog and pointed. "She ate it."

Ruth gripped her hips. "Seneca, go get your progress report."

"Oh, alright."

Seneca moped from the kitchen and pounded up the stairs to her room. The puppy flopped to its side on the floor. Ruth tilted her head and looked at it. "I suppose you'll need some food."

The puppy lifted its brow in reaction to her voice. Ruth pulled the grocery items from the bags and placed them in their proper places in the cabinets, freezer, and refrigerator. She was down to her last bag when Seneca returned to the kitchen, holding out the slip of paper. Ruth slipped the report from her fingers and read. The expression on her face shifted slightly and she looked down at her daughter.

Seneca is a bright, articulate child, but she has a propensity to use inappropriate language during class discussions. Last week, during science class, she told another student that Tyrannosaurus Rex is named so because if he shit on your head you would be "wrecked." When questioned where she heard this, Seneca

*replied: "It's true. That's why dinosaurs had to become birds, so when they 'shit' on people's heads, they wouldn't be wrecked."
In all honesty, I had to contain my laughter. Seneca is clearly a very intelligent little girl; however, her language for the class needs to be curtailed or I will have to begin sending her to the office for these offenses. Other than that, Seneca is a an enormous pleasure to have in class. I will continue to send home weekly progress reports on Seneca's language.*

Ruth reread the comments to Seneca, while Seneca sucked her bottom lip.

"Am I in trouble?" she asked her mother.

"Seneca, you can't use this kind of language in school. Now, what do you think an appropriate consequence should be for this?"

"I don't know."

"Well, the puppy is going to be a big responsibility. I think that you should prove that you're able to handle that, so the puppy is going to have to go back to Amos for two weeks until you can improve your language."

"But—"

"No, buts. Two weeks. If you don't get in any trouble with your language, then you can have the puppy, okay?"

"Okay, but do we have to give her back right now?"

"No, honey. Let me finish putting these away and we'll go get some treats for Ariel."

Seneca's expression ignited with joy. She dove to the floor and crawled on her hands and knees to the puppy.

NINE
Amos

Logan's, the windowless, cement bomb shelter where Caleb and Amos collected a pay stub, was one of the few bars left in town that hadn't been shut down for too many stabbings, fights, or cars being torched in the parking lot. But Tommy didn't call the cops when those things happened. He called Amos and Caleb. The bar was always dark. A lack of windows prevented any natural light from slipping in. It also gave Tommy the privacy he wanted after hours, after he'd shut the bar down. He'd built the bar in the center of the room against the back wall, with an island in the middle. A narrow path between the island and the back wall gave him access to the small basement room where he kept a hyper-vigilant supply of firearms and ammunition. The walls were drab, gray-painted cement. Tommy didn't like decorations, except during Christmas, but he kept a price list above the bar.

Beer—$38.00
Liquor—$38.00
Allen's Coffee Flavored Brandy—GFY

Tommy only used the prices he'd listed when he didn't want someone in the bar or someone he liked needed to be cut off. He also felt that anyone who mixed milk or half and half with their liquor should be shot, so coffee brandy, the staple drink of Maine townies, was never on his liquor order. Tommy considered himself a townie, but he thought men and women should drink their booze like adults. When Tommy wasn't wearing a flannel, which was rare and only ever behind the bar, he wore sleeveless T-shirts revealing prison tats flashed up and down his arms that had faded to turquoise smudges except for the one on his throat. There, a half-dollar-size clover tattooed below his Adam's apple pulsed and bulged when he spoke. He always wore an orange beanie. Half of his right pinky finger had been cut off—a process he'd endured as an act of revenge from a boy he'd beaten savagely in his youth for being a suspected homosexual. He constantly used the nub to rub the corners of his mouth where a gray goatee spread around his lips. His eyes and hair shared the same gray color as the ashes from the cigarillos constantly at his lips or between his fingers.

"Tom-A," Caleb called when he sat at the bar. Amos leaned against the wall. Tommy turned, adjusting the fold on his beanie. The other patrons at the bar lifted their drinks.

"Well, if it isn't my favorite hell raisahs." Tommy put two shots of Turkey on the bar followed by two pints of Shipyard. A rack of pool balls broke behind them. One of them gurgled into a corner pocket. "Happy birthday, kid." He shook Amos's hand. "Looks like that hairline's receding even more now."

"Are those the guys?" Caleb pointed over his shoulder with his thumb at the two men shooting pool.

"Yeah. Goddamn tweakers. I figured you guys could use a little recreation."

"How do you want us to get rid of them?" Caleb asked.

Tommy laughed. "Be creative. Not too messy though. They've been looking for a game. Why don't you take some money off 'em first then that other shit they got on 'em. Back left pocket."

Caleb walked over to the two strangers. He took a sip of his beer but tipped the glass too much then sprawled his upper body and flung his arms out to avoid the spillage. He wiped his chin and placed his pint on a high-top table. Tommy leaned against the bar resting his chin in his palm. The nub twitched against the corner of his lip. His other palm moved two rolls of quarters back and forth over the bar. Caleb turned to Amos and nodded. Tommy winked and Amos scooped up the quarters.

"Try not to break a cue this time, hunh," he whispered.

Caleb spoke to the guy in the brown Ford-logo baseball hat. The other guy, hair shaggy and covering his eyebrows, wrung his hands around the end of his pool cue. They both watched Amos approach. Nine ball. Fifty bucks a rack. Amos put a roll of quarters on the edge of the pool table. Ford-hat pulled his cash from the front pocket of his jeans and put fifty on top of Caleb's. They flipped for break, and Ford-hat took it, sinking the three ball then missing his shot at the one.

"Nice." Caleb chalked his cue.

"Why are you two all dressed up in suits in a pool hall?"

"I sell pool lessons."

Ford-hat smirked.

"Where are you two from anyway?" Caleb asked.

"Houlton."

"The county, hunh? Nothing but broccoli and potato farms that far north." Caleb comboed the one and hit the nine into the side. He slipped the cash from the edge of the table and stuffed it into his pocket. He turned and gripped the quarters. "You guys have pool tables in the county?"

Ford-hat's partner kept snapping his head to shift his bangs from his eyes.

"Yep." He spit tobacco juice into a plastic cup. "We got pool tables."

Caleb moved to stand next to Amos across the table from them. "So you guys want another game?"

"Sure."

Ford-hat tossed down another fifty and pushed his quarters into the table and gathered the balls as they rolled into the end. Some patrons had moved to one side of the bar for a better view of the game. Tommy leaned against a beer cooler watching with the rest of the customers.

"So what brings you guys all the way down here? You two looking for a job at Walmart?" Caleb asked.

"We came for the hospitality," Shaggy said.

"Oh. I guess we haven't been hospitable enough," Caleb shook his head and laughed. He moved around the table closer to Ford-hat, rested the butt of the cue on the floor, and leaned on it. Shaggy placed his against the wall and put his spit cup down. Caleb moved between Ford-hat and Shaggy, keeping Shaggy close to the wall. "I've taken your money and I don't even know your names." Caleb turned and winked at Amos. Shaggy saw it and cracked his knuckles. Amos moved around the table to stand beside Caleb and tightened his grip on the thin end of his pool cue. "Let me guess," he turned and pointed to Ford-hat, "Bubba and," he pointed to Shaggy, "Bubba. So tell me, Bubba. If your parents get divorced, will they still be brother and sister?"

Shaggy threw a punch. Caleb blocked with the cue and slammed the roll of fist-wrapped quarters into his teeth. Shaggy flailed back and fell against the wall catching blood and a few teeth in his hands. Ford-hat stepped away from Amos toward Caleb, but Amos swung the butt end of his cue up and it connected against Ford-hat's windpipe. He fell to his knees holding his throat. Caleb threw Amos the roll of quarters and he dug into Ford-hat's front pocket for his cash. Amos slipped his hand into Ford-hat's back left pocket and pulled out a few bags of meth.

"What's this, chalk?" Amos dropped the small baggies and ground them into the floor with the toe of his shoe.

Shaggy tried to get up, but Caleb grabbed him by the neck. He squeezed and Shaggy's pale forehead flushed maroon. A few of the patrons pounded their glasses against the bar.

"Now, in case you didn't notice, you're not welcome here. If I see you in here again, I'll squeeze your neck until shit comes out your ears." Caleb released his grip and the boy gulped in gasps of air. His friend helped him to his feet, both of them coughing as they scurried through the door. Tommy threw Caleb a towel for the blood on his knuckles and poured them two more Turkeys.

Amos tossed Ford-hat's cash on the bar. "That should cover a round for everyone."

Tommy laid out the shot glasses. Caleb put the glass of Turkey to his lips where it chattered against his teeth, his hands twitching from adrenaline. Tommy slid the bottle of Turkey back to its place between a bottle of Jack and Jim Beam on the island behind him. He tapped the ashes of his cigarillo against an ashtray resting on the rows of rocks glasses in front of the liquor bottles.

TEN
Ava

For six weeks Ava Metzger had kept herself in the small room at her aunt's house. The flower-print wallpaper she'd helped her aunt hang when she was a little girl was still on the walls. The seams were still true and twice a year her aunt washed the walls so the paper had lost some of its glossy sheen over the small yellow daisies. Not much had changed in her aunt's house since she was a girl, and she hadn't ventured out since her return, so Ava couldn't really tell how much had changed in the town. The corner store, what used to be Provo's, was barely running. They no longer had a deli and the items they carried were random and sparse—toilet paper, Zig Zags and car freshener, cans of corn and motor oil, ninety-nine-cent can openers and Drano. Ava's image of the town in her mind reflected the store that was once Provo's. She wondered if the people who still lived there had deteriorated similarly.

Years before, her parents moved her away from Maine when they discovered she'd given it up to a construction worker's son; they were as miffed as if the son had taken a shit on their thirty-thousand-dollar Persian carpet. It didn't matter that he was the son of the man who'd built their house or that the boy went to church with them. It didn't really matter that she lost her virginity. It did matter, to Ava's parents, that she was fucking the son of a laborer. It mattered that, despite the man owning the business, and that he could have built a house twice as extravagant, she was pursuing the son of a man who made his money with his hands.

Her mother was the first to show her the clipping of Amos Swain, neatly cut from their hometown newspaper. *Top Bowdoin Student Heads to Prison.* Ava cupped it in her hands like her first dead pet while her mother sneered over the photo of Amos being led from the courtroom. Her mother wanted to say something, but she didn't or Ava didn't hear her, but it didn't matter. After five years, they had the validation they'd hoped for, vindication against the five years of disdain Ava had held for them. She'd kept the clipping folded in her yearbook, which she had open on the bed in front of her. Ava looked up at the mirror above her dresser, worked her jaw.

After six weeks of being holed up in her aunt's house, she was ready to see more of the town, more of the things she hadn't had the chance to see change. She showered, shaved her legs, put on matching bra and underwear. She pulled three dresses from her closet, and after holding them up against her body in the mirror, she reminded herself of where she was going, which made it easier to pick out a pair of jeans and a T-shirt. From the box in her nightstand, she pulled out a tourmaline necklace Amos had given her one hot summer day on his father's boat. She paced in her room allowing her nervousness and excitement flutter through her body and into her fingers.

Ava took a cab to the bar where Amos worked. The tone-deaf voices of karaoke shambled through the night air like the drunken gait that would lead the singers home when the bar closed. The bar was full and the people packed into the space and the yelling and smoke and droned, drunken voices made her head throb. She was about to give up before she'd made half a dozen steps toward the bar, convincing herself that he wouldn't be there on his birthday. She panned the room, and as people shifted and reached for drinks or hugged their friends, she saw him, suit clad, an older face, stone jaw and eyes dark enough to pierce the dimness of the room. He lifted his drink, shoulders tense.

ELEVEN
Amos

By ten o'clock the bar was packed. Caleb and Amos had moved to a table. Tommy had set the stage for karaoke after a line had already formed at the sign-up sheet. Caleb made a pyramid with empty shot glasses. Tommy's new barback scrambled among the tables to retrieve empty beer bottles and glasses. The boy was thick— probably sweating it out daily at the gym and pumping shots in his ass to bulk up, his jaw bricked into flat edges and he possessed the grace of a cement block lumbering down a hill. He bumped into Caleb on his way by, his fingers twisted between empty bottles.

"Whoa. Excuse you." Caleb wiped bourbon from his cheek.

The barback looked at Caleb, made a passing glance, and kept moving through the room.

Caleb stood, and Amos grabbed his forearm.

"That little fucker's gonna get smacked," Caleb hiccupped.

"He ain't so little."

"Fuck him. I'm going to find some snatch."

He left the table. Amos sat alone through another horrible song. The barback bumped into more people with the same smug reaction he gave Caleb. It saddened Amos to watch people step on stage and belt out their favorite country songs as though a talent agent were lurking in the corner waiting to discover the

43

next Tim McGraw or Bobbie Gentry. Somehow, being there for four minutes gave them an escape from the misery of living in a town that bullied them into hangovers every weekend. Amos was about to head to the bar for another drink when he saw her approaching.

"I want to hear *you* sing." She sat in the chair across from him. Familiar brown eyes locked onto his. A sharp nose and high keystone cheekbones planed down into her lips. Below that, a green emerald-cut piece of tourmaline that he'd bought in high school for the only girlfriend he'd ever had hung around her neck. "Been a long time, Amos."

Every noise, breath, blink, heartbeat, watch tick, swallow, foot tap, stool swivel, pool shot, ice clink, sizzle of cigarette drag, everything, stopped. He'd thought about Ava every day since the last day he'd seen her. He'd imagined seeing her in different places: the supermarket, coffee shop, music store. He remembered her. He remembered telling her he wanted to hear her sing while they were in church—the day he finally got the balls to talk to her. And, he remembered the summer before their senior year when she left to attend a private school for girls in Oregon when her parents caught them under her sheets. A feeling of panic came over him and his heart and eyes quivered. All the things he thought he would say if he saw her again came to him at once, but he didn't say anything.

"It's a little noisy right here. You want to sit at the bar?" she asked.

Amos followed her and stared at her body looking for things he remembered. She'd changed, more curved and smooth—polished marble—jeans too tight to slip a book of matches in her back pocket. Caleb hustled a stout girl with crooked teeth in the back corner. Ava approached the middle of the bar but changed her direction as Amos headed to his usual corner. She ordered a beer and Tommy gave Amos another Shipyard. Amos thanked him, and Tommy gave a discreet thumbs-up.

"Can I buy you a shot for your birthday?"

"Only if you do one with me."

She leaned toward the bar and ordered two shots of tequila. Her tongue slipped into the corner of her lips while she waited. When the shots arrived she wished him a happy birthday and they drank. Her face puckered when she sucked the lime and Amos wanted to be a piece of fruit mangled by her teeth. She'd cut her hair short, tapered from front to back, with bangs hanging over each side of her face like the sharp, curved edge of a battle axe.

"How have you been?" he asked.

"Well," she started pulling the corner of the beer label from the glass. "Good, I guess. I lived in Seattle for a while after college. I was a teacher. Now, I guess I'm just looking for a change. I missed the East Coast."

"So you came here? Funny. What did you teach?"

Caleb slammed into Amos before she could answer, almost knocking him off the stool. He wrapped his arm around Amos's shoulder and handed him a shot. "Happy birthday." He tapped his glass and drank. "Damn. Who's the..." Caleb hiccupped. "Spinner?" He yelled and his eyes were barely open.

"This is Ava," Amos said.

"Shut the fuck up, man. She's gone. Flied away like a little bird. Sorry, hun," Caleb said to her. "He's still in love with some girl from high school." He got closer to Amos's face and spoke slowly. "Like a little bitch." He raised his eyebrows and closed his eyes. "Don't worry though," he said to Ava. "You're way hotter." His body swayed, and he shuffled his feet to maintain his balance. "Wow, I am wicked fucked up." Caleb wavered on his feet as he stumbled away.

"You two are still best friends, I see."

"Yeah. I'm usually in worse shape than he is."

"Oh, really? It's *your* birthday. Shouldn't you be on the floor by now?"

"Probably."

She tapped her fingernails against the neck of her beer bottle.

"How about another shot?" she asked.

Moaning and cursing erupted in the background. Amos turned and Caleb had sprawled out on a pool table and passed out on the felt. The beer in his hand slipped from his fingers and broke against the floor. The men around the table tossed their cues and made their way to the bar. The crowd had thinned to a few scattered groups of people trying their best to ignore the countdown to their departure when they would have to sleep and wake up and look to the next work week to make up for their overspending that night. Ava seemed to grow more comfortable around him—laughing loud over other conversations and music and touching his hands and knees. Occasionally, he would say something unintentionally funny, and she would giggle and rest her cheek against his shoulder. At the bar, things grew quieter until the drops of water falling from melted ice somewhere behind the bar competed against the quiet echo of their conversation.

"You know," she paused to suck on a lime. "You are the best dressed criminal I have ever seen." Her face went solemn. "I'm sorry. I shouldn't have said that." She placed the gutted lime into the shot glass with a slow, methodical motion and wiped her fingertips on a beverage napkin. The patron who'd been sitting at the corner since Caleb and Amos ran out Tommy's pests earlier that day changed his expression for the first time that night, and Tommy paused halfway from pulling a cigarillo from his lips. Ash fell to the toes of his boots.

"It's okay. But, don't say it too loud." Amos leaned closer to whisper to her until his lips were touching her ears, and he could smell perfume on her neck. Even over the smoke, a delicate hint of gardenia. "I don't want anyone to know."

Amos tried to look serious. After a moment, she erupted in laughter. He leaned back into the wall. Tommy frowned, tossed a soiled towel into the corner, and moved across the bar. "So how'd you know about that anyway?"

She looked away at the row of beer bottles on a shelf above the bar. "That day you came up to me in church and said you wanted to stand next to me while I sang, I thought I was going to die. I almost started crying I was so happy." She swallowed like she'd been chewing powder and went back to scraping the corner of her beer label with her thumbnail.

He didn't want to think about how she'd left. "How about one more?" he asked, waving two fingers at Tommy. They took two more shots and finished the pyramid. "Do you still go to church?" he asked.

"When I need to clear my head."

"I go to the beach for that."

"Yeah?"

"I had my fill of church."

"How about me?"

"I'm just getting started with you."

She leaned toward him until her lips were touching his cheek. "Are you too drunk to drive?" She kissed the corner of his mouth.

"Yes. I am. It's a good thing I live around the corner."

"That's convenient."

"You ready to go?" Amos pushed himself from the wall.

"To your place?"

"Where else?"

"You're awfully assumptive."

"I'm lonely."

She slid her fingertips down his stomach. "Okay," she whispered into the mouth of her beer bottle. "But I have to use the bathroom first."

Amos dropped two bills on the bar, and Tommy slipped him his piece after Ava walked away. Amos looked at Caleb on the table, and then back to Tommy, who shook his head.

"Are you joking, kid? Get out of here. I'll put him in the back room."

"Thanks."

Amos stopped by Caleb and shook him. "Tommy's got you tonight."

He groaned. "Happy birthday, fucker. I'm sorry I got fit-shaced."

"Good night."

Ava thread her arm through Amos's elbow.

"Good night," Caleb sighed. "Good night little girl that Moss thinks is Ava." He chuckled into the drool on his shirt. Amos took Ava's hand and they staggered into the cold toward his apartment.

TWELVE
Bobby

The sutures in Bobby Sisk's ear were ugly. Part of it was gone, nothing but mist that had sprayed over the curtains and table and the money Amos Swain took from him. He knew before the gunshot, when he looked up and saw the reflection of the masked face behind him and saw those eyes, not even eyes, the shadow of eyes. Bobby threw the small vanity mirror to the other end of his couch.

He tried to stand to test his balance, but his equilibrium was still off. He'd tried for hours to walk, but his body would lean to his right and he'd crash into a wall or an adjacent piece of furniture. The ringing had dulled into a roar, like the amplified rush of sound from a seashell. Bobby looked over to his kitchen floor as he dropped back to the couch. The blood had darkened and dried into the shape of a melted hand.

The cops had come, almost a half an hour later. Report of gunfire. They'd found him holding the side of his face, leaning against a kitchen counter. The ambulance came minutes later and carted him off to the hospital. They asked him questions he wanted to answer, but a snitch is a snitch. He kept his mouth shut as if the missing piece of his ear had silenced the part of him that wanted to speak and the cops didn't need any more of an excuse not to give a fuck.

Bobby listened to the roof of his trailer moan from the weight of the snow pushing down on it. In the center of the living room, where he sat on his couch, the ceiling sagged in the middle. The strip of wood used to conceal the seam in the ceiling had broken from the stress and Bobby stared at the jagged break touching the edge of his ear and comparing the texture of what he felt to what he saw. He leaned forward and pulled the shotgun from the floor and placed it on his lap. He pulled the box of shells from the end table and dumped the shells onto the cushion next to him.

While the nurses cleaned up his ear and the doctor ran the stitches around the wound, he thought about how he had to fix things. How he could make himself somebody who didn't have to worry about a bouncer telling him where he could move his product. But he had to get his name known on the street first. Bobby pushed the shells into the receiver of the shotgun. He worked the action, pumping a double aught round into the breach. Amos Swain was going to pay because Bobby Sisk was a name he wanted people to be afraid of.

Bobby let the gun rest across his legs. He lit a cigarette and started working through his plan. He'd move on him at Logan's when Amos made his way through the parking lot. He'd have to do it during the day, which presented certain risks, but night time would leave too much room for error. Swain was always with his partner at night, and the parking lot at Logan's would be too hard to get out of then. The last thing Bobby was prepared to do was shoot his way out of that parking lot.

Ash fell from Bobby's cigarette onto the soft skin on the back of his hand and he turned up the volume on his television. He resumed his movie, *Scarface*. Pacino lifted his head from that enormous desk, his face powdered, a cone of white extending off his nose. Bobby lifted the shotgun and took aim at his television, hovering the small bead at the end of the barrel over Pacino's face. Bobby took a long drag from his cigarette and let the smoke cloud in his mouth. He dropped the cigarette in the glass of water on the end table and stood up. His balance was better, but he was still wobbly. He sat back down. A few minutes later he stood again. Bobby repeated this through the night, until he was pacing the matted carpet in his living room.

THIRTEEN
Amos

Ava and Amos made it to the steps of his apartment building, a brick, three-story fortress with four apartments and two office spaces on the first floor, one of which was the former head-quarters of his father's construction business. Like most business property in the town, the spaces in the building were empty and the windows boarded before they became targets for rocks or bottles or television sets. Amos owned the building but kept it in Tommy's name. Some nights, he'd go into the empty, first-floor space and stare at *Swain Construction* painted on the glass. The building sat on the edge of the pond, and he'd taken the apartment closest to that side of the building.

Ava stopped him before he could step into the stairway and he hoped she wasn't changing her mind. Her bangs stuck below the edge of the radar cap she wore and covered the eyelid of her left eye. Amos touched her cheekbones with his thumbs while she bunched the flaps of his jacket into her fists.

"You motherfucker." She pushed him hard into the brick.

Her lips and tongue came at him hard, and it took him a few swirls to catch up. They moved up the stairs kissing and stopped in front of his door. He flung the door open and it smacked against the inside wall and vibrated. She smiled with her tongue still touching his and they moved into the apartment.

Their fingertips dug into each other—back, arms, neck, and ribs. In the middle of his living room, they stopped. She looked at the floor, pulled a few strands of hair from the corner of her mouth then brought her hands to his chest. His fingertips fanned his pants. Her hands slid up over his shoulders beneath his coat and it slipped to the floor. Then her fingers patted the handle of the 1911 .45 tucked into his belt. Amos kept it on the left side of his body, butt out. A cross draw was quicker for him when he wasn't wearing a hoodie.

"Some things have changed since I saw you last," she said.

"About thirty pounds, facial hair, and a receding hairline."

"You're handsome. That hasn't changed." She looked away from his face down at his pistol. "Do you have a permit for that?" she asked, sliding her index finger over the thumb guard and drawing her hand away.

He shook his head. "It would be in a holster if I did."

"What makes you think I was talking about the gun?"

"I wasn't talking about the gun."

She gave him a playful bite on his lip and looked him over— her gaze like a thick brushstroke over his face and down to his chest.

"So tell me, Amos Swain, is what Caleb said true? Am I the girl you're still in love with?"

People say things about love they don't really mean when they're drunk, but if he had said *yes* he may have meant it. Romantic love was something he hadn't felt for a long time, and he had only the memory of what he thought that was. The excitement that her presence brought was enough for him to confuse what he may have genuinely felt. She kissed him again and he led her to the bedroom. In the night, his thoughts softened him to love, a feeling he'd only ever felt for her but had forgotten. The feeling returned, unexpected, like an abrupt change in temperature—the final clothes-shedding frenzy of a hypothermia victim. Amos reached over and rolled the piece of tourmaline between his finger and thumb, wondering. She kissed differently than he remembered. He wondered for a moment how many men she'd kissed and how many other men had twisted that piece of tourmaline between their fingers.

You're supposed to run, he reminded himself, when you hear sirens.

When he got out of bed to answer his phone the next morning, he stepped on the heel of one of her shoes. Amos bit the curses off the end of his tongue. Ava stretched along the edge of the bed—the sheets coiled around her body from her ankle to the back of her hand where her temple rested. A smile snuck to her lips when he kissed her cheek and left to get Caleb at the bar. He'd lost his keys and was too hungover to walk to Amos's place.

The bar door was open. Caleb strode through it pulling his piece. Amos glanced in the rear window of the car he was passing and saw Bobby Sisk swing the barrel of a shotgun toward him. Amos lunged forward grabbing for his burner, but Bobby had already pulled the trigger. Amos spun around before crashing to the cement. Pieces of glass fell down around him cutting the back of his neck. His arm and shoulder went alight with the sensation of burning probes where lead burrowed into his flesh. Caleb's shoes rushed toward him. A tear of gunshots and empty shell casings sparkled as they passed through the sunlight. Amos blinked when a few of them hit his nose and lip then clinked on the cold asphalt.

Bobby Sisk dove into the front seat of his truck and roasted the tires through the parking lot. The truck fishtailed into the street, the driver's side door flapped forward and shut. The rear quarter panel slammed into a blue postal box and tilted it on the cement block it was bolted to. The scream of tires cut through the air and Amos spit gravel and broken glass from his lips.

FOURTEEN
Detective Jones

He'd meant to say goodbye, but the news that Amos Swain had been shot flushed away any appropriate manners he should have remembered before he left the funeral. Jones braked the car to a halt at the police line outside of Logan's. Caleb rested against the trunk of a cruiser answering questions for one of the beat cops. Tommy Logan was near the entrance of his bar doing the same. Both of them shook their heads and shrugged while Jones approached two cops on the line.

"Victims?" he asked the cop, a rookie, crew cut, rigid, mirrored sunglasses, typical little-man-syndrome douchebag that made Jones hate being a cop at times.

"Victim," the cop answered. "Singular. He got clipped in the shoulder. EMTs took him to Goodall."

"Shooter?"

The cop pointed at a middle-aged woman at the other end of the parking lot watching the procedure. "Didn't see the shooting. Heard the gunshots and then saw the truck speed out of the parking lot. She got the plate number, though. Dispatch says the truck belongs to a white male, Sisk, first name Robert."

"Shit."

"Shit is right, Detective. Shit aim. Fucker couldn't even drain that piece of shit Swain from twenty feet away with buckshot."

The cop paused. Then he chuckled. "Drain Swain...Get it?"

Jones scowled for a moment then relaxed his expression. "Call dispatch and tell them to tell whoever escorted the EMTs not to say a word to the victim. Not one fucking question until after I've spoken to him first. Got it?"

"Roger."

Jones turned back to his car before the rookie thumbed the call button on his radio.

He drove to the hospital, thinking back on the Kesslers, the day he'd met them. He was still a beat cop back then, a few solid busts from making detective. The robbery came over the radio and Jones was three blocks from the pharmacy. Sirens on, he felt the adrenaline scream through his veins while the engine surged as he weaved around cars. The suspect's vehicle pulled down a side street, and Jones drove down a narrow alley. The suspect sped past the opposite end and Jones felt pavement yank at his tires as he made the turn coming out of the alley. The suspect sped on and took a right into a residential neighborhood.

Jones pulled off the chase, followed protocol to preserve the safety of civilians, but that junkie fuck still crashed. Jones heard the crushing of metal, probably would have heard it over the sirens if he hadn't turned them off. As he came onto the scene, the suspect's car was turned on its side against the sidewalk after deflecting off a Volkswagen Bug, and the other car, Mrs. Kessler driving, smashed into a parked, full-size pickup. He saw her hair draped over the airbag. The suspect climbed from the opening in his torn windshield.

Jones rammed the suspect's vehicle, tossing him to the ground. Jones scrambled over the pavement and broken pieces of headlights to handcuff the suspect before he could make another attempt to flee. Jones put the other cuff on him, pushed his face into the pavement with his knee for a solid three minutes, until the edge of the sidewalk had taken layers of flesh, until Mrs.

Kessler stumbled from her vehicle screaming for the limp child slumped against the dashboard, until he realized the piece of shit on the ground couldn't feel anything.

The suspect had a mouth and he knew about a burglary that was a shoe-in felony for a DA with a political agenda. In the course of legal proceedings, what should have been a slam conviction for Bailey Mitchell turned into a hand-over-hand plea deal that set him free. The Kesslers' tragedy drifted away like a summer morning mist because they couldn't pull the plug, and there isn't a homicide without a death. They thought God would bring their boy back, but God was busy with other things, and any justice that should have been served that day was restrained with Bailey Mitchell. It wasn't surprising to Jones. He'd seen it before—the system played like a juvenile game without consequences that left the true victims, those who suffered more than material loss, without justice.

Jones testified at the trial that got Bailey Mitchell sent to rehab with five years probation. He went to the trial where Bailey Mitchell testified against a promising, mini-Ivy League student who'd just lost his father. Shortly after, Jones, despite his disgust with the shortcomings of the legal system, made detective and transferred to a place that needed a pissed-off cop, to a place every other cop was trying to leave. He transferred and waited for Amos Swain.

FIFTEEN
Amos

For almost a full day, his father's coffin had sat in their living room. Amos spent that time sitting next to it wiping his sweaty palms on his pants, wondering how a man hardened by struggle and labor could be reduced to something so immobile. He'd sat until delirium fooled him into thinking he saw the dead man's eyelids twitch or that the dead man had whispered his name. Amos's father had fallen from his boat and struck his head on the edge of the pier before plunging into the water. The water had cradled him until it sucked his life away and swept it out to sea with the tide, leaving his body bobbing in the ebb of the frigid Atlantic.

Detective Jones leaned on the doorknob of the exam room, watching the nurse. Amos's arm stung with the burn of buckshot-torn flesh and moving it sent electric jolts through the bone. The nurse had gentle fingers which did little for the forceps she used to pull pieces of lead from his shoulder. She took shallow breaths through her mouth and forced them through her nose, a cadenced rhythm that was annoying more than the pain pulsing through Amos's arm.

"How are you feeling?" Jones asked.

"Spry."

"At least your sense of humor is still intact. Ironically, I just left a funeral that I need to get back to."

"Don't let me keep you."

He shook his head and reached into his pocket for a pack of gum. He slipped a piece of Doublemint from the pack and crammed it into his mouth.

The forceps dug into Amos's arm and he winced. "Last one," the nurse said and dropped the lead fragment into the stainless-steel container. She handed it off to Jones on her way out.

He took a few steps closer, swirling the fragments in the container, and exhaled through his nose. A line of sweat made a subtle, downward arc across the chest of his white shirt and he smelled faintly of cigarettes. His fingernails were chewed down and the tips of his fingers were calloused.

Amos took a breath.

"This is a fucking mess, Swain. You let this shit get ahead of you and you're heading back inside, you know that, right?"

"Yeah, well, what did you want me to do?"

"Probably should have put one halfway to his other ear."

"That changes things."

"This," Jones held up the stainless-steel bowl and shook the pieces of lead. "This changes things."

"Yeah, it does."

"Tighten up, kid. All professional courtesy, if we can call it that, aside, we have a problem. I'm three months from pension. Three months until your case gets passed off to Curry, and we both know how much he likes you. That's three months you get to make moves and the party's over. But right now, this moment, you got a guy who's going to suck a dick to take a deal, and we all know how well those deal makers do against you. Not only that, but if word gets out that you're the one rolling dealers, and not just one of Tommy Logan's leg-breakers, you're not going to be safe anywhere. This is sloppy shit, and you have very little time if you have any time at all."

"Well, fuck it then. Maybe I should just skip out. This life is a fucking waste anyway. This isn't what I was supposed to do."

"Supposed to? You're still reaching for a dead man in the water. Whatever life you had before this is gone. That's something you'll never get back. Live with it. You're in this. You're standing in the middle of it looking around trying to find all the good in evil. Do what you do. Do what you did to Bailey Mitchell and give yourself some room to breathe. Do it, because if you don't, that little sister of yours will be waving you goodbye out of a courtroom."

Caleb burst through the door before Amos had a chance to say anything else. "Hey, Detective, the lawyer's on the way."

Jones licked his lips and adjusted his expression. "You must spend a lot of time in front of the mirror, Swain, because you really think you're cute."

"You spend a lot of time watching me. Maybe *you* think I'm cute."

"One of my officers will be in to take your statement." He punched Amos's shoulder. Amos grabbed for it to squeeze out the pain. "I'll see you around, Swain." Jones took a step toward the door and stopped. He looked at Caleb. "Do you wear the same fucking clothes every day?"

"Only when I spend the night at your ex-wife's house."

Jones shook his head and looked back at Amos. "Only a matter of time before you're back where you belong." He left the room.

For the first time since Jones had burrowed his way into Amos's life, he was worried. Of course they'd offer Sisk a deal when they found him, and Sisk would undoubtedly do whatever he could to stay out of jail. The neat little package that held Amos's deeds was being kicked around. But that wasn't all that worried him. Jones was poking around in his life more than usual, and eventually, someone was going to wise up about their interaction. He still had a chance. All he had to do was find Sisk before the cops did.

Caleb shook his head as he spoke. "You have to be the luckiest motherfucker ever. The cops said if those pellets hadn't deflected off that car they would have taken your arm off. Feel lucky I was too dehydrated to piss and waiting for you by the doors. The cops took my gun. They were pissed I had it. Tommy has your shit. He's still down at the bar answering questions. What are you going to say in your statement?"

"Same shit I always do. Caleb is my hero." Amos batted his eyelids and hopped off the table to reach for his shirt.

Caleb had a concealed weapons permit, which had come in handy more than once. Amos wasn't even supposed to touch a gun because of the felony on his record. Collecting debts for Tommy Logan and robbing dealers wasn't good Samaritan work, so not carrying a gun because it was illegal didn't make much sense to Amos.

"Well, that was one hell of a birthday. Crow wants to talk. I told him you had to deal with something else."

"No, let's get that shit over with."

"You sure?"

"Business as usual, Cal, with one new priority on the agenda."

"I'm already on it."

"Good. Can you go by my place?"

"Yeah, why? Is that girl still there? Did you let a woman spend the night at your place? Fuck. This is practically catastrophic to your reputation."

"You mind making sure she's all right."

"No. Who is she?"

"Ava Metzger."

His grin vanished. "Shut the fuck up."

SIXTEEN
Ava

The wail of sirens pulled Ava from sleep into a foggy realization of where she was. She shut her eyes, squeezed, and opened them again. He smelled the same as she remembered and she took a deep breath of him from his sheets. She could still see the lines in the fabric where it had been folded inside a package. His bed, centered between two large windows that streamed light onto the carpet, began to feel strange to her. She sat up and leaned against the headboard, pulling the sheets to her shoulders.

As she peered around the room, taking in the things that Amos had collected, a torrent of loose, sordid feelings began to subdue her. She thought about Amos's hands on her the night before, the strength in them, and how gently his fingers seemed to settle in the spaces between her ribs. She thought about them moving down and how perfect the ridge of his hand between his thumb and forefinger seemed to fit and lock on her hips. She remembered wanting to fuck him, but that part of her, that desire, tightened everything from the insides of her thighs to her throat. She sensed him feel it, too, and he loosened his grip. They kissed more, his mouth fitting against her jaw and collarbone like wax melting in the contour of a votive and she let the tightness drift, but Amos kept to her skin, exploring it with his hands until, until…She didn't remember falling asleep.

SEVENTEEN
Amos

The cop had come in for the statement, but all Amos could think about was Jones. Amos had come out of prison like a nail that had been pounded clean through wood. Prison does that to some people, makes them angry their place in the world is the mess that's been swept into a corner. Amos had already lost everything he cared about, except Bailey Mitchell. Caleb was working for Tommy and Lucas Fraley, who'd become a cop when Amos got out, and Caleb wanted to bring Amos into the fold. That first night out, while Amos bit blood from his lip while he stood at the bar in Logan's listening to Tommy talk about guys on probation turning into canaries if they got pinched, he could only focus on the snitch that put him in prison. Amos didn't mind prison. He got to read. He hated the fact the guy who'd put him there practically killed a kid and was free, breathing air that didn't smell like industrial laundry and hooch farts. Then Tommy told Amos if he wanted in he'd have to prove he wouldn't be soft. Amos told Tommy to stop talking shit from behind the bar. Tommy stopped talking and went to the back with Lucas. They came out with Bailey.

Caleb handed Amos a note from Ava when he picked him up

from the hospital. "She was gone when I got there. That note was on the door."

Amos looked down at the paper. The last note Ava wrote him said, *Goodbye*, just before her parents moved her to the other side of the country. Amos wrote letters, but they were all returned. Just before he opened the note, Amos began to feel the disappointment settle in his gut.

Amos, did you forget I was in your bed? Call me.

"When did she come back to town?" Caleb asked.

"I don't know. She surprised me at the bar last night."

"Did you fuck her?"

"Don't worry about it."

Caleb adjusted the heat on the console. The fans hummed louder, and Caleb cleared his throat. "I've got some ears on the street listening for anything about our earless friend."

Amos felt tension in his stomach, like Jones was in the back seat with both hands on his shoulders. If they didn't find Sisk soon, those hands would clench around his throat along with Tommy Logan's and countless others.

Caleb's house, the inheritance he received when his grandmother died, bore the eccentric cloaking of a shut-in elderly woman whose only grip on life for the last decade that she lived was the worry of who would feed her cats. The cats were gone, but the macrochet animals clung to the walls near old calendars on the wood paneling. The only improvement Caleb made was having the floors carpeted. He'd bought his own furniture, sleek, modern black leather, but the rest of his grandmother's life's collections still littered the house.

Crow was half drunk and sunken into Caleb's sofa. The heels of his basketball sneakers rested on the edge of Caleb's coffee table and he tapped the insteps together. He sat up when they came in, scratching a space between his corn rows.

"Shit, man." He pulled a cigarette from his pack. "I heard what that punk tried to do."

Amos sat on the couch. Caleb brought Turkey and glasses

from the kitchen and handed them to Crow, who poured half a glass of bourbon for each of them.

"So what's up? I know you didn't come all the way up here just to see how I was."

"Some guys are moving in from Revere. I need some heavy hittin' MVP motherfuckers to handle it. It has to be done soon before they recruit some locals. Two of my guys just got pinched and I need to do something before I lose ground." He forced a jet of smoke from the corner of his mouth.

"What are they moving?"

"Yey, probably. Maybe H."

Caleb took his suit coat off revealing the sleeveless black shirt he had on, a red tie and suspenders and hung the jacket on a nail. He pulled a pack of cigarettes from his pocket and packed it against the fleshy part of his palm.

"Watch their moves. Find out when they get a supply and how much. In a couple weeks, we'll roll them. If a couple of weeks isn't that long for you to wait. Otherwise, there's not much I can do." Amos looked over at Caleb. "What the fuck are you wearing?"

"What? The sleeves were too tight."

"You look like a hobo stripper."

Crow leaned forward and put his glass on the coffee table. "You do look like a stripper."

"You look like a burnt smurf." Caleb shook his head and put his jacket back on.

"Aight. That's some fucking racist shit, man."

"Let's save that argument for a later date. Get that info, and I'll let you know what we can do," Amos said.

"Man, I appreciate it." Crow killed his bourbon and stood up. For a moment he hesitated, looking off somewhere like he'd realized something or some great idea came to him. "I better get going. I'll see you boys later."

Crow left and Amos took another swig of bourbon. The great thing about drugs is that they would always be around.

There would always be dealers. If they got rid of one, there would be another to take his place. The problem was they wouldn't always have Jones around to feed them the scores that kept them obscure. Caleb stood in front of Amos, glaring at the empty glass Crow left on the table beside the coaster. "Hey," Amos said and Caleb shifted his eyes. "Did you buy that tie at Walmart?"

"Up yours, shithead. I'm bringing you home."

EIGHTEEN
Tommy

He lit her cigarette. Ruth's hands shook as she pulled it away from her mouth. Initially, she'd started talking about Amos calmly, but her voice level increased the more she talked about what happened. Her hands trembled more, too, until she had to practically chase the filter of her cigarette with her lips. Before he drifted back to a memory of Amos, he noticed the tears forming in the corners of her eyes.

Bailey Mitchell had squirmed into the corner when Tommy and Lucas entered the beer cooler. His hands were bound, his mouth gagged with a small handful of chalk squares that Tommy had shoved into his mouth before they left him prone against the floor. They lifted him to his feet, dropped a cheap backpack over his head, and walked him out into the bar.

Caleb rolled out the plastic drop cloth and they put Bailey facedown again. Amos stood there staring as Lucas and Caleb hung blue tarps as a backdrop around the plastic Bailey lay on.

"You got a lot of spice in your speech," Tommy said to Amos. Tommy then set out glasses for the four of them. He turned again to grab the bottle of Wild Turkey. "Maybe a finger or two of bourbon will help to even that out."

Caleb led Amos to the bar, where Lucas stood at the end near the wall. Tommy poured the shots and slid the tumblers to each of them. Tommy lifted his and waited for Amos to let his slip down his throat before he took it.

"What is this supposed to be?" Amos asked.

"This, my formerly incarcerated friend, is Wild Turkey 101" Tommy said, tapping Lucas's arm as he moved toward Bailey. "And this is murder one-oh-one."

They lifted Bailey to his feet and Caleb pulled a chair from an adjacent table. He slammed the edge of the seat into the back of Bailey's knees, and Tommy snatched the bag from his head. The patter of piss flowed from the seat to the plastic drop cloth.

Tommy went back to the bar, pulling a .45 from under his flannel shirt, and put it next to the glasses.

"This is what we call a throwaway. You put a body on a gun, you get rid of the gun. Now, three years in prison because of this fuck…What are you going to do, Amos Swain?"

Ruth put her cigarette out in Tommy's ashtray. "Have you listened to a fucking word I've said?"

Tommy rubbed his temple with his half-digit. "No, Ruth. I haven't. I was thinking about your son."

Ruth's expression, which had been docile, changed to a stern, unforgiving look of rage. "I have an eight-year-old daughter at home right now, and a son in the hospital who's just been fucking shot, Tommy. Is that brief enough for a recap?"

"Moss's got a flesh wound. We'll take care of it. Go home to your daughter."

"Go? Go home to my daughter? Where do you—"

Tommy stood. "Last time I checked, Ruth, this is my fucking business. You work for me and so does your son. What the fuck do you want me to do, file a workman's comp claim? This isn't even a setback, and instead of making moves to find out where this piece of shit is, I have to sit in here with you and listen to you rant about Amos. If you fucking care so much, show it to him, not me. I love that kid like he was my own son. So curl up that fucking finger you're pointing, tuck it into your fucking too-good-for-this-shit suit and go the fuck home. I'll let you know when I have more weight for you to move."

Ruth took a deep breath. "You're right. I'm sorry. I shouldn't have come here."

"No, you shouldn't have. The only reason I didn't kick you in the ass is because your son got shot in my parking lot and you have a legitimate reason to show up here wanting answers. That being said, think about how oddly fucking peculiar it would look if one of these shitbag, beat pigs sees us on one of our drops. Maybe this is a guy who's looking to make a name for himself and he starts following one of us during his off time. That's how people get fucking pinched, Ruth. Moss is fine. He'll take care of this. For fuck's sake, sometimes I think you forget who your son is. Now go home to your daughter."

Ruth collected herself, twined her fingers together and squeezed, then grabbed her things and left the bar.

NINETEEN
Amos

Amos called Ava to explain what had happened that morning. She arrived at his building in minutes—shoes slamming on every other step to the apartment. She came in holding her purse by one strap leaving it to hang open. The things inside were about to fall out. A thought made her eyes tense and blink, then she sat next to him on the couch.

"Are you okay?" she asked.

"Yeah. It's not a big deal. The doctor said I should be fine in a week or two."

"What happened?"

"Hunting accident."

"Shut your face."

Amos pinched the top of his ear and turned it, scrunching his nose and mouth and squeezing his eyelids shut. "Is that closed enough?"

"You're silly. Really, what happened?"

"Some guy shot me."

"Did you sleep with his girlfriend or something?"

"Not that I know of."

"Were you doing something illegal?"

"I tried to last night, but you weren't in the mood."

"Stop. I'm not going to give it up on the first date. Ha. That wasn't even a date."

"See. You were off the hook. Besides, you already gave it up."

"That was ages ago." She paused for a moment and sucked on her bottom lip. "Did that ruin your birthday, aside from getting shot?"

"Not getting laid? Of course not."

"I'm glad I ran into you."

She curled up next to him on the couch tucking her toes under his thigh. He looked over every part of her—from the tips of her eyelashes to the bluish green veins along the side of her foot.

They found a movie on TV that had been slaughtered by commercials and editing. After, Ava went to the bathroom to gather gauze and bandages. She changed the bandage on his arm and brought him to bed. When he woke from a dream that his arm was on fire, she was on the couch writing in a notebook. Amos watched her, quietly, through the doorway and the sound of her pen scrawling on paper almost put him to sleep. Her small silhouette in the shadows of the room made him wish he could trust her again.

In the morning, the wind blasted against the windows and rattled him from sleep. Ava began moving dishes into the cabinets. Music played—a man with a voice that sounded like he sang into a Pringles can. Sad music, the kind someone would play after a breakup when they were lonely and sitting in a dark room asking themselves, *what if?* Amos crawled from bed and pulled a pair of sweatpants on with one arm. There was a moment of frustrating difficulty while he reached across his body to pull the waistband over his ass cheek. With a few flutters of the knees, it slipped over to its place around his hips and he walked into the kitchen.

"Well, hello there, buckshot," she said.

"That's fucking hilarious."

"I was kidding," She moved around the corner and wrapped her arms around his waist.

"What's up with the music?" he asked.

"You don't like it?"

"I like Tool. This shit makes me want to turn my face inside out with a shotgun."

"You're grumpy this morning." She went back to the dishes. "You can turn it off if you want."

There were two large paper sacks from Marshalls on the counter. She hummed with the song and Amos stood there debating whether to go back to bed. "What's in the bags?"

"I got you some new sheets and a comforter. The sheets you have are not comfortable." She dried silverware and tossed it into the drawer. Metal on metal chimed at the end of her statements.

"I usually sleep on the couch."

"Well, maybe now you'll want to sleep in your bed more." *Ta-ching.*

"How much more are you going to be in it?"

"You feeling lucky?" *Ta-ching.*

"Yeah, my luck's been wicked good lately."

"At least you're alive."

"That's what I meant."

She tilted her head to the side. "You shouldn't say things like that."

"I was kidding."

"Okay. Are you hungry?" *Ta-ching.*

"Starving."

"I'll make some breakfast. You should take a bath." *Ta-ching.*

"I'd rather get a kiss."

"Maybe later." She slid the drawer shut with her hip.

Amos went to run a bath. The hot water helped him massage the tightness from his arm. The burning was still there but fading to an annoying sting. He slid his hand over the scars he'd gotten over the years, a thin white line above his hip and the deeply chewed gnarl on his lower back from blades, the dark, U-shaped smile on his elbow from a hatchet, and the vague circular raises of skin on his thigh from a .22, the horseshoe scar on the side of his hand from a Doberman, and the slash just above his eyebrow from a beer bottle. None of them could remind him of the pain as significant as her leaving or his father dying. That pain burned its way through him from the inside, and he could never corner it to catch it and make it stop. She was a dream that allowed the nightmares to fade and as long as he stayed in the tub, she'd be in the kitchen cooking and he could step out and see her there then that moment would pass and he'd have to move on to the next. The water went cold and the smell of bacon and the sound of Springsteen brought him from the tub.

Ava slid the tip of a pen over the page of her book while they ate. Her journal, she told him, when she put it away. Amos ate standing at the counter with a towel wrapped around his waist.

"What are you writing about?"

"It's a journal. I don't talk about it. I should thank you though, for influencing me to write."

"How so?"

"I tried to write a letter once, but all I could write was—"

"Goodbye?"

"Yeah." She stared at him and scratched the corner of her mouth with her pinky. "What are you doing this weekend?" She took a bite of ketchup-drenched scrambled eggs.

"I don't have any plans."

"Will you go to church with me, for old times?"

His jaw froze in mid-chew. The thought of going to church almost forced him to laugh. Her stare pulled his eyelids down and he swallowed. A quick memory of her in a flower-print summer dress came and tied knots with his guts.

"I understand if you don't want to go."

"I'd love to go," he lied.

TWENTY
Caleb

Stevens held the door for an elderly woman moving out of the store hunched over her purse, stuffing a handful of scratch tickets inside and withdrawing her car keys with shaky hands. She gave him a broad smile. Stevens let the door close and pulled the lid from his cup of coffee. Steam rose against his face. Caleb felt the pain return to his stomach. He hadn't thrown up that time, but he wished he had. The burning in his stomach rose into his throat as Stevens sipped his coffee, replaced the lid, and leaned against the cage of propane tanks in front of the store.

He thought back to Amos and the night with Bailey Mitchell. Tommy had just pointed to the gun he'd put on the bar before Amos's first shot of Wild Turkey. Amos walked over to it as easily as anyone would walk to their car to unlock it. He picked up the gun. He walked back over to Bailey and stood in front of him. He put the gun to Bailey's head and looked around, at Caleb, Tommy, and Lucas. Amos lowered the gun, released the clip and ejected the bullet in the chamber. He put the clip back in to balance the weight and he gripped the barrel like the handle of a hammer. When it was over, when Amos was done, he walked over to Tommy and took the bottle of Wild Turkey, holding the gun out for Tommy to slip it from his hand. Caleb had never witnessed so much violence, or learned how much it took to crack a human skull. He wondered if he'd ever have to watch Amos approach him with the same darkness in his eyes.

Caleb climbed from his car and walked toward the store, passing the man, who continued to look straight through the parking lot toward the intersection on the corner. Caleb bought a pack of cigarettes and packed them at the entrance, giving the man enough time to get to his car and get in. Caleb had backed into a space next to the man's vehicle. The first drag of his cigarette soothed his stomach briefly. Then he got out and sat in into the front seat of the man's car.

The man took a sip of his coffee and looked at Caleb. "Almost lost your boy I hear."

"Moss's a fucking machine." Caleb looked at the man. "If any of us make it out of this, it'll be him."

"Well, we'll cross that bridge when we come to it. How will business proceed?"

"I'm not so sure that it will."

The man placed his coffee in the cup-holder between the seats. He reached into his jacket pocket and pulled out his wallet. He flipped it open. "You remember who you're talking to, right?" The man tapped the golden shield on the open flap of his wallet with his finger. "Federal Fucking Agent is what this says."

"I know what the fuck it says."

"Then I'm sure I don't have to remind you of how we met."

"No. You don't."

"Good. Do I need to remind you of our deal?"

Caleb spit onto the pavement between the cars. "I keep Moss on the street, you don't bust me for interstate commerce."

"Interstate commerce is just one ingredient in the marinade. You forget all the other splendid seasonings as well."

"I don't forget anything."

"As I'm sure Amos Swain and Tommy Logan don't either. And I'm sure that they won't forget if I have to push the paper-work through. Now, what do you have lined up next?"

"We got a guy who says he's getting crowded by some

competition. He wants Moss and I to take care of it."

"That's fantastic. You might be worth your weight in gold."

"I'm sure that's going to depend on what your cut is."

"Are you complaining? This is the way life should be. It even says it on the sign when you cross the border. It also says, open for business."

"Maybe for you, Stevens. But I get my snitch mark, and I won't be in business if this shit gets out. Whether that shit's carved on my face or not, it'll be there. Then what?"

"What are you talking about? You have a legitimate job as a bouncer."

"Yeah, in the fucking drug hub of New England."

"That's true. Maybe you should try your hand at washing dishes if you're so worried about it, or maybe," Stevens reached for his coffee, "you shouldn't be such a fucking twat about it. Put some money away. Move some place warm. Eventually, you're going to get pinched anyway."

"Only dealers get pinched, Stevens. You should know that."

"Already you forget. You got pinched, dipshit. I'm keeping you afloat. We'll talk in a couple days."

TWENTY-ONE
Amos

Ava's presence helped him pull away from the piercing expectations of his life. When panic, chaos, and the unresolved should have been drilling screws into his spine, he felt himself drift to a simplistic calm when she was around. Despite the daunting presence of the struggle he'd submerged himself in, and despite the absurdity of actually attending church, her closeness helped him forget, briefly, who he was. On Sunday, Ava wore a light blue dress, matching shoes, and a black wool jacket. Her skin was toned a golden wheat color. Amos could barely stand to be away from her lips for more than a second without wanting to kiss her again—the groping need to surface from the depths of a plunge too deep for the body to handle.

"You look very striking," she said, adjusting his tie on the way into the church.

"You don't look so bad yourself." Amos slid his hand down her back onto her ass and gave it a quick squeeze. She spun toward him, her hair lashing his chin.

She pressed his chin with her finger. "Behave." She leaned in to kiss the corner of his mouth. "For now."

"Please tell me you're going to fuck me in here."

"Jesus, Amos."

The walls were bare, windows with no shades, a cross behind

the podium where Pastor Roberts spilled some bullshit about the downfall of ignoring God's will. Amos had seen his name on the haughty sign in front of the church advertising hours of worship. Blood vessels in his neck protruded and worked down his neck like the gorging burrow of worms while he chanted: *Praise Jesus! Praise Jesus! Praise Jesus! Amen!* His face was red, and sweat ran down the sides of it as he yelled into the microphone. Amos noticed Roberts's suit was nicer than his. The pews were wooden, scratched, and uncomfortable. Sitting through a sermon on them was a test of faith in itself, and Amos wanted to watch a wrecking ball streak through the row of them.

The only thing that took his attention from Ava and brought him back to his thoughts about Bobby Sisk was the collection plate. He followed the plate down each pew, watching parishioners drop their tithing without question or wonder. With more people using credit cards and checks, a decent cash score became more difficult to find. Then he saw the prize. Sitting in the front row by the aisle was the last person to drop offering, Kenny Kavanagh.

Kenny was the biggest supplier of cocaine north of Boston. He was a ghost. Stories would surface about him, murders, but nothing was ever connected to him. Most people wouldn't know him from any other asshole standing behind them in the grocery store. Amos wouldn't have noticed him if he hadn't dropped three envelopes in the plate or Amos hadn't seen the tattoo across his fingers or subtle burn scar that rode up his face like a dent in a beer can.

Pastor Roberts talked about the church needing a new chimney and how the next Sunday was Easter, the busiest church day besides Christmas Eve. He asked everyone to bring someone and check their piggy banks. Roberts chuckled after he said *piggy banks,* and no one in the room realized they were being shook down. The envelopes Kavanagh threw in the plate weren't for a new chimney. The two men that had run the collection plates up and down the aisles met at the front of the church. Pastor

Roberts said a prayer over the offering and the men brought the money into the office to the left of the podium. One moved behind the desk and knelt. Before they shut the door, Amos caught a glimpse of the slate-gray color of the safe.

When he lost his scholarship at Bowdoin, Amos cracked a safe in the basement of a local restaurant. Amos had done the job with Bailey Mitchell. There was nothing he could have done about Mitchell, but that was only because the cops got to him first. Amos sat in prison for three years waiting for his chance to get to him, dumping every miniscule ounce of rage he had ever felt upon Bailey with the butt end of a pistol. When Amos did get him, he wasn't worth a bullet, and Bobby Sisk would have to get more than he was worth if Amos didn't want to get dropped into the prison system again.

At the end of the sermon most people took their time moving from the pews to hug one another or shake hands—a last gesture of goodwill until the next week. Kavanagh moved through the people to the side exit. Through the windows, Amos watched him walk to a black Monte Carlo. As he stared at Kavanagh, a sickening feeling came over him. The three years he'd spent in prison weren't enough for him to ignore the score. That conscience came back again, throwing its temper tantrum on the auditorium floor in front of a million synaptic spectators and Amos noticed Ava had followed his gaze through the window.

"What are you looking at?" he asked her.

"Nothing. I was wondering what you were looking at." She grabbed her purse from beneath the pew in front of her and they left.

At some point during their time inside the church, she'd made some distance from her previous affection. He first noticed when she pulled her hand from his when he tried to touch it on the way home. The one-word, terse responses to innocuous questions were another indication. She bore a vacant look on her face and made small, throat-clearing vibrations.

"What is your problem?" he asked when she pulled to the

curb outside of his building.

"Nothing."

"Obviously."

"Moss, I have a lot on my mind and things are happening between us at a ridiculously fast pace. I just need some time to think about this."

"Ridiculous?"

"I didn't mean it like that."

"Then what did you mean?"

"I don't know."

"I guess that's a fair answer considering you came back into my life. It wasn't the other way around."

"What's that supposed to mean?"

"Well, why were you at Logan's? It's not like you were out for a night on the town. You came in there looking for me."

"What makes you think that, Mr. Bowdoin?"

"Women like you don't go into Logan's by themselves. You lived here once. You know that."

"Yeah. You got me all figured out. I came looking for you, Mad-dog Moss. Swain's Pain. The—"

"Fuck you."

Amos got out of the car and slammed the door.

TWENTY-TWO
Ava

Ava slowed her car to a full stop, slamming it into park on the street by her aunt's house before it had stopped rolling. She tried to shake her frustration. Amos had done nothing wrong, but while she sat with him in the church, she couldn't shake the feeling of resentment for him because of how she felt. After a couple deep breaths, she emerged from the car and walked across the street to her aunt's.

Her aunt met her at the door, a look of worry draped across her face. She was a marathon runner. Well into her fifties, the woman's body was a flow of muscle, molded from the sweaty miles she pounded away. She had a narrow face, much like her niece. Her lips had thinned with age and the thin-framed glasses she wore gave her an intellectual elegance, even though she'd spent the last nineteen years at a manufacturing plant in the town's industrial park where intelligence wasn't a necessary quality in employees.

Ava slipped past her into the house. Her aunt stood on her porch peering up and down the street, searching for the cause of her distress.

"Honey, what's wrong?" she asked after she'd closed the door.

Ava pulled a beer from the refrigerator, a light pilsner that her aunt kept a good stock of. "Nothing," she answered.

Her aunt cocked an eyebrow, tilted her head, and looked over her glasses at her niece. "Nothing?"

"I really don't want to talk about it."

"Ava, if there is a safety issue, that's something we need to discuss."

"Oh, God. It's not that, Aunt Kim."

"Well?"

Ava walked toward her aunt into the living room and sat in the papasan in the corner, beside the stone owl statue and the side window. "Why am I still so fucking wrapped up in this hatred of men, and why is my attraction so strong to this thug, townie fucker?"

Kim relaxed her posture for a moment, then crossed her arms over her chest. "You've been seeing Amos?"

Ava took a sip of her beer. She caught her aunt's eyes for a moment, then looked away.

"Well, I didn't think it would take long before that curiosity of yours got the better of you." Kim moved to the footstool in front of her niece and sat. "Ava, I'm not going to tell you what to do, but I'll tell you something about Amos Swain. Last summer I saw him put two men into the pavement in about three seconds. You've never seen violence like this man can produce."

Ava thought about her last comment to Amos, how the serious, inquisitive look on his face flashed to a brief sweep of sadness before his eyes narrowed. "Do you think he's the kind of man who would hurt me?"

"I don't know Amos enough to know what he would do to anyone. I hear a lot in this town, and the one thing I have never heard is anything about Amos hurting someone who didn't probably deserve it. But, a man like that, a man that violent, might be the kind of man who determines who deserves it."

"How does that happen to people?"

"What?"

"How does someone who's so gentle and nice become a ball

of rage and violence?"

"Prison, Ava."

TWENTY-THREE
Amos

His anger wore off by the time he reached Paras Pizza. He walked there, feeling the air seep into his clothes and warm itself against the wounds in his arm. Just before the pizzeria, he passed a bum with a torn, brown corduroy jacket. His shoulders were pushed forward, toward his chest as if he'd spent his life huddling from the cold. The bum hacked and pulled the jacket tighter around him. The shirts he wore underneath were tattered, torn in enough places that Amos could see his dirty skin through the rips. He slumped against the building and leaned over to rake his fingers through an ashtray for a cigarette butt long enough to smoke. Amos went in to place an order then waited for Caleb outside, twisting a thread of fabric in his pocket. The bum crossed the street to another building's ashtray and continued his scavenging. Caleb's car rumbled to a halt at the sidewalk.

Caleb stepped around the front of his car. "How was church, choir boy?"

Amos shook his head and opened the door for Caleb. Shelly, the woman who ran the joint, put the pizzas Amos had ordered on the counter.

"Hey, Shelly," Caleb said scooping up his pizza. "Wanna go out this weekend?"

The straps of her apron pressed into her breasts. White flour formed handprints on the pockets of her ass. George, the owner, sat in a chair against the back wall reading the paper. He wore an apron as well, but he didn't slave around the ovens anymore.

"Caleb," she said, putting her hands on her hips. "What makes you think I'm going to say yes today?" She moved her eyes to Amos's. "I heard you got shot on your birthday. How do you two idiots manage to find so much trouble?" She walked to the back.

"It was the day *after* my birthday, but I'm fine Shelly. Thanks for the concern. George, how are you?"

George looked over the paper. Caleb grabbed the pies and followed Amos out to the car. The house special, Amos's pie of choice, was salami, pepperoni, ham, sausage, green peppers, onions, and mushrooms stacked on a ten-inch crust and came out of the oven as dense as a manhole cover. He stretched a pinch of meat from the pizza and dropped it into his mouth.

"I saw Kenny Kavanagh at church today."

Caleb's eyes drew wide. "Why would he be there?"

"I think he's running money through it. There's a box in the office."

"You don't seem very excited about this. We are taking this down?"

"I don't know."

"Why, because of Kavanagh?"

"No."

"Because it's a church?"

"It's not that. It's who brought me there."

"So now we're not taking jobs because of your ex?"

"That not as much. It's a box. I don't like boxes."

"Blow me. You got ratted out."

"I still spent three years inside."

"That was your own fault. If you had called me instead of doing the job with that piece of shit, you'd have been fine."

"I know, Caleb."

"Look. You want Seneca's college fund secure, right?"

"Already is. That was the first thing I took care of."

"Whatever. What about the boat and getting out of here?"

"I'll find a different job."

"You know as well as I do that we'll never find something this big around here."

"I don't even know how big it is."

"Bullshit. It's huge. This is what we've been waiting for. We do this and Crow's thing and we're set for a while. You can get on your little boat with your girl and chase the fucking sunset."

"Since you put it that way—No, Caleb."

Caleb sat back in his seat, crumpled a napkin, and tossed it on the dashboard. "You're a fucking pansy. All the years I've been with you, and you're going to turn this down because some bitch you haven't seen in ten years comes back into your life. First of all, who's going to tell her? Are they going to have an announcement? Who was there when she split and you were devastated for a year? How many times did she come to visit you in prison? Who looked out for your baby sister when you were away? Who was there for you when your father died? Who got you in with Tommy? And let's not mention the trigger action I put down for you just the other day, which probably kept that piece of shit from getting another one off in which case, we wouldn't be having this conversation. Fuck you. We're not going to do this? You're a fucking asshole. I need this."

Amos finished chewing, swallowed, and wiped the grease off his fingers with a napkin.

"Well, motherfucker?"

He wondered why he told Caleb. Part of him knew he needed Caleb to talk him into it. He thought about Ava, how she'd been gone for ten years, how his father was gone forever, and there was nothing Amos could do about people leaving and never coming back.

"Fuck it," Amos said.

"Thank you. Now what about Crow's thing?"

"I'm more concerned about that other thing."

Caleb pushed out a wide grin. "About that. I think I found him."

"Yeah?"

"I'm going to verify it later. Do you want to move on it tonight?"

"The sooner the better. Make sure, Cal. I have to go. My mother left me a message about the dog."

"I told you she'd be pissed."

"What else is new?"

Ruth sat in her living room fixed on an infomercial. She held the phone against her thigh. The heel of her stiletto drew small circles in the air as she rotated her ankle. She didn't look at Amos when he entered. A faint smell of fingernail polish drifted through the house. Amos put the pizza in the fridge then sat on the couch next to her. The man in the commercial sliced through a tomato with a knife then asked what Amos thought was the dumbest fucking question ever: *Did you see that?*

"Are you thinking about buying some knives?"

She sighed. "We'll see." She adjusted the hem of her gray skirt then flicked a few pieces of lint from the matching top. Her business suit getup was always the same, always a skirt suit and heels and jewelry and makeup and a smile. The smile though, she rarely used in front of Amos.

"Where's Seneca?"

"*Your* dog is in the upstairs bathroom. I have an open house and I want the dog gone before I get back."

"Is Seneca not taking care if it?"

She stared at the television. "No. Seneca is caring for the puppy quite well, actually. But Seneca has a problem with her language."

"What the fuck is wrong with her language?"

"Is that supposed to be funny? You're missing the point, Amos. You should have asked me before you decided to get a puppy and give it to your sister. You're always doing things like that, giving her things. Sometimes, I think you do it just to spite me or make me appear to be the bad guy. You've done enough to spite me, Amos. I want the puppy out of here." She sighed. "What happened at Logan's? I read about it in the paper."

"Target practice."

"I don't understand you. You had it all." She looked at him again. "Now, you've reduced yourself to nothing but a leg-breaker for Tommy Logan. You dress in nice clothes to try to fool people, but you don't fool anyone. It's pathetic really. I almost pity you." She stood, turned the television off, and went upstairs to her room.

Amos bit into the side of his cheek. His ability to keep squashing his anger after Ruth's diatribes began to fade. Ava's words cut back into his mind. He sat on the couch for a while with his head back staring at the ceiling and stretching his throat until Ruth came back down the stairs.

"I forgot to tell you." She slipped a large silver hoop earring through her left lobe. "The puppy's name is Ariel. And she likes to chew suede. She ate my favorite pair of Loeffler Randalls."

She slipped the other earring in and pulled herself back up the stairs by the railing. Amos had no idea what Loeffler Randalls were.

The bathroom had been redone. The solid white tile running up the walls blinded him for a moment. The puppy panted behind the toilet. She lifted her head with an ear cocked to look at Amos and squeezed between the porcelain and the wall to wobble over and sniff the tips of his shoes. It had no idea the wrath it had escaped—first, the woodstove, then the destruction of something unnecessarily expensive. It sneezed. The shudder echoed through the bathroom before Amos scooped her from the floor and left.

TWENTY-FOUR
Vassar

Vassar climbed from the bed where he'd left Farrah sprawled on the mattress. The sheets were bunched around her shoulders and head. Her fingers twitched and slowly, she moved her hands down to her thighs where the bruises were already beginning to form. Vassar lit a cigarette in the kitchen and went back to the doorway of his room. Farrah searched her legs for the tender places he'd punched her. She drew one of her hands from her legs and pulled the sheets from her head.

"How was that, baby?" Vassar asked her, blowing smoke into the room.

Farrah moaned. "Did you have to hit so hard?"

"Making up for lost time, baby."

Farrah turned on the mattress so she could see him in the doorway. "I love you, too. When are they getting here?"

"Should be any minute now."

Vassar stepped into the room and grabbed a pair of jeans amid the clutter on the dresser. An overturned ashtray left crushed cigarette butts and the dusting of black ash on the torn construction pay stubs and various pieces of unfinished whittling projects. He slid his jeans over his legs and left Farrah in the room to wait for his supplier.

Vassar had lit his third cigarette when their Cadillac inched up the driveway. He shook his head. Three men climbed from the car and tip-toed around the patches of exhaust-stained snow and tire tracks. They pranced up to the door, two of them, the two who Vassar knew, Richard and Avery. A third guy moved slower behind them, a kid practically. His nose was bandaged, and his eyes were blackened like the rotting knots on a dead tree. Vassar let them in and cleared the soiled paper plates from his picnic table in the kitchen.

Avery nudged the kid. "Give him the stuff."

The kid held out a package, freezer paper bound with masking tape that looked no more conspicuous than a package of meat from the butcher.

"What the fuck happened to your face?" Vassar asked.

"Fucking cunt supplier of ours put a piece of firewood upside his head," Richard muttered.

"Fishy-woman-hole bitch," Avery added.

"I guess you guys didn't make that good of an impression." Vassar pulled a serrated steak knife from the counter and pierced the package. He tested the product from the tip of the blade then stabbed it into the table. He held his head back for a moment. "Shit's good." Vassar turned toward the sink and knelt. He opened the cabinet and reached for a box of SOS pads where he kept his cash. He pulled out a stack of bills and tossed them over to the kid. "So what'd you guys do to the bitch?"

"What do you mean?"

"What did you do to her after she fucked up your boy, here?"

The kid spoke up as he handed the money to Richard. "They didn't do shit."

"What could we do?" Richard asked.

"Should have fucked that bitch up. Probably would have been easier if you weren't a couple a queers."

"We don't like to use our hands that way."

"Oh, right. I always forget that the only thing you two beat are dicks."

"You're never very nice to us, Vassar."

Vassar cringed at the sound of his name lisped into a pissing sound.

"Maybe you guys should hire someone. Teach that cunt a lesson."

"And you know people like this?" Richard threw his hands up. "Of course you do. I don't even know why I asked."

"I know a guy who does that sort of thing. Probably wouldn't cost you too much."

"How much?"

"Depends on what you want done. You want her intimidated, a grand or so. You want her fucked up, broken arm or leg, maybe, five grand. You want her damaged, ten and if you want her dead, it'll be at least fifteen. But I don't recommend that unless you have another supplier."

The two men looked at each other. One of them crossed his arms and bit the fleshy part of his index finger. The other put his hands on his hips and tilted his head to the side, waiting for the other to make the decision. But the kid, Vassar noticed the kid more. The kid had spread a vengeful grin across his face, hoping.

"What's it going to cost us to have you set it up?"

Vassar spooned out a pile of blow from the package onto the cutting board. "How about you throw in one of these packages."

"Fuck no."

"Well, I guess you'll just have to handle this on your own."

The kid's expression twisted into a petulant scrunch. "Look what this bitch did to my face."

"Oh, Seth, calm down. The ladies like battle wounds."

"I'm sure Seth doesn't like being the beat-bag for a couple of fag dealers who can't handle their business."

"Okay. But not a whole package. Twenty-five percent."

Vassar shook his head. "I got exclusive guys. Reliable. Perfectionists. Seventy-five percent."

"Fifty."

"Deal."

"Payment up front."

Seth was on his way to the car before Vassar could finish.

"You got any information on this bitch? Name? Address?"

Richard shook his head. "Nnn—ooh. Business card."

He slapped Avery on the shoulder. Avery gave him a blank look. Richard jutted out his chin. "Business card," he whined.

Avery shook his head and pulled his small, purple purse around his body from the small of his back.

"Jesus fucking Christ," Vassar whispered.

Avery flipped through the series of cards he had. He made another run through.

"For fuck's sake, you can't have that many cards in there."

Avery scoffed. "They're alphabetized starting with C and I don't remember her last name."

Vassar shook his head.

"Found it." Avery jerked the card from the purse and presented it to Vassar, unfolding his arm toward him like a drawbridge.

Vassar slipped the card from his hand and read the name. "Ruth Archer. She sounds like a fucking cunt. Okay, so what do you guys want done?"

Richard clasped his hands together. "What were the options again?"

Seth rushed back into the house with another package as Farrah stumbled into the kitchen pulling her robe around her. Seth directed his attention toward her as he handed the package to Vassar.

"Christ, kid, you want a piece of ass, all you have to do is ask," Farrah said.

Seth broke his stare and glanced at Vassar with embarrassment. Vassar took the package.

"Hey, baby," he said to Farrah. "Why don't you take this kid back into the room and show him how deep your throat is. I need to talk business with the fags."

Richard and Avery crossed their arms in unison. Farrah smiled at Vassar and then Seth. "Come on, kid. I suck the best cock in Southern Maine." She took the kid's hand and pulled him toward the bedroom despite his confused expression.

TWENTY-FIVE
Amos

The puppy sniffed around furniture and end tables in Amos's apartment. Its paws clicked over the linoleum of the kitchen as it continued to sniff around table and chair legs before it disappeared into his bedroom. Amos sat on the couch and stared at the pigeons flying back and forth to broken windows in the mills across the street. His thoughts circled around Ruth's pathetic comment. He wondered if her bitterness toward him came from his attempt to hold on to something she didn't want to remember, memories of his father. It was easier to deal with the shit parts of life if there wasn't anything good to compare it to. He guessed that's how she felt, that the best parts of her life died with his father, and he was just the searing reminder of what she'd never get back.

Amos left the apartment and walked down to Logan's. Caleb had perched at the bar trying his best to work his way into the pants of some local girl who didn't look old enough to be in there—pale, young face without the droop of frustration or accepting a going-nowhere life. Caleb ditched her and followed Amos to the darker corner of the bar past the pool tables.

"Another great conversation with your mother?" He lit a cigarette and handed it to Amos as they sat at a table.

"Stellar." Amos took a drink and chased it with a drag.

Smoke wafted into his eyes from the ashtray, and he rubbed the burning from them. A black line worked its way up the cigarette. They sipped in silence and Caleb burned through more cigarettes. Two couples shot pool at the table closest to them. The women dressed in tight jeans and camisoles, clothes they thought they still fit into. Their hair curled into wiry scribbles against the smoke floating through the bar. The men wore sleeveless T-shirts flashing spindly arms. They tried to give pointers to their girlfriends on shots they couldn't make themselves. One of them stared at Amos and whispered to his girlfriend. Laughter followed.

"Hey," the guy said. "What's with the hood? Who the fuck are you supposed to be?"

Caleb turned in his chair with a cigarette dangling from the corner of his mouth and shot a jet of smoke from his nostril. Both couples stopped to look at Caleb and Amos. Amos slid his palm over his head to pull the hood down. The other guy put his beer on the edge of the pool table and moved to his friend.

"Those are the bouncers. Shut the fuck up."

"Man. I'm sorry. I didn't—I thought you were someone else." The couples finished their beer and went to the bar, leaving the remaining balls motionless under the light. Caleb turned back toward Amos and tapped ashes from his cigarette. "Fucking townies."

"Speaking of townies. Anything?"

"He's holed up in a seasonal rental in Old Orchard. The Grand Beach Motel. It's a quiet place and they don't ask a lot of questions. They don't even ask for an ID to get a room. He's got a room on the end. The one next to his is vacant, so I doubt the cops know anything. Freight train rolls by every couple of hours. So does the Amtrak. Loud as all fuck and shakes the building. Should be pretty easy."

Amos thought about Bailey Mitchell again and his claim that Amos had bullied him into taking down that restaurant safe. Amos remembered Caleb sitting in the back of the courtroom, his chin lowered to his chest, scowling at the entire procession.

"We should go. If we can find out where he is, the cops will find him soon." Amos finished his drink and swallowed his nervousness to kill a man. It hadn't been there the first time.

Cold dropped out of the sky like an obnoxious, shuddering sneeze. It tortured and curled everything outside like the gnarled fingers of a corpse. Caleb and Amos pushed hand warmers into their socks and the insides of their clothes that had stiffened in the cold. Shivers had long abandoned their bodies and they stayed tight in the wool blankets Caleb had stowed in the trunk of the Monte Carlo, a hunk of steel born in the eighties, rusted, a typical heap that blended well with the other winter renters' vehicles parked in the under-lot of the Grand Beach Inn. The smell of damp floorboard carpet lingered inside, a static crunch emitted each time they shifted their feet. Amos held a pistol in his hand, the barrel threaded for the silencer under the seat. They shed their breath under the collars of their shirts, the windows slightly cracked to keep them from frosting over too much.

Bobby smoked on the balcony of his room. He stood against the building, ducked in the shadow of the roof, but emerged slightly every time a car slowed on the street. The television flashed through the room behind him. He was going to die, and the last pleasures in his life would be the mindless entertainment of a television show and the comforting drags of a cigarette.

Caleb checked the time. "Train should be coming through soon. Better thread that burner."

Amos reached under the seat and pulled out the heavy metal cylinder. In the dark, he found the tip of the barrel and turned the silencer. Nothing but the rub of metal.

"Shit," he mumbled.

"What is it?"

"Fucking threading is condensed from the cold. You got your lighter?"

Caleb fumbled in his pocket and slipped the lighter across

the seat to Amos. He pulled the blanket over his head and put the flame to the metal. When the flame had stolen the air from beneath the blanket and Amos began to have difficulty breathing, he tried the silencer again. Still just the rub of metal. Again, he put the flame to the metal and let it burn until the lighter ran out of fluid and the rumble of the train began to move the fabric of their clothes into a tickle over their skin.

TWENTY-SIX
Bobby

Bobby tossed his cigarette off the balcony and slipped back into his room. He stood in front of the monitor by the patio door, where he peered out into the parking lot. The cold had latched onto his skin, even through the layers he wore. He worked his fingers into fists, the movement painful and awkward from the rigidity the cold had forced into them. He scanned along the walkway on the second floor that led to the other rooms and shut his eyes to break the strain that pulsed in them.

The rattle of plastic cups in the bathroom warned him of the coming train. He shed his jacket, giving up on any relief from warmth and pulled his backpack off the bed. He went through it, again, more than two dozen times already, checking to make sure he had what he needed. The shotgun rested on the bunched polyester comforter. When he finished checking his bag, he picked up the shotgun. He held it with both hands at his waist and practiced drawing it up toward the door, the patio. Bobby climbed into the bed, sitting against the headboard, and practiced again. In the few short minutes Bobby had swung the gun, his eyelids felt heavy. The green digital display on the cable box read 3:08 a.m. Even the headboard was cold against the back of his skull. He worked his toes in his boots, trying to circulate blood for some warmth. The vibration in the mattress shook the tense muscles in his legs and back. He repositioned the shotgun on his lap and shut his eyes.

The knock was faint, but Bobby pulled his eyes open in the dull blue glow spewed from the television. He wondered if it were just delirium creating sounds in his mind. The knock came again, and his heart roared into a humming throb. The mattress springs squeaked as he swung one leg off the bed, then the other. The clock display read 3:11 a.m. The floor creaked as he stood. Another stiff knock made him almost pull the trigger. He kept the shotgun pointed at the door and slipped his arm into his jacket. The passing train rattled the dresser drawers and he slid the patio door open.

Knocking came faster and harder, and it continued. The cold outside slipped around his shoulders and put an icy grip around his neck. The sound of the train growled and rose over the building. Bobby backed out onto the patio, the saliva on his lips froze into a flaky spread of ice. He lifted the bag and let it fall over the rail. Bobby turned and Amos was there, standing on the walkway, his arms held together in front of him, pointing, the roar of the train louder than anything Bobby had ever heard. Amos Swain's wrists twitched. Weight thumped against his chest simultaneous with a tiny flash and the sound of the train was gone. His body warmed and went weightless like the steam-filled air over a hot bath.

TWENTY-SEVEN
Amos

Amos would see Bobby Sisk randomly, arching in the snow from the bullets he'd sent him, and it would turn out to be a kid building a fort or a dog rolling over. The first time he'd killed a man, Amos had enough bloodlust built up from prison that he only set out to punish him, to inflict pain. Murder, killing, what he had done was an afterthought. When Bailey Mitchell was dead, Amos realized exactly how much rage he'd contained and released, but he didn't think about it much before or after. Bobby Sisk was different. There was no rage. Bailey Mitchell created the sequence of events that ended his life. Amos created the events that ended Bobby's. After he shot him and watched him wither into the dim blue glow of his room, that's when Amos felt rage. More than he'd ever felt. Angry that he had to kill Bobby. Angry that all the choices he thought he'd made for himself had been made for him, and there were no excuses any longer.

The wounds in his arm began to itch and Amos bloodied his shoulder in an attempt to relieve it. Despite the healing that was progressing, the ache and tenderness level rose. It bothered him more that he pushed the blame for it on psychosomatic reactions to killing Bobby, and he felt encumbered by the haunting that Bobby's murder was inspiring. Amos had no emotional or moral reservations about killing, but murder was a class entirely on its own. Bobby had his shotgun in his hands when Amos killed him, but he was clearly attempting to flee from Caleb knocking on his door, and murder was the defining label of killing someone helpless or weaker, someone who didn't deserve to die. Had Amos shot Bobby in the parking lot when he'd been ambushed, perhaps his perspective would be different. But Bobby was trying so hard to live, and no doubt in other danger because Amos had rolled him, and Amos felt like he'd killed something innocent.

Friday before Easter, Ava asked to take him to dinner, an apology, she said, for the names she'd called him. Amos almost said, no, his feelings for her had shifted to detachment, and he didn't really care about grasping that part of his past. He also didn't like it, and a part of him, that aggressive little nag in his mind ripped off a list of questions: *Why did it not bother her that I got shot? Why is she back here? What is she doing? Why does she want to spend time with me? Why does she call me out on who I am? Why did she show up to the bar that night? Why, why, fucking why? What is she hiding? What does she want? Where has she really been?*

While Amos got ready, places deep in his arm burned and itched. Dressing with the cumbersome coordination of his injured arm was discouraging to the point of tantrums, and his temper forced him to throw random, breakable objects against the walls. His feet shifted from side to side in his shoes as he paced the room because he wasn't able to tie them tight enough.

Amos locked the puppy in the laundry room before Ava got there. He didn't want her *goo-oohing* over the animal. When she arrived, she called out to Amos. The heels of her shoes clunked at the doorway as she kicked them off and her footsteps moved through the living room toward the bedroom. She stopped at the doorway and put her back against the side of the doorjamb.

"Hey there." She lifted her left leg to put the heel of her foot beneath her ass. Her black dress slid up and exposed most of her inner thigh.

"I need a kiss," she said. She reached above her head to

stabilize herself and pulled Amos in when he walked over to her. Both of her hands cupped the back of his head as their lips mashed. Her fingernails scraped his neck. Amos nibbled her earlobe and listened to her moan as she squeezed her thighs against his wandering fingers. Pain shot through his arm and reminded him that it was injured.

"Damn it." He backed away to the bed holding his shoulder.

She moved into the room with her palms facing him. "I'm sorry. Did I hurt you?" On the bed she kissed the bicep of his injured arm. She helped Amos with his shirt and tie then hurried him out of the building and drove to the restaurant.

It was a cloth napkin type of place. Most of the things on the menu were French. Polished silverware, candles, low light, romantic. They even had good toilet paper in the bathroom, not the tire-sized industrial rolls. The hostess showed Ava and Amos to a table. Most of the people wore suits, ties or at the least, a collared shirt. The three men at the table closest to them wore their Ivy League sweatshirts, Harvard and Yale, over their gingham or white cotton dress shirts. They all looked basically the same to Amos—slicked Rogaine-grown hair held in place with Propecia, the smooth faces of privilege and a budget for spa treatment and facials and Botox—the absence of stress or worry about breathing from one moment to the next. Amos hated them before they gawked at Ava. They'd stopped talking when she passed until she leaned over to place her purse against the leg of the table and Mr. Yale whispered, "Look at the tits on that one." They pushed their heads closer to the middle of their table and laughed quietly.

"What have you been doing?" she asked when Amos sat.

"Trying to figure you out."

This waitress is pretty pathetic, Mr. Yale said.

"What is that supposed to mean?" Ava asked me.

"Just curious why you got so distant."

"Amos, I'm sorry. I have a lot of pressure on me. And besides that we're getting very close very quick."

"I remember when we were close."

"It's been a long time. Things have changed."

"Tell me about it."

Excuse me, waitress. I need another drink, Mr. Yale said.

"Amos, I'm sorry. I don't know how many times I can say it. I want this to work but you're not the guy I typically date."

Again Amos thought of her with other men. He also thought of his fault in expecting things from people, the reason Caleb was his only real friend. *If you never expect anything, you're never disappointed.* The words of his father, his generational hand-me-down wisdom had little practical application in Amos's life. He wanted people to be loyal, especially in what they did. Ava's fickleness bothered him. The waitress finished taking the drink order for the Ivy Leaguers and came to their table.

"Good evening," the waitress said. "Can I get you a beverage while you look over the menu?"

A busboy broke a glass behind Amos and he flipped the knife through his fingers into his palm.

"That's what I'm talking about." She pointed at the knife. The waitress stole a quick glance at his hand and looked back at Ava.

Waitress.

She turned.

"He needs a drink, too." Mr. Yale pointed to his friend across the table.

The girl bit her lip.

"Get us when you get back," Amos told her.

"Thank you." She practiced a smile and stabbed her pen behind her ear.

"This guy is beginning to piss me off," Ava whispered over the top of her menu.

The waitress returned with the Ivy Leaguers' drinks. "Why is it taking so long for our food?"

"Sir, I'm sorry. We're short staffed in the kitchen and—"

"I don't want to hear it. It shouldn't be that hard to write something down. Think you can get us some more water?"

"Jesus, I hated waiting on guys like that," Ava said.

"You waited tables?"

"Yeah, for five years. It was the worst. People are such ass-holes when they think you're their bitch."

"Is that what this guy thinks? That she's his bitch?"

"Pretty obvious, wouldn't you say?"

The girl returned and filled their water glasses. Amos stood and pulled his chair to the corner of the Ivy League table and sat. Ava crossed her arms in front of her on the table then lifted her hand to the side of her face. Amos pulled a wad of cash from his pocket, thumbed off the rubber band, and peeled away two hundred-dollar bills. He placed the wad back in his pocket, his movements slow and deliberate. He kept his eyes on his money, averting eye contact with the men at their table until the right moment. Amos forgot about the pain in his arm. The tables surrounding them went motionless and quiet.

"Hun," Amos said. "You need a break. Grab me a Turkey neat, whatever that beautiful girl needs, and keep the change."

She shook her head slightly, not sure what to do.

Amos leaned back in his seat and motioned with his head. "Go ahead. This asshole will be here when you get back." Amos looked through Mr. Yale's steel-framed glasses. "Maybe."

People at the tables closest to them allowed a nervous chuckled. Even Ava let out a little giggle. But that bothered Amos even more. He felt anger pulsing beneath his fingernails. An easier response to the whole situation, one that he wanted out of, was to smash the guy's lips and hold his bleeding head over the pressed white linen. But people don't like that. Blood makes them queasy, but they're all for the guy who'll stand up to the bully. And none of them understand that that's where violence comes from. It comes from the guys pissed off at the self-entitlement they have to witness, guys tired of taking shit from their boss or peers or wife or kids or the asshole behind a counter or the condescending prick who thinks the world is his red carpet and anyone close to it as he strolls by should be scrambling to flatten the kinks. Mr. Yale shook his head and stared at Amos. He was scared. His eyes jerked around the table at his buddies looking for one of them to speak up so he wouldn't have to.

"Can I help you?" he asked Amos, quietly.

Mr. Yale's hands palmed the table to keep them from trembling. Amos had to relax. Staring Mr. Yale down until he shut his mouth would only keep Amos from maintaining his cool. He had to talk, play nice at first, make threats, then humiliate Mr. Yale without going physical. All the things he hated.

"Yeah. I think you can. My lady friend over there, the one with great tits, is trying to have a discussion with me but the pathetic service in this place is causing quite a bit of a distraction. So, I need a favor. I need you to pretend like the service is outstanding and bring it down a few pegs."

Mr. Yale moved his head slightly and his left eye twitched. His lips parted to say something.

"Before you tell me to fuck off, I want you to think about it." Amos leaned closer to Mr. Yale so only he and the men at his table could hear. "Think about how long it will take for a broken collarbone to heal, especially one that's been ripped out of your fucking chest."

"Look, man. We don't want any trouble," one of the other men said. "Charlie, just let it go."

"You have smart friends, Charlie. They must have gone to Harvard or something."

Charlie's head wobbled. The manager floated behind the server with her arms crossed and a finger tapping on her chin. Relief dropped from Charlie's shoulders as Amos pulled his chair back to the table, but he didn't sit. He stepped back to the Ivy League table and leaned close to him. "There's one more thing. Your waitress needs an apology. My lady friend, too. Okay, Charlie."

"Yeah, okay."

"Thanks a bunch, Charlie. I really appreciate it."

Joe Ricker

Ava locked her eyes onto Amos's. When he sat, she leaned over the table to whisper. "You have no idea how badly I want you to fuck me on this table right now."

Before Amos could respond, Charlie interrupted. "Ma'am. Excuse me, ma'am."

Ava looked at him, curious.

"I'm sorry," he said.

She righted herself in her seat. "Oh thanks, doll. You gentlemen enjoy your dinner."

She'd called Amos *doll* in the halls of the high school when he walked her to class. He thought he remembered there being pressure then, the inability to function properly with juvenile angst tormenting him. At that dinner table, the pressure was much heavier. Amos already knew what losing her felt like, and it seemed he was only moving to a place that he would lose her again. Ava shook her head at him.

"What?" he asked.

"You're fucking amazing." She reached over the table to touch the base of his jaw. The waitress brought their drinks and took their order.

Ava insisted on paying. Amos was going to let her, but Charlie beat both of them to it. They'd skipped dessert and had already left so Amos didn't get a chance to thank him. On the way home, Ava placed her hand on his knee. "That was the most amazing thing I have ever seen," she said. "What you did for that girl was very sweet."

"I didn't do it for her. I just wanted to eat in peace."

"You did too. You have a big heart, Amos. You always have." She slipped her hand to his crotch. "Among other things."

She turned to him. Amos pushed back in his seat and closed his eyes, focusing on the soft, fine pressure of her fingernails scraping his inner thigh and then the pressure of her palm pushing against his dick. He got hard and she drew her hand away.

"Anticlimactic," he said, stiffening in his seat.

"Be patient."

106

"So where are you living?"

"I'm staying with my aunt down on High Street."

"She still lives down there?"

"Yeah."

"Let's go there."

"You're crazy. No way. She'd freak out if I brought you back there."

"I guess I'm quite the celebrity around here."

She nodded. "Yeah."

The fire escape on Amos's apartment overlooked the pond. He'd lived there since he got out of prison and had never been on the fire escape with other women, afraid that they would become clingy if shown the view of anything except his bedroom. He waited out there for Ava while she poured them a drink. She came out wrapped in one of his thick leather jackets.

"It's beautiful out here," she said.

"Yeah, at night."

Porch lights from the houses around the pond reflected against the ice. Booming shook across the lake as ice expanded. Their breaths came out in hot mists between sips of whiskey. She rested on his good shoulder, moving her head once in a while to rub her nose against his jacket.

She held her breath and moved her finger around the rim of the glass. "Amos, I have very strong feelings for you." She took a breath and looked out over the ice.

"But?"

She stroked her hand over his head. "Let's go inside." She leaned forward into a kiss.

She took off Amos's jacket and shirt and sat him on the bed. The light behind her formed curving shadows over his torso and as he reached for her, she slapped his hands away. She bent her limbs along the savage and torn scars on his body, twined them around him like the grip of something brutal. The flat scrape of her teeth worked along his skin as she pushed his pants off. She turned, sat on his lap, and reached over her shoulder to hold the back of his head. She raked her dress up over her waist with her free hand then guided Amos inside her. Her terse grip tightened his throat. She leaned back into him and held his head with both hands, working her hips slow and circular. A line of sweat beaded on her spine and Amos's ears collected her moans.

She breathed heavier as he ran the tips of his fingers hard down her ribs. She turned to face him and kissed his mouth and moved down his neck biting and thrashing her hips. Her arms squeezed tighter around his neck. They came together, both of them gripping and biting and shuddering—the clash of full bottles shattering and mixing into one shredding, liquid concoction. She collapsed into his shoulders and he held her until the pains in his lower back spiked their way up his neck.

Amos's need to grasp things from the past made him think of all the things he was doing wrong—what others thought was wrong compared to their own morals. Good and evil. He thought about his father and the choices he'd once had. Right and wrong are determined by choices. Amos thought about Bobby Sisk for the last time and the pain in his arm was gone.

PART II

Fierce, seraphic, savage-eyed
With the shadows I shall glide
Back across the bedroom floor,
Back into your life once more...
—Baudelaire

TWENTY-EIGHT
Caleb

Caleb parked along the sidewalk that ran against the retaining wall on Kennebunk Beach. Agent Stevens had followed him from the airport in Sanford when he made his turn down 99. He was moving closer and closer to home, and Caleb felt the smothering of his presence like a torturous hiccup or a cough that kept people awake at night. When Stevens got out of his car and shut the door, Caleb pulled the car from the sidewalk and drove around the bend to the next stretch of parking spaces along the beach and parked there. A spray of waves burst over the rocky beach and he waited for Stevens to pull in behind him again.

Caleb made it through two songs before killing the engine and climbing from his car. He moved to Stevens's vehicle and got in the passenger seat.

"You're fucking cute," he said to Caleb. "Real fucking cute. What do you have for me?"

"Nothing."

"You don't come to coast without Amos unless you're casing sites."

"Yes, Special Agent. That is true. I was casing sites."

"Well, we're making an adjustment to your business practice."

Caleb bunched the knees of his pants into his fists. "I can't give you more than I already do."

"That's not what I meant. There's too much heat on construction right now. These local dipshits are pulling over everyone with construction materials and asking for receipts or the contracting job. Boosting construction sites is over for you."

"What the fuck? How am I supposed to dump sites?"

"I don't know. I don't give a shit. Make something up. You want to be on the street, don't risk a small-time bust over this bullshit. You're supposed to be working in a streamlined manner until our little deal is done."

Caleb's lips parted. He felt the movement, despite its slightness, and Stevens noticed.

"You have something, don't you?"

"Crow's thing is the only thing we have right now. We just dumped a lot of heat back home, but there will probably be more coming down. This local detective has a fucking hard-on for Moss."

"Jones, right?"

"Yeah."

"What's his partner's name again?"

"Curry."

"That's right. I keep thinking Rosemary for some reason."

"Well, when he gets back shit's really going to be tight."

"Why's that?"

"I don't know if he knows about Moss, but Moss is one of the guys who fucked his wife."

Stevens laughed. "I love salacious gossip."

"Yeah. Apparently, there were a couple of cops, too."

"Wow. What a piece of shit."

"Moss?"

"No, the wife."

"Yeah, well, we went to high school with the guy. Typical fucking douchebag with no other options but to become a pig."

"If they were smart, they'd make you and Moss cops. What's with Jones? Why does he have it out for Moss?"

"I don't know. He's been on Moss since he got out of prison.

It's strange how relentless he is, but Moss takes it in stride."

"Cocky fucker."

"Not really, and Moss respects Jones, for some reason. Other cops, though…Moss says they became cops so they wouldn't have to think for themselves. If they weren't cops, they'd be inmates; criminals too stupid to get away with it. They're nothing but uniformed sociopaths with a legal right to carry a gun."

"That's a harsh judgment on his part. He went to prison."

"Moss got ratted out. He was in the clear, but that fucking piece of shit took a deal for running that kid down while he was high on Oxy and the system decided Moss was more of a threat to society than some junkie fuck who killed a kid. He gave up the money, though, so they gave him the minimum and then he got out on GB."

"I thought you said he fought a lot in prison. Doesn't sound like good behavior to me."

"Yeah. Almost every day the first six months he was in."

"I guess he established himself."

Caleb stared at Stevens for a long time. "It made him a fucking animal. He wasn't the same after. I know they say prison changes a man, but Moss. That motherfucker came out like a heavyweight splitting maul. Believe me, he's someone you should be worried about."

Stevens moistened his lips and swallowed. He checked his mirrors and scratched his throat. "We're done here."

TWENTY-NINE
Amos

Amos's eyes were still dry and tired. Caleb bounced a ball off the brick above his living room windows. The puppy sat beside the coffee table watching the ball soar over its head. Ava passed Caleb on the stairs, and Caleb's first comment entering the apartment was how her ass looked like breakfast in bed. The tag hanging from the sleeve of his navy, pin-striped suit jerked and fluttered as he tossed the ball.

"Did you get a new suit?" Amos asked.

"I've had it for a while."

Amos sat on the couch next to Caleb and looked down at the calf-length white socks he wore. "Are those the kind of socks that have the colored rings around the top?"

"Blow me."

"I'm going to take a shower." Amos slapped Caleb's leg and stood up. "It's nice to see you've taken an interest in finer clothes."

"I checked out those sites this morning."

"Yeah? What do they look like?"

"Both of them have residents."

"What?"

"There are people there. Maine plates on the vehicles."

"Why would Vassar give us sites with residents?"

114

"Probably because of all that shit he puts up his nose." Caleb tossed the ball over his shoulder and shook his head. Ariel lunged after it toward the fridge. "I'm ready to get out of this suit. Do you have anything I can borrow?"

"You know where the closet is."

He pushed himself from the couch and went to the bedroom. Metal hangers shrieked across the aluminum pole in the closet. The water didn't sting like it had for the first couple days, and the small scabs were getting smaller. Spots that had been difficult to reach with Amos's bad arm were becoming easier to wash. Usually, it never took him very long to take a shower or do anything in the bathroom because of how vulnerable it is. He'd wash his face in the sink, because worse than being naked was being naked with soap in your eyes while you were in the shower. There was a stainless-steel .38 beneath the towels stacked on the windowsill above the toilet. The small window opened up to the back parking lot three stories above a dumpster.

Water dripped from his hair and ears and places he couldn't reach with the towel. Caleb sat on the counter cutting a rectangular piece of fabric from the inside of the sweatshirt behind the stomach pocket.

"I didn't already do that?" Amos asked.

Caleb pulled a sleeve up and bit the plastic holding the price tag. His teeth ground a little and it made Amos cringe. Caleb held up the tag and spit a piece of plastic toward the trash can. Cutting holes in their sweatshirts allowed that extra edge if they needed their burner. Put a hand in the pocket through the hole and the gun is in hand. Then, a simple upward pull of the sweatshirt and the gun is out, ready for use.

Caleb ordered food. The puppy chewed the TV remote while they waited for it. Her tiny teeth broke off small pieces of plastic and rubber buttons that Amos took from her while Caleb cheered her on. She lost interest in the remote when the food arrived and pawed up both of their legs yelping as they ignored her. She licked rice and other pieces of food from the floor that they tossed to keep her quiet.

"At least I got something out of those sites," Caleb said, halfway through the meal, and pulled a diamond-studded Rolex from his pocket.

Amos stopped chewing for a moment when he put it to his ear and listened to it purr. "Where'd you get that?"

"I helped some yuppie change his tire. He took it off and put it on the roof of his car and I snatched it."

"See how much you can get for it." Amos handed the watch back to Caleb. "I'm going to head up to Vassar's to see why the fuck he gave us bogus sites. You want to go?"

"I don't think so. Maybe we should just forget about sites for a while. I mean, with what just happened, maybe we should lay off."

"That's not a bad idea. I thought you needed the money?"

"I do, but we're not going to make much if we get pinched lifting materials from jobsites."

"Okay, whatever. I'm still going to talk to him, though. At least let him know his information's off. Since you're not going." Amos paused to swallow. "Watch the dog for a little while. I should be back in an hour or so. We'll go check out the church later tonight."

"Do I look like a dog sitter to you? I hate animals. Especially this bitch." He pointed his chopsticks at her nose. Ariel flicked her tongue at them.

"You sure as hell don't seem that way considering the women you sleep with."

Amos pushed the small white cartons to the side to retrieve Caleb's car keys. "I'm taking your car. There should be some rope in the junk drawer. Take Ariel for a walk around the pond. It'll be good for you. Plus, that puppy's a pussy magnet. We both know you need all the help you can get with that."

"Ariel?"

"Yeah. That's her name."

"Why do you have to take my car? What's wrong with your

truck?"

"Nothing. I feel like driving something fun today."

Caleb had sat on the sleeve of Amos's hoodie and made no effort to shift his weight as Amos pulled it from under him. He leaned back, picking small pieces of pork from between his teeth with a skewer and glanced at the dog then back to Amos with the same anxious, bewildered look the puppy had. A box of lo mein rested between his legs. Ariel weaved her head between his knees smelling the air.

Caleb whispered to the puppy. Amos pulled the hoodie over his head and reached through the pocket to adjust his burner. As he left, Caleb leaned over to let Ariel devour the lo mein. He rubbed her ribs and coached her, "Good puppy."

Jones was parked across the street from the apartment when Amos left. Amos waved to him when he climbed into Caleb's car. Jones pulled out to follow him in the rearview. He took the long way to Vassar's, allowing the car to writhe along the road between the yellow and white lines through the tight uphill turn past the fried clams restaurant, a village market, and down to the foot of the Mousam Lake, careening over the bridge past a trading post toward the fairgrounds. The back tires shoved the car forward in aggressive bursts after shifting. An empty glass bottle rolled beneath the seat toward the rear of the car until it clinked against something metal. Just before the fairgrounds, when Amos was well out of Sanford, Jones hit the lights on his cruiser.

THIRTY
Special Agent Stevens

The flicking sound of Crow drawing a pick through his hair began to irritate Stevens. Crow winced and yanked the comb through his tangled hair, corn rows that he'd released for retro trend afro. Stevens had his elbow propped against the door, resting the side of his face against his palm.

"Maybe a boot brush would work better," Stevens said.

"A what brush?"

"Never mind. Explaining the joke would be a waste of time." Stevens mumbled something incoherent and adjusted his posture by gripping the wheel with both hands and pulling his body forward. "Tell me about this crew that's moving in."

"Ah, fucking cub scouts. I got no enforcers, so these soft-ass motherfuckers are pushing on corners three blocks from me. I dropped it to Moss. He said to get what information I could. I'm just waiting on my guys to get it."

"And then what?"

"Moss and Caleb fuck 'em up."

Stevens scratched his chin. "You're not getting any more construction materials."

"What the fuck? I get a lot of paper from that."

"Well, not anymore. It's too risky. I can't afford you getting pinched."

Crow smacked his lips. "You're on some bullshit, man. You fucking buggin'."

"Yeah, I be *buggin'*."

"So what the fuck am I supposed to tell Caleb? I ain't going to fence his shit? He's going to give it to the fucking Irish."

"Caleb's not going to have any more materials for you."

"What are you talkin'?"

"This move you're having Amos and Caleb do for you, this is going to be their last."

"Hunh?"

"Do I have to color you a fucking picture? Let Caleb and Moss do the job, then you take them out."

"I can't fence materials because it's too risky, but you're okay with me pushing for a murder charge."

"Nobody's going to get you on anything. You're not going to be there."

"Where the fuck am I going to be?"

"With me. Look, Caleb's getting pushy. It's time to find another mark."

"Caleb is the only one I have who's moving enough to make it worth it."

"This next job will be enough for you to take some time to find someone else. These guys are too heavy for us to push this anymore and keep things quiet. It's time to cut it loose."

Stevens pulled an envelope from his pocket, stuffed and barely sealed. He handed it to Crow. Crow took it and ripped the corner with his teeth.

"Is this all of it?"

"And a little more for being such a good sport. I told you I'd come through."

"Yeah, it's about time."

THIRTY-ONE

Amos

Amos pulled the car onto a side road and parked behind a warehouse. The engine calmed, slipping a soft vibration through the chassis. Jones got out of his cruiser and walked toward the GTO.

"How's it going, Swain?"

"Pretty good."

"Have you taken care of our friend?"

"It's taken care of."

Jones pulled a pack of cigarettes from his jacket pocket. He offered one to Amos. Amos shook his head and watched him pull one from the pack and put it back in his pocket.

"You got real lucky on this one."

"Maybe."

"You ever heard of Kenny Kavanagh?"

"Yeah, I've heard of him."

"Guy's a fucking ghost."

"What's your point?"

"Word on the street is that Bobby Sisk was one of Kavanagh's dealers."

"Okay. So?"

Jones gripped the edge of the doorframe and bent down. He blew smoke into the car. "Rumor has it that Bobby took off with Kavanagh's money, but he tried to rob Logan's first."

"You have quite the talent for telling stories, Detective."

Jones shrugged.

"So, I guess we're in the clear."

"Yeah, well, Kavanagh finds out you rolled his boy none of my stories are going to help you."

"I'm not afraid of ghosts."

Jones chuckled. "I know." He looked toward the edge of the forest near the back of the lot and sighed.

"Something you want to tell me, Detective?"

"Curry's back. Suspension's over."

"Awesome."

"Well, you brought on some heat from this Bobby Sisk shit and Curry wants to nail you bad."

"You think you could get me some breathing room?"

"How do you suggest I do that?"

"You and him should pay me a surprise visit. I'll think of something. Does he know about me and his wife?"

"Jesus, Swain." Jones shook his head. "I'm really looking forward to my pension."

"What the fuck are you going to do with retirement?"

Jones pushed himself from the car. "Fuck, I don't know. Drink less. Go fishing."

"Sounds like a whole lot of boring."

"You might want to think about moving on to boring. Who's the girl?"

"An old friend."

"She might like boring. Look, Curry's on a short leash, but he's already yanking on it hard. You keep your shit together."

Jones walked away from the car and Amos pulled out from behind the warehouse and back onto 109. He continued toward Vassar's feeling a slight sense of relief. Kavanagh was weaving through his path far too much. Amos started to feel some reluctance in taking on the score. But the more he thought about it, the less it mattered. He'd already stung Kavanagh. He'd want to sting back. With Jones out of the picture, Amos's breathing room condensed. He'd have to start looking elsewhere for jobs, unless the church played out enough to let him sit on the sidelines for a while.

Vassar sat in the doorway resting his head against the edge of the sliding glass door. He was smoking a cigarette and naked except for brown, paint-stained work boots. Vassar stared into the trees beyond Amos, ignoring his approach. The edges of his nostrils were raw and scabby. His eyes remained fixed and not blinking, dark yellow circles around them. Amos stopped beside him and leaned his shoulder against the house waiting for Vassar to acknowledge his presence. After two glances of his watch, about three minutes, Amos leaned closer to him. "Vassar."

"Shhhhhhhhh." He didn't move his gaze, but held up his index finger and left it pointed toward the sky. Again, Amos looked at his watch, debating whether he should leave. "Can you hear it?"

Amos's eyes felt heavy—dense and drying into clumps of parched earth. He rubbed them and looked in the direction Vassar was staring. "Hear what?"

Vassar's cigarette burned into the filter and his fingers. The tiny black hairs between his knuckles coiled and withered to white then disappeared. He looked at Amos's mouth, shook his head, then dropped his chin to look at his hand. He lifted it, extending his arm, and let the burning filter drop to the ground. Cracking came from his knees and elbows when he stood and entered his house.

"You coming in?"

Amos took a breath and followed.

"You want to fuck her?" He pointed over to Farrah who was naked and asleep on the couch. Her hair was strewn across her face. One of her feet, the bottom dirty, rested on the armrest. The other pressed into the floor. Her skin was pale, almost translucent, with dark purple bruises on her ribs and thighs that seemed to hover just above her skin. She looked like Vassar had dragged her from a ditch somewhere. Amos walked closer to her to make sure she was still breathing.

"I'm good. Thanks though." Amos looked through the door at Caleb's car outside.

"You sure?"

"Yeah. We need to talk about those sites."

Vassar perked. "Fuck the sites. I got something better."

His grin was disturbing, wide. Amos could see the rawness of his gums. He pulled a business card from a cupboard and held it up.

"What is that?"

"Some guys need someone to teach somebody a lesson."

Amos took a step closer and looked at the card. *Richard* was scrawled on the back of it, grooved dark letters that Vassar must have gouged into the paper with a pencil.

"You want me to fuck up some guy named Richard?"

Vassar pointed at him. "No. Richard is the guy who wants you to fuck up some cunt that's shaking him down."

"Cunt?"

"Yeah. I told him it was extra because it was a woman."

Amos stepped back. "I'll pass, V. Tell Richard to handle the woman himself."

Vassar frowned, as exaggerated as his grin. "You sure?"

"Yeah, man. I don't—fuck this. I'll see you around."

Amos squeezed back through the door and left.

THIRTY-TWO
Amos

Caleb sat on the steps of Amos's apartment building with a long piece of rope attached to Ariel's neck held beneath the heel of his boot. Ariel sniffed the cracks of the sidewalk pulling the slack tight. Amos pulled to a halt in front of the building and got out of the car.

"That was quick." He flicked a cigarette to the sidewalk in front of him. Ariel turned her head toward it. She approached it slowly, sniffing. Her nose drew a circle in the air as her head rotated and she sneezed then backed away sideways.

"You should have come. I think Vassar would have let you nail Farrah."

"Really? Why was she there?"

"I don't know. She was passed out, practically fucking dead and Vassar was morphed."

"Did you say anything about the jobs?"

"I started to, and then he tried to commission me on some wrench work."

"Sweet. Who? When?"

"I turned it down."

"Why? That's easy money."

"It was a woman."

"Oh. Fuck." Caleb scratched the side of his face.

"Anyway, I left within minutes. He was too gone to talk about anything seriously. I'm thinking we should just cut this jobsite shit right out. Focus on the next couple runs and then take a vacation."

Caleb shrugged. "A vacation would be nice. Where are you thinking, Florida?"

"Fuck Florida. I don't know. I've never really thought about a vacation. Maybe buy the boat and just anchor off the coast for a month, just far enough out so I don't have to see land."

"You going to invite me or Ava?"

"Neither of you. I said I wanted a vacation."

"You're a dick. What time do you want to go check out the church? I won't be around until after ten."

"Eleven, then. It's rural. There's really no reason to have to wait until three in the morning. What do you have to do?"

"I have a date with a bartender."

"What's his name?"

"Piss off. She works down at the beach. I bet she's a freak."

"Why do you say that?"

"Because female bartenders are either dykes or freaks. We have a date, so I'm guessing she's a freak."

"You going to wear one of your suits?"

Caleb shook his head behind his cupped hands as he lit another cigarette. "Take your bitch." He stuffed his lighter into his jacket pocket and lifted the knotted coil of rope. "She likes crotch, by the way. When she's not sniffing other dog's piss and shit, that's where she heads." He stood and slapped grit from his palms against his pants.

"I guess you can skip the foreplay with the bartender."

"True." Caleb crossed the road to his car. Amos took the dog upstairs.

Ariel lapped fresh water from a bowl he put in the bathroom for her before he left.

* * *

Tommy sat at the bar rummaging through receipts and loose cash. The barback swept cigarette ashes off the pool tables. Old English lettering tattoos ran down the backs of both of his forearms. Something ambiguous and vapid like "family" or "pride" or "respect" but Amos couldn't make out the words.

Tommy spun from the barstool and stood next to Amos. "Justin, come here, I want you to meet Amos Swain."

Justin paused and looked up across the room. "What up?" He continued working.

Tommy shook his head. "Kid's got a little attitude problem."

"I can see that. He pissed Caleb off the other night."

"Guess he's lucky to be walking."

"Can we talk for a minute?"

"Business?"

"Yeah."

"Hey Justin, go sweep off the walkway."

"I already did that."

Tommy's voice hurled into the air toward the kid. "Fucking do it again."

Justin grumbled on his way toward the door and grabbed the push broom and his jacket on his way out. Amos took a stool next to Tommy. The heating vent pushed warm hugs of air over them. Corners of receipts and cash waved off the bar. Tommy pushed them into a pile off to the side and lit a cigarillo.

"What's up?"

"There's a church up on 202 past Alfred. I think Kenny Kavanagh is filtering money through it."

Tommy lifted his eyebrows. "Kavanagh, hunh?"

Tommy got up and poured them two shots of Turkey. He placed the bottle next to the receipts then climbed back into his stool. He sighed, lifted his shot glass and they drank. Amos shook the burn down his throat. Tommy cracked his knuckles. "Wow. That's fucking genius. A church? You sure it was him?"

"Positive."

"Who's the pastor?"

"Roberts."

"Roberts?"

"Yeah."

"Sounds familiar. Anyway, you think Kavanagh is running his money through that?" He fingered a loose eyelash from his eye.

"I think it's where he's stashing. I didn't see him leave with anything. I'm almost positive the money's in the church."

"As long as he doesn't find out it was you, you'll be fine, obviously. If he does you two will have a major battle on your hands. Kavanagh's no joke." Tommy put his cigarillo out and lit another. "What were you doing in church anyway?"

"Girl."

"Oh. I see. Not that gorgeous little spinner with you on your birthday, was it?"

"Yeah."

"Good job, Amos. She's a cocker. Just remember what I told you about women. They have the best and worst things to happen to men."

"Mouth and pussy, Tommy. I remember. I'll see you later."

Amos grabbed a newspaper from the bar and passed through Justin's glare outside.

He laid out the paper for Ariel. There was nothing important she could chew so Amos left her sniffing around the house and took a nap on the couch. Jones's words crept into the unrest of his situation, his life. A vacation, the thought of one, leaving temporarily and coming back felt unsettling.

Caleb pressed his fingers against Amos's nose to wake him. A sweet, sweaty smell polluted his nostrils. Amos opened his eyes and slapped Caleb's hand away. Caleb grinned like he'd tied the corners of his lips together with a string around his head.

"Told you she was a freak." He chuckled.

Amos stretched the compression from his back and sat up. "So you fingered her. Most girls like that. How does that make her a freak?"

"Not that. She started blowing me. Then, she stuck her finger in my ass."

"Did you like it?"

"No. I freaked out. Guess what she told me after that."

"What?"

"That if I didn't like it, it made me borderline gay."

"What?"

"Exactly."

"So, because you don't like something in your ass that makes you borderline gay?"

"That's what she said."

"Christ, Caleb. Where do you find these women?"

He shrugged. "Usually shitfaced and close to passing out."

He slumped on the couch next to Amos. Another odor began to settle in Amos's throat. A gag pressed against the back of his tongue. "Man, what is that smell? Where else did you put your fingers? It smells like shit."

"Check by the door. I think you need to work on house-breaking the puppy."

Amos looked over Caleb's shoulder at the brown, soupy puddle big enough to make him wonder how something that small could release such an amount of shit and odor. Amos had to pull the neck of his shirt over his nose to keep from puking and used the newspaper and a towel to clean up Ariel's mess.

Caleb had his feet on the coffee table and his fingers laced behind his head. "Must've been the Chinese. I had to stop on my way to that girl's house." He dropped his feet and hands and turned to Amos. "It was similar in texture." He laughed.

"Asshole." Amos shook his head and tossed the bag by the door.

Ariel was in the bathroom lying beside the toilet. Amos could still smell shit and after looking around his room, he found another puddle centered on the inside of Caleb's new suit coat on the floor. The sleeve was torn. A broken hook from a plastic hanger lay beside it. Amos balled the coat up and carried it into the kitchen. The smile on Caleb's face faded.

"Is that my coat?"

"Yep."

"Fuck."

"Must've been the Chinese. It was similar in texture."

"Oh, that's…" He crossed his arms and shook his head. "Are you serious?" He slapped the armrest and cushion simultaneously. "Are you fucking with me?"

"Oh. I'm serious. Do you want to see for yourself?"

"No." He held his palm toward Amos. "I hate animals."

Caleb bitched about his suit coat all the way to the church.

While Caleb and Amos trudged through the snow at the rear of the church to check it out, Amos began to think of how Ava would react if she found out the church she'd brought him to was robbed. There was the chance that she wouldn't find out, considering whose money they were taking. Roberts probably wouldn't report it. Amos knew he could explain after, how the money wasn't really the church's.

THIRTY-THREE
Amos

Easter Sunday morning, Ava climbed into his bed, approaching him for a kiss when Ariel found her way from beneath the sheets. Ava crawled over him and scooped up the puppy. She squinted and let Ariel drench her face with slobber. Minutes later, she put the puppy on the floor, washed her face in the bathroom, and began undressing. The whisper of fabric over her skin and the quick snaps of static electricity opened his eyes. He rolled toward her as she crawled onto the bed. Her lips went to his neck and she kissed him. More kissing followed over the tattoo across his collarbone, then down his sternum and over his stomach. Her fingernails followed on either side of his body scraping down his ribs to the ticklish parts of his skin between the bottom of his abdomen and hip bone. He was throbbing—feeling her chin and the sides of her face rub against his hard-on. She came back up, kissed the other side of his neck, and repeated the process. Amos reached for the clasp on her bra, but she stopped him, laced her fingers into his, and continued kissing.

The puppy whined at the foot of the bed. Ava gave a final kiss and a vixen smile, then climbed off Amos to scoop up Ariel and hold the puppy against her face. Amos thought his dick was going to explode and curl down like a shotgun barrel fired underwater. Ava sat at the corner of the bed with her legs crossed. Ariel panted over her shoulder at him and he gave her the finger. Her tongue spilled out of her mouth and a line of drool wet Ava's bra strap.

"When did you get a puppy?"

"It's my sister's. My mother doesn't want it at her house."

"Oh, but it's so adorable. Does it have a name?"

"Cunt."

"Shut up. What's her name?"

"Oh, the puppy?"

She gasped. "Did you just call me a cunt?"

"I would never. The puppy's name is Ariel."

"That's precious." Ava and the dog rubbed noses. Small muscles in her back flexed as she moved the puppy to cradle it and scratch beneath its chin. She placed it back on the floor and curled up against his ribs.

"So, happy Easter."

"Yes, happy Jew-zombie day."

She lifted herself with an elbow and looked at him. Her eyes moved back and forth across Amos's. "When did you get all your tattoos?"

"When I got out of prison."

"Oh yeah." She placed her head back on his chest. "The Bowdoin thing."

"So you know about that."

"I read a few of the articles. Someone testified against you, but they recovered the money so you got a lesser sentence. Why'd you do it?

"Tuition."

"Seriously? That worked out well. Where'd you learn to break into a safe, anyway?"

"College."

"What else did you learn, besides that and how to fuck?"

"Whoa. The language on you, woman."

Ava bit her lip and looked up at him. "I'm not that little high school girl anymore."

"I noticed."

"Which is why I'm not so sure about this, Moss."

"What?"

"You're dangerous. Sometimes, that scares me. I don't want to be scared anymore."

"What do you mean, anymore?"

"Forget it."

"No. What did you mean?"

"I don't want to talk about it before church. Go take a shower so we can get some breakfast."

When Amos was ready, they only had enough time to grab coffee and a couple bagels. At the church they shambled into the congregation among the elderly with their walkers and pacemakers and middle-aged couples with their children taking reluctant steps. The volume of people moving into the church made it difficult for Amos to keep his patience. They sat four rows from the back between an elderly woman who smelled of mothballs and cats, and two young children who, throughout the procession, swung their feet kicking the pew in front of them.

Because of the amount of people entering the church and taking a while to find seats, Pastor Roberts started his sermon a half hour late. And, because it was Easter, it lasted an extra hour and a half. Enough time for Roberts to pass the offering plate around four times instead of the usual two. Ava caught Amos putting pennies in the plate and glared at him. She didn't offer anything. He threw a ten in the last time it came around. Fuck it, he thought. He knew he'd get it back later. Most of the service he checked for exits, motion sensors, if the windows were locked, and Kavanagh, who wasn't in attendance.

Roberts dragged through the sermon, most of the time holding his arms outstretched and mimicking the cross behind him. Amos only half listened, catching bits and pieces of the rant. During that time, he looked for cops who may have been there watching Kavanagh. Every parishioner seemed too intent on the sermon to be a cop. With Kavanagh not in church that day, Amos gave up trying to spot them.

Roberts opened his closing prayer with *the sun sets day by day on the just and the unjust alike.* Amos had a thing for quotes and pushed them into his memory like sticks in the mud. The people who were *just* worked nine to fives and had mortgages and families and responsibilities. All of them struggled to make a better life hoping their children would make an even better one for themselves. The *just* were the people who got cancer and died in car wrecks; they fell from boats and drowned. They wandered through their despair with a hand reaching up to God to help them. Faith is funny that way—able to soften the pains of living just enough to make life bearable until death.

Total crock of shit.

Ava and Amos sat in her car waiting for the elderly to back out of their parking spaces—the slow, blind, backward move where they expected other drivers to pay attention to their driving as well. Sometimes, he hated the elderly. The only thing they had left to wait for was death, like the rest of them, but their wait was shorter. Ava rested her palm over his knuckles and quietly sang the song playing on the radio while they waited.

"Let's go do something," she said.

"Like what?"

"I don't know. I want to go do something."

"How about the beach?"

"Still obsessed with the ocean?"

"Yeah, but I don't think of it as an obsession."

She shot him a wink and pulled her car out and got onto the road. Amos was tired and his back hurt from the pews. He worked out the details of the job while she drove to Kennebunkport, down the road from where they'd had dinner. Amos directed her to the boatyard and they got out.

"What are we doing here? I thought you wanted to go to the beach."

"I do, but I'd like to show you something first."

She took his hand and he led her to the back corner of the lot where his father's boat was kept. The white cover was drawn tight. Amos ran his hand down the hull and wondered why he'd brought her there. Maybe he thought she would be as nostalgic as he was.

They were sixteen when the tension of dry humping and mauling each other's genitals through their clothes put them at a borderline level of violence. They were on the boat and Amos's father had gone to get some things from the store. Ava had kept Amos at bay for almost a year. They sat across from each other on the deck after an aggressive bout of groping with their flesh sticking to the boat. The sun was directly behind her. She had her head down running her fingers over the tourmaline necklace he had placed around her neck earlier that day. Without saying a word she stood, took his hand and led him below deck. It was clumsy and confusing. They didn't know how to make their bodies move together. He assumed it would have been as simple as how he'd thought about it, but it was awkward, like pushing his legs through heavy, wet jeans.

"I remember this boat." She kissed Amos's cheek.

"Too bad it's covered."

She grabbed his hand with both of hers.

"My mother sold it when my dad died."

"Why the fuck did she do that?" She pulled her hands from his.

"I don't know. I'm buying it back."

"Then what are you going to do?"

"Put it in the water and get the fuck away from here for a while."

She bowed her head, a brief look of disappointment swept across her cheeks snatching the smile from her face.

"What do you mean?"

"I don't want to be *Swain's Pain* for the rest of my life."

"Who do you want to be?"

"I was thinking I'd teach kindergarten. I think I'd enjoy nap time."

"Not *what*, Amos. Who?"

He couldn't think of an answer.

THIRTY-FOUR
Caleb

Caleb spent the morning pacing in his living room. He was ready for the job that night, but the prospect of freelancing himself for a job that Amos turned down seemed far more betraying than hiding the extortion his FBI friend inflicted on him. As much as that made him feel like a coward, wrench work on a woman disgusted him with his current position. Four months ago, he'd have never entertained the thought of hurting a female. He felt his choices dwindling. Jones would eventually get them on something, unless they laid things to rest for a while, let the surge of dealers rise again, easy pickings. He had to shake the fed, get him to a point that it wasn't worth squeezing him anymore. They'd lay low, hang out at Logan's and pick up again in a year. For now, though, Caleb needed the money, some breathing room, a chance to confess to Amos. He pulled his jacket from the nail in the wall next to his door and went out to his car.

Two boys stood at the door in white cotton shirts, clip-on black ties, heavy parkas, and a book in each of their hands— Jehovah's Witnesses—wide-eyed and frozen in shock at Vassar who was standing at the door with a shotgun when Caleb pulled in the driveway. They turned to walk away as Caleb got out of his car, but Vassar hopped down from the doorway and ran in front of them. Caleb wondered, for a moment, about the witness part of their title. It seemed sinister, especially in the context that he thought of witnesses. They were certainly about to witness fear.

"Hell, no. You boys want to come to my house to tell me shit about God then let's have it. Bring your Bible-thumping asses in here."

The boys stopped walking and looked at each other. Their breathing was heavier, chugging from their mouths and over their shoulders like the grim, billowing smoke of a house fire. Both of them looked at the other for an answer. After a short moment of bulging eye movements and Vassar's corralling with his shotgun, they moved back to the house with their hands clenched around their Bibles.

Vassar looked at Caleb. "You're just in time for the sermon." He grinned and widened his eyes then guided the boys to the couch.

They sat close to each other, wiped the palms of their hands on their pant legs, and then placed them back on the Bibles resting on their knees. One of them had eyebrows as pale as his hair and unsettling light blue eyes that dumped a gaze over Vassar like a bucket of frigid water. The other boy parted his hair and struggled with the onset of acne that was making its way down his neck. He rubbed his thumbs in circles on the bound corners of his Bible.

"You guys want a beer?" Vassar asked as he put the shotgun on the table in front of Farrah.

They shook their heads. Farrah dropped her cigarette. It rolled through one of the cracks on the table to the floor. She bent down to try to retrieve it. Vassar leaned over her to do a line, humping the back of her head and sticking his tongue out at the Jehovah's. He tapped the plastic tube against the phone book and did another. Words came from him almost too difficult to make out as he held his nose with his head back.

"So tell me. What is the purpose of you going door to door

to convert people to your religion?" He snorted hard and shook his head, gagged, snorted, hocked, and then swallowed.

"Our purpose is to share our knowledge with others," the blue-eyed kid said, softly.

"Oh, really, Blue Eyes. Then why not just stick your magazines and pamphlets in their mailboxes? Why do you have to knock on the door?"

Farrah finally reached her cigarette. Caleb sat at the table and faced the boys sitting on Vassar's sofa.

"We feel that person-to-person contact is important in spreading the Word," Blue Eyes said.

"I have a few words." Vassar stood in front of them. "Fuck you and your fucking Jehovah bullshit."

Blue Eyes didn't flinch. His answers had been quick. He wasn't nervous or scared. The other kid was probably on the verge of shitting himself if he hadn't already, but Blue Eyes didn't release the faintest hint of fear. In fact, his hands were clasped and resting on his Bible. His shoulders were relaxed. He was poised with his chin extended in confidence.

"Sir," Blue Eyes said, "this is your home. I meant no disrespect to you or your friends." He waved his palm toward Caleb and Farrah.

Vassar pointed to them, the end of a cigarette bobbing in his mouth. He lit it as he spoke, cupping the flame. "These guys? These guys aren't my friends. This little cunt right here…" Vassar palmed her head and shook it aggressively. Her hair flailed and she slapped at his forearm. "Is just a little fuck toy and she sucks a mean cock so I let her hang around."

Vassar gave her head a shove and she cursed him and stormed into the other room.

The Jehovah boys were fucked. They didn't know what to think about that, not even Blue Eyes. His face tightened and he moved his shoulders back and forth to relieve his discomfort. Caleb felt discomfort, too. He wanted to leave. He didn't know what Vassar was going to do and he didn't want to be around to witness it.

"You guys do drugs?" Vassar asked.

"No," said Blue Eyes.

"Um. No," said the other.

"Not even coke? Fuck. You two don't know what you're missing. You two ever been laid?"

"I'm sorry?" Blue Eyes swallowed.

"You know. You ever stuck your dick in a nice hot piece of cunt. I bet you guys got a lot of that fresh stuff running around. All nice smelling with those fucking fourteen-year-old starter tits. C'mon. I won't tell on you."

"No. We haven't."

"But you've thought about it. Yeah, you have. Don't lie." Vassar chopped his fingers at them.

They pushed back on the couch. Blue Eyes placed his Bible on the cushion beside him. Caleb fixed his attention on the boys, waiting for them to tell Vassar something that mocked their purity. Blue Eyes looked down then at Caleb.

"Well, there is one girl," he said.

"Ha. See. I knew it. You slipped your hand up her shirt yet?"

"No. Nothing like that. We just sit together at service. She is hot."

"Blonde or Brunette?"

"Redhead."

"Even better. Fire crotch. But in a good way." Vassar held his palms toward the boys. "Stay away from the other kind. They'll give you a great fuck and then your dick will leak like a broken faucet."

Blue Eyes gave a confused look.

"Well, at least you're not a fag. What about your buddy?"

"No, he doesn't like any girls."

"So he's a fag?"

"No. I mean he likes girls just none at our church."

"You sure. You never know. You don't take showers together after gym, do you?"

"No."

"If you do, keep your back to the wall. Your buddy might get jumpy with a finger or that third leg. If you want some pussy just let me know. There's a good piece in the next room you can have for fifty bucks."

"Fuck you, Vassar," Farrah yelled.

Vassar laughed and mouthed fifty to the boys holding up his hand with outstretched fingers then nodded and thumbed toward Farrah.

"We're fine. Thanks for the offer."

"Fuck you, too. You little faggots," Farrah yelled again.

"Do you guys jerk off?" He leaned against the chair making masturbation gestures with his cigarette hand.

"No."

"Fucking liars." Vassar made large swooping movements with his hands. "Okay, okay, enough with all that. So why do you guys try to stay so, I don't know, righteous?"

"Because we want to go to Heaven."

"Yeah, but a piece of ass isn't going to keep you out of Heaven, is it?"

"Maybe. Maybe not. We know that God is always watching us."

"Even when you jerk off?"

The boys smiled and there was almost the hint of laughter hidden in their throats, but they managed to hold it back. Caleb lit another cigarette. Vassar did another line and the boys peered at the phone book.

"Why do you do drugs?" Blue Eyes asked.

"Good question." Vassar took a drag and exhaled toward the ceiling. "Because it keeps me from killing little purified fuckers like you." He snorted away a line. "You two ever shot a gun?"

"I shot my friend's shotgun once. It hurt."

Vassar pulled a Ruger 9mm from the silverware drawer. Smoke shot from his nose as he turned back to them. He put the cigarette out in the ashtray then his eyes came back up to

Caleb's and locked like gears fitting into place. Silence. Caleb shuffled his feet in discomfort. Vassar didn't blink. In his eyes there was nothing—not the hint of humor or passion or even anger, simply dark irises focused on some distant point. He blinked and looked toward Blue Eyes.

"You two come on outside." Vassar tucked the gun into his belt. He lit another cigarette. The boys followed him.

THIRTY-FIVE
Amos

Detective Jones and his partner Alex Curry were parked in front of Amos's building when he and Ava arrived. Jones and Curry approached them as they got out of Ava's car.

"What's going on?" Ava moved behind Amos.

"Nothing. Just bullshit."

"Amos, I see you've found more attractive interests. Where were you this afternoon?" Jones asked.

"The beach."

Detective Jones swept an open palm toward his partner. By the color of Jones's teeth, he hadn't been drinking anything but coffee. "You remember my partner, Detective Curry?"

Curry cleared his throat and pointed at Ava. "Is that where you found this little spinner?"

"Actually, I was making sure the tide was high enough for your wife to surface. I heard she's been going down a lot."

"You are a funny guy." Curry pulled the flap of his jacket behind his pistol.

"So you're back now, Alex? Ready to stop crime?" Amos asked.

"Something like that."

"Baby steps, right?"

Curry squinted.

Jones spoke. "We found him."

"Who?"

"You know who we're talking about?"

"No, I don't. Are you talking about one of the twelve cops who fucked Alex's wife or the other twelve guys who aren't cops?"

"Bobby Sisk. You know, the guy who clipped you."

"Congratulations, Detective. I hope you're going to charge him with attempted murder."

"He's got a lot to say." Jones's left eye twitched. "We highly recommend you come down and talk to us. Last chance to give your side of the story."

"I'm a little busy right now."

Jones shook his head. Alex hadn't stopped staring at Ava. She squeezed Amos's hand.

"Good looking girl, Amos," Alex said. "Boy, I'd really like to have something nice like that to come home to. Nice hair. Nice eyes. She even has a nice mouth." He reached over Amos's shoulder toward Ava's face. Amos was about to break his arm when she spoke up.

"You touch me, asshole, and I'll knock your fucking teeth out." Her eyes had narrowed, and she'd moved her right foot back as if she were preparing to throw a kick.

Alex drew his hand back and covered his mouth. "Tell me, hun. How much does it cost for a good call girl these days?"

"Why would I need to pay when I could just swing by your wife's house and stand in line?" Amos said. "But, then again, if she saw me then I wouldn't have to stand in line."

Alex clenched his jaw. Ava's grip on his hand relaxed.

"I'm kidding, Curry. Relax. There was never a line." Amos spit on the sidewalk. "But I did fuck your wife in the ass one Wednesday morning right before you two went to your marriage counseling session. She wore her yellow Victoria's Secret bra and panties that day."

Ava dropped her hand from his and folded her arms. Amos

slipped his right hand into his pocket. A vein throbbed on Alex's temple.

"But she didn't wear the panties to your session, because I took them." He pulled a yellow pair of panties from his pocket and held it in front of Alex's face.

Alex whipped out his pistol and slapped the trigger guard against Amos's right eyebrow. His head snapped back and when it came forward the barrel of Alex's Glock was inches from his face. Ava grabbed and squeezed his knuckles. The wallop lingered for a minute then a small line of blood seeped onto his eyelid. It forced him to blink. It had been exactly what he needed to get some space from Curry.

Jones grabbed Curry's shoulder. "Let's fucking go."

"Keep runnin' that mouth, Swain." Alex drew his gun back and holstered it and the two of them walked away.

"You know, Detective, maybe I should come down to the station and file a complaint. I even have a witness this time."

"We're a little busy today," Jones said over his shoulder.

The blood began freezing against the hairs of Amos's eyebrow. His hands were steady. Jones looked over his shoulder at Amos then to the ground behind Alex's feet.

When he made eye contact with her, Ava was glaring at him.

"What?" he asked her.

"Are you fucking kidding me right now?"

"I used a condom."

She clenched her teeth and balled her fist in his face.

"Holy fuck, Ava. I'm kidding. I just said that shit so he would lose his cool and I'd have some leverage so he'd leave me the fuck alone."

"Then whose panties are those?"

"Do you really want to know?"

She put her hands on her hips.

"You remember that old bitty sitting at the end of our pew? Well, when I went to the bathroom she followed me into the..."

Ava punched his chest. "Shut the fuck up. Let's go. I'm cold."

In the apartment, Ava touched the gash in Amos's eyebrow with her pinky. "He can't hit you like that. Even if you did fuck his wife."

"Those are the perks."

"You might need stitches."

"I'll be all right. Let's go upstairs."

Amos crawled onto the bed and put the clean side of his face on a pillow. The puppy yapped at the foot of the bed and Amos tossed the other pillow at her. It spooked and ran under the box spring. Thoughts of the score flared in Amos's mind. He was so close—close to having options. He could take the jobs he wanted and leave the nickel-and-dime shit to someone else. Ava went past him into the bathroom. She rummaged around for a minute then came out with some peroxide and a towel. She stood there scanning him from head to toe.

"Roll over." She sat on the edge of the mattress and crossed her legs. She dabbed the towel with peroxide and cleaned the blood away from Amos's face. Her eyes moved from his to the wound. Mostly they stared into his.

"What are you staring at?"

"You're trouble," she said, finishing up. "I'm getting tired of fixing you up, stud. I'm not a corner man." She stood and brushed the straps of her dress off her shoulders and let it slip to the floor. She killed the light in the bathroom and climbed into bed.

Post-coital, Amos stared at the textured ceiling and listened to her pen grind against the paper in her journal. He'd never been a fan of writing things down, but watching Ava write with him close to her gave him comfort. When she finished, she dropped the notebook on the floor and smoothed the bed sheets over her stomach.

"My aunt asked me if I'd seen you."

"Did you tell her, naked?" Amos curled strands of her hair around his index finger.

"Right. That would have gone over well."

"She's a huge fan then, hunh?"

"She thinks you're dangerous, but I'm sure she won't say anything to my parents."

"Yeah, I think I get it. Your family hates me."

She rolled to her side to face him. "Moss, I'm sorry. I didn't mean it to sound that way."

"Then how did you mean it? I don't expect your aunt to invite me over for dinner. I understand I'm not liked. I don't need you to remind me constantly."

"Maybe I should go."

"Really? I don't want to listen to you tell me how much your family hates me, and that makes you want to leave?"

"Goddammit, that's not what I was trying to say. I don't like it when you raise your voice. It scares me."

"We're back to that, now. Are you even going to tell me what's going on with you, what you were talking about earlier?"

She bit her lip. "I've been hurt, Moss. It's hard for me to trust men."

"Yeah, well you hurt *me*. Should I trust you?"

"That was fucking high school, and I didn't have a choice. Do you actually blame me for that? For my parents making me move?"

"No. I don't. That was a shitty thing to say to you. I'm sorry. But it did hurt. Actually, it fucking killed me inside to lose you."

Her voice lowered. Her eyes went moist. "I should go."

An ache drenched through his chest. "Ava…"

"What?"

"The door's right behind you."

THIRTY-SIX
Caleb

Caleb followed Vassar and the boys outside, keeping his hand on his pistol. If Vassar killed them, which Caleb was sure was about to happen, he'd have no choice but to put bullets of his own into Vassar. The sun was setting just over the trees behind Vassar's house, burning the clouds to pink mist. Vassar pointed at a metal sap bucket roped to a tree branch twenty yards behind the house. Blue Eyes held his hand over his eyes to block the glare. Vassar busted off five rounds. A flock of small birds fluttered from the trees to the right and flew straight up then arced down and dropped. Small chirps and the rattle of red squirrels emitted from dark places in the trees. Blue Eyes studied the gun Vassar held out to him then passed his Bible to the other boy and grabbed the pistol. He held it, rubbed his fingers over the steel as if the gun was as vulnerable as the things it could damage. The muzzle wavered as he held it aimed toward the bucket until he shot. The animals became quiet. He handed the gun back and took the Bibles. Vassar handed the gun to the other boy who shot twice. Vassar flicked his cigarette and took the gun. He took aim at the bucket and fired the last two rounds. The bucket spun when he hit it. Vassar hit the slide release and the chamber slapped shut.

"How was that, boys?"

"That was cool."

"That's not going to send you to hell, is it?"

"No."

"So you're both going to Heaven, right?" Vassar tapped the muzzle against his leg and the change in his pocket. His lips parted slightly. Behind his glare, Caleb could see the lack of compassion he had for anything, especially life.

"Well, we hope so."

"If you died right now, would you go to Heaven?" He tapped faster.

The boys looked at each other. The other boy moved behind Blue Eyes.

"What do you mean?"

Vassar took a step toward Blue Eyes and put the barrel against the boy's head. "I mean, you fucking smug, Bible-thumping motherfucker, if I pull this trigger right now and blow your fucking brains all over your buddy behind you, are you going to go to Heaven?"

The boy stuttered, "I-I-I-I."

"Answer the fucking question," Vassar shouted. His voice boomed over the quiet and sent silence retreating into the darkness with the animals. "Are you going to go to Heaven? I know I'm not going. I'm going straight to Hell with this mother-fucker, so if I blast pieces of your skull all over what remains of the snow on the ground nothing different is going to happen to me."

Tears ran down Blue Eyes' face. His entire body quivered. Tiny spasms shook his shoulders and the Bibles fell to the ground at his feet. The sides of his nose sucked in as he panted. His body was in a state of panic—confused—trying to breathe in and out at the same time. The boy behind him took in thin, raspy breaths. The gun was unloaded, but only Vassar and Caleb knew that.

"If you can't answer that question then you should rethink your faith because one day you will be dead and there won't be a chance for you to reevaluate the time you've wasted believing in some bullshit you're not even sure of."

"Vassar, cut the shit, man," Caleb said.

"Tell me Blue Eyes, are you ready to die?"

Blue Eyes squinted and more tears ran. Vassar pulled the trigger and the firing pin clicked. The boy dropped to his knees. Vassar stepped back. "Get up and walk." He motioned him up with the barrel of the gun. Vassar went back inside.

Caleb tucked his piece away and went to Blue Eyes to help him to his feet, pulling him up beneath his arms. He scooped up the Bibles and tossed them in the back seat as the boys climbed into the car. The other boy lunged for them and pulled them close to his chest.

Vassar erupted in laughter when Caleb entered the house. Farrah slammed things around in the back room. "How was that for some Easter entertainment?" Vassar asked.

"You're fucking twisted, man."

"Yeah, I know. What the fuck are you doing here anyway?"

"Well, Moss said you offered him some wrench work. I want it."

"Just like that, hunh?"

"If you haven't already shopped it."

"Nope. But what is Moss going to say?"

"Let's just keep this between us, alright."

Vassar tapped his pockets and lifted the various items on the table. "Where the fuck did I put that card? What did Moss tell you about it?"

"Said it was a little too grimy for his taste."

Vassar snickered. "Fucking guy sees himself wrapped in the American flag holding the Bible, doesn't he?"

"Nah. I just think he's a person of higher moral character than you or me."

Vassar had moved to the cupboards. "Where the fuck did I put that fucking card?"

"You need some help looking?"

"No. Fuck it." Vassar ripped an envelope in half and wrote a number on it with a broken pencil. "Call this guy. His name's Richard. He'll fill you in."

"How much?"

"I told him ten and then, of course, there's a finder's fee."

"Five percent?"

"Ten. And I'll have Farrah suck you off."

"I'll suck his cock for free you piece of shit," Farrah called from the back room.

Vassar shrugged.

"I'd love to, Farrah," Caleb called. "But I have to get back to town. What's the timeline on this?"

"Yeah, you better call him tonight. He wants shit done soon. Tomorrow, I think."

"Jesus, that's quick."

"He's not a patient guy."

THIRTY-SEVEN
Amos

Amos drifted in and out of sleep. The puppy found a resting spot between his legs again. The sound of Caleb's car thundering in circles out in the parking lot pulled him from bed. Ariel began an attempt to scratch behind her ear with her hind leg but missed and scraped the inside of his thigh. Caleb tromped up the stairs and came into the apartment. He tossed the sheets over Ariel and her body wobbled as she found an exit and moved toward Caleb.

"Why the fuck are you in bed?"

"Because I was fucking in the bed."

"When are we leaving?"

"I need coffee."

"What the hell happened to your eye?"

"Foreplay."

Amos kept the apartment dark and watched the sporadic traffic outside. Caleb packed the tools and other essentials for the job. A pellet pistol, ice pick, two power drills with backup batteries, drill bits, mini sledgehammer, two punch rods, flat bar, ski masks, an extra duffel bag, gloves, pepper spray, ASP batons, and voice controlled two-way radio headsets. They scrambled into coveralls, loaded the truck, and left.

Cigarette smoke filled the cab of Amos's truck before they

151

were halfway to the church and Caleb cupped his hands over the cherry to keep them warm. He hadn't exhaled anything but smoke. The coveralls bunched in Amos's crotch and armpits, where it fit tighter over the layers of clothing. Headlights, black tar, yellow and white lines and ice creeping from the snowbanks onto the shoulders were the only things on the road. When they got to the church, Caleb smoked another cigarette before they made their way through the woods.

At the edge of the woods, they watched for movement until Amos's knees began to ache. Caleb leaned against a small pine scanning the buildings across the street. The windows of Pastor Roberts's house showed murky reflections of the iced-over tree branches. They skirted the edge of the dark out of reach from the floodlight on the back of Roberts's house and moved to a window at the back of the church. Caleb moved to the edge of the building and watched around the corner while Amos stood and shot a hole through the window with the pellet gun. The slapping sound of the discharge echoed against the trees and the back of the church. He put the ice pick through the hole and moved the latch enough to unlock the window. Amos slid the window up and crawled into the darkness.

Inside the church, he fit in the earpiece of his two-way radio and turned it on. Caleb inserted his, then moved back to the edge of the woods and continued scanning. Amos sat beneath the window allowing his eyes to adjust and listened for anything outside. There was a picture on the wall, but he couldn't tell what. A picture of Jesus? Churches didn't have many pictures besides that. The room was carpeted and smelled like damp cement. The safe was in the next room.

After a deep, solid breath, Amos tasted the mustiness in the room and moved through the door into the congregation area. The pews sat long and open like rows of coffins. The office door was locked. Before the doorknob finished rattling, Amos kicked it open. Screws through the hinges ripped from the jamb and the door teetered backwards on the bottom corners and fell to the floor. Papers fluttered on the wall.

The desk drawers were empty except for a few scattered pens and pads of yellow legal paper. The safe was bolted to the floor along with the desk, so he had to squat beneath it holding a pen light in his mouth. The metal was cold and tasteless like something a dentist would use. Saliva seeped from the corners of his lips. After spinning the dial to the try out numbers, combinations pretty much universal with safe manufacturers, and no luck, Amos clamped the drill brackets on the safe and started drilling into the lock face.

The first few seconds of the drill grinding instantly placed him inside the cold office of that restaurant where he'd taken down the first safe. What he thought about the first time he did a safe he began thinking about again—his father and the last time he'd seen him alive.

They'd sailed the entire morning without speaking. The only sounds that morning were the wind thudding into the sails and the slapping of the bow cutting through the waves. His father's calloused hands and mangled fingers worked the helm to maneuver the boat between lobster buoys. Sunlight shimmered off the sweat of his shoulders and frozen cones of light in the waves. At midday they dropped the sails and anchored off the Isles of Shoals. Seneca was only a few weeks old, and Amos's father needed the quiet. Amos kept his face in a book by Celine until night came and the starlight stabbed through the black skin of the sky.

His father spoke then, only to point out constellations—a ritual they'd had when Amos had been a kid. When Amos was a kid, though, his father pointed them out through the fourth-floor apartment window. They were poor and Amos's mother spent nights cutting coupons—humming while the crisp slice of the scissors saved his parents' money and gave his mother more hope that his father would marry her sooner. His father would point out Ursa Major, Hercules and Scorpio, the beast that killed Orion. Amos would stare into the sky and follow his father's thick finger as he pointed out every star.

Amos's neck cramped from being ducked beneath the desk. The tightness worked its way down the muscles along the edge of his spine. After a few short minutes he had the door open and pulled stacks of cash from it. He'd hoped the safe was empty. Things would have turned out better. Kavanagh came to mind and the duffel bag grew with heft. People had crossed Kavanagh, and they'd paid. They'd ended up with their bones pulverized and in a heap of garbage or they disappeared. Nobody had ever robbed him successfully.

Amos had one leg out of the church window ready to duck through it when headlights hit the trees behind the church. Tires crunched against the gravel. The tools in the duffel bag dug into his back when he rolled back inside the church. The sheriff's cruiser was behind the church before Amos could reach up and shut the window. His heart pounded against his chest like it wanted to jump from his body and leave him there. Another pinch for robbery put Amos in a cell for ten to fifteen. The engine cut off and the lights went out. Confusion. Cops didn't cut their engines off when they arrived on scene, but it was a county officer and in that area they were invalids who couldn't direct traffic on a one-way street.

"Bail," Amos whispered.

"Fuck off. I'm not leaving. There's only one."

The deputy's uniform stretched open between buttons revealing his white undershirt. He spun out of the door, removed his jacket and gun belt and placed them on his seat. A young girl climbed from the passenger side—the wispy fabric of her clothes too thin for the temperature. Both of them got into the back seat of the cruiser. The girl shut her door and the deputy left his open. She opened his pants and went down on him. Palm sweat drenched Amos's gloves.

He pressed his back against the wall. A wind picked up and came through the window whispering in the corners of the room. Sweat chilled the skin behind his ears. A grunt came from outside and the deputy's shoes kicked over stones. A door closed. Footsteps moved around the car then another door opened and shut.

"Son of a bitch," Caleb whispered.

"What?" Amos asked.

"He's staring at the window."

The girl's voice called, "Hurry the hell up. My father will kill me if he finds out I'm gone."

The deputy's footsteps were quieter as he approached the window. *Click.* A light jumped into the room shining on the small canvas painting of Jesus's crucifixion. Despite his arms being stretched and his ribs crushed, the grin and the angle of his head looking down gave no sense of suffering. Instead, he seemed to be content in his fate as if those around him would suffer one much greater. It was a smile of revenge. Amos clunked through his mind for a thought but there was only the drone of fear—the thumping pulse of a knock underwater. He closed his eyes and pulled a slow breath through his nose, held it, counted to three, exhaled, and pulled the canister of pepper spray from his back pocket.

He pushed closer to the wall and pulled the ski mask over his face. The circle of light grew smaller with each footstep until they stopped, and the end of the deputy's Maglite poked through the open window. The deputy's breath blew against the glass with a slow, quieted wheeze. The light lowered and the deputy's hand poked beyond the sill. The beam moved from the far corner of the room to the other and the deputy's arm, up to his elbow, was inside the room. Amos figured, half hoped, it had been enough time for Caleb to move closer. He dropped the pepper spray and stood, grasping the deputy's forearm with both hands and yanked. The deputy's face came through the glass. He let out a yelp just before glass and wood shattered and splintered. Shards clinked against gravel.

The deputy drew back and dropped the Maglite to clutch his face. The light cart-wheeled over the sill and thumped against the carpet. A half-moon beacon shined at the wall below the window and blood was spattered on the carpet and baseboard. Caleb's footsteps shuffled closer. The smack of an ASP baton silenced the deputy's groaning and he collapsed to the ground. The metal objects of his uniform tinged against small stones. Amos swept the broken glass from the windowsill with the cash-filled duffel bag and pulled himself from the building. Caleb moved toward the cruiser where the girl sat.

Cuts and stripes of blood painted the deputy's face and neck. His cheek mashed into his teeth from the weight of his head against the ground. Exhaled breaths pushed bubbles of blood through the corner of his mouth. His shirt was untucked, arms folded beneath his torso at angles verging on fracture and his shoes were pointed inward. The cuffs of his pants were ruffled and pushed high on his calves. Specks of blood dotted his white socks. Amos's breath was hot against his cheeks as he breathed into the fabric around his mouth. Caleb pulled the girl from the car by her ankle. She screamed and clawed and kicked but when he pulled, her body jerked from the car like a hand from the burn of a flame. Her screams became whimpers and sobs as Caleb held her down.

Amos dragged the deputy to his cruiser. The heels of his shoes made paths in the gravel that widened and narrowed in the shape of hourglasses. Amos tossed an extra set of cuffs from the beacon light over the roof to Caleb for the girl, and he used the deputy's cuffs to secure his wrists. They wrestled the two into the back seat of the cruiser.

The girl whispered, "Please don't kill me."

Amos grabbed the duffel bags and looked up at the lights shining in Roberts's window.

THIRTY-EIGHT
Ava

Shortly after she'd fallen asleep, Ava woke. She wanted to blame it on her dream, but she knew it was just the thoughts preceding that. A new preoccupation took hold, and all the feelings she had that relieved her anger were now abandoned for a sadness so new to her, she'd forgotten how it felt after so many years. In the end, her parents were still right. Moss was not the man she could be with. This, mostly, was the reason she climbed from her bed, dressed, and went back to his apartment. She, like every other time in her life, couldn't accept her parents' vindication. She had to decide for herself. As dangerous as he was, she felt safe with him. For the first time that she could remember she felt safe.

Ava had already told her aunt that she'd be in for the night, so she did her best to slip quietly from the house, which did little to keep the hyper-vigilant woman from sensing the surreptitious movement through the house. The aunt slipped into the hallway behind Ava.

"It's a little late to be heading out, isn't it?"

Ava released the tension she held in her shoulders as she tried to sneak toward the staircase. "Yes, it is." Panic of being caught that she hadn't experienced since she was a teenager reminded her of Amos. She turned to face her aunt with a slight smile on her face.

"Where are you headed?"

"I was going to see Amos."

"It's late."

"He doesn't exactly keep a nine to five schedule."

Her aunt frowned. "Make sure you lock up."

Her aunt went to bed and Ava made her way through the house and outside, abandoning her clandestine attempts to make it out in silence. She shivered in the car as she drove. Amos wasn't home when she arrived, and she thought about heading to Logan's to find him, but the bar would have been closed then. The puppy bounced around her feet playfully and she scooped her up. For a long time, she thought about Amos, about trusting her feelings, especially the sudden turn of them. She swirled her finger around the puppy's ear as it rested on her chest. Eventually, the puppy began its puttering snore.

The living room light went out, and it woke her. The darkness of the apartment was immense, and she could only hear the slow movement of a foot taking a step. She strained to hear in the dark, waiting for another footstep, but her concentration only allowed the rising pace of her heartbeat to throb in her ears. Ava wanted to say something, *Moss? Hello?* But her throat had dried. She stayed motionless in the bed, her sweaty palms clinching the edge of the sheets. The bedroom door was barely visible as she waited for a silhouette to break the plane of darkness. The bathroom light came on behind her and she turned her head slowly, blinded by light, staring, horrified at what stared back.

THIRTY-NINE
Amos

They didn't pull their masks off until the back tires of Amos's truck chirped against the tar. They hadn't spoken until then, just moved in unison through the trees to the truck.

"What the hell was that?" Caleb asked.

"Bad luck."

"It could have been worse for us," he said over a cigarette he was trying to light. He took it out and handed it to Amos then lit another for himself. "If that pig had had his gun…"

The smoke burned in Amos's throat behind his tongue and the taste of it was charred meat.

"How bad do you think you fucked him up?"

"I think the real bitch of it is when someone finds him hand-cuffed with that girl."

They cruised down the road passing small neighborhoods lit up with streetlights. The lights would fade, and Amos and Caleb would become mired in darkness again. The wind blew and the trees swayed as if they were whispering secrets to each other. Amos's face flushed with the green light of the instrument panel. The tires hummed down the road and the engine vibrated through the accelerator and every so often, when another vehicle passed, the window would rattle. All of those little noises with the absence of voice were soothing to Amos.

Then Caleb spoke. "So how are things with Ava?"

"She's yo-yo. One minute she's all over me, the next she's distant, especially after sex." Amos answered so quickly, the question felt as though he'd been waiting the entire night to answer. "She says she's stressed. I don't know."

"Think she has a boyfriend?"

"I hope not. That's bullshit I don't need."

"You spent the night at her house yet?"

"She lives with her aunt."

"She good looking?"

"Her aunt? Actually, yes. Why, do you want her to stick a finger in your ass?"

They laughed for a minute. An occasional chuckle broke on their way back to Caleb's. The two of them moved bills through their fingers until cramps had set in their palms. While they counted, Amos looked around Caleb's house at the things he owned—the items left to him by his grandmother along with the house when she died. He thought of Caleb's attachment to them, why they held on to the past as if it would vindicate the suffering they'd experienced in loss. The count came to $38,800. Amos pulled five thousand from the stack, put it in an envelope, and tossed it over to Caleb, who fumbled it around in his hands.

"What's this for?" he asked.

"It's not all drug money. Make a donation."

He shook his head. "Good score, man."

"I guess I should thank you for convincing me to do this."

"Why would he keep this much money in a church?"

"Who would rob a church? You want to grab something to eat?"

"I'm beat. I'm going to crash. I'll pick up my car tomorrow." He looked away for a moment then snapped his head back to Amos and stared at his T-shirt. He'd finally noticed that Amos had worn a *Jesus Christ* T-shirt. The red shirt's white lettering mimicked the Coca-Cola logo. "I can't believe you wore that.

You're a true shitbag."

"I couldn't find the one that said *Jesus is my homeboy.*"

"Did you get that just for this job?"

Amos shrugged his shoulders.

"Save a seat for me in Hell, will ya?" He shook his head.

They split the cash and put it in paper grocery bags. Caleb gave Amos short, brooding glances during the process. He carried his paper bag into the basement and Amos left.

The light ahead turned red. A police cruiser pulled next to Amos in the turning lane. Through the corner of his eye, Amos watched the cop pull fast food from a bag and put it to his mouth. The cops in town harassed high school kids and skaters or kids who played their music too loud in their cars and wore their hats backwards. Usually, the cops would find some beer in the car or a joint and arrest the kid. Cops were incapable of preventing real crime, and even if they weren't, most of them didn't really give a fuck anyway.

The light changed and they went opposite ways. The cruiser's taillights faded to small red dots in Amos's rearview. His apartment was only a few blocks down and he parked the truck across the street. Another cop drove by and slowed. Amos draped his hoodie over his arm and the paper bag and crossed the street, stopping abruptly before he stepped up on the sidewalk. The kitchen light was on. He never left the light on.

His heart raced and he took each step up to his apartment slowly, one at a time. At the flight of stairs a floor from his apartment, he lifted the first step of the riser and pulled the riot gun from its hiding place. He dropped the bag of money in the step and covered it before heading up to his apartment. Feet twitched beneath the sheets. When he got to the door and pushed it open a few inches, he slipped the barrel into the opening and hit the lights.

In complete darkness, it's best to shut your eyes. Keeping

them open will only eliminate the ability for your other senses to take over. When he got out of prison, Amos spent a lot of time moving around his apartment in the dark. It took him months until he could finally sleep in the bedroom. A person lying in wait in the bed is the smartest way to kill someone. Nobody expects it. They lose their fear, the fear they would have if someone were sitting on the couch or rifling through the drawers in their kitchen. A person in the bed, though, a drunk who wandered into the wrong apartment, a friend who couldn't call, but nobody expects someone to be in there with a shotgun under the sheets. That's all Amos could see behind his eyelids as he made his way into the bedroom.

When he turned on the bathroom light, he barely had time to lower the shotgun as Ava turned her head toward him. She sat up in a white sleeveless undershirt. Her hair was pinned back over her ears and there were faint red lines on her face from sleeping against the wrinkles of the pillowcase. She winced at the sight of the shotgun and scooted up in the bed. The tan mound of her belly showed at the top of her light blue cotton pants. Ariel moved around beneath the sheet.

"It was probably a stupid idea to come here like this," she said, staring at the far wall.

"I'm not so sure it was the smartest idea. You should have told me you were coming over."

"I thought I had some things to talk to you about."

"Not anymore?"

"I'd rather do that when you don't have a rifle in your hand."

"It's a shotgun, baby."

Amos rested the shotgun in the corner by the bathroom door and sat on the edge of the bed. Ariel dropped to the floor, sniffed at the toes of his boots.

"What's on your mind?" he asked.

"Us. This. How difficult it is to make a rational decision."

Amos turned slightly to face her. "And?"

"I don't really know how to say it. I thought I did, but now I don't think I have the words."

"This is a recurring thing with you."

"It's not easy for me. None of this is easy. I can't decide what I want to feel about this or how I should feel about you."

Amos looked up toward the ceiling. When he was finally comfortable to sleep in his bedroom, he spent a lot of time staring at the ceiling, trying to make sense of how the things in his life had settled around him. He had similar questions, but the ambiguity was easier to deal with without waiting for her to make up her mind. He'd been to prison. He'd killed a man. He had a dead father and a mother reluctant to let him see his little sister. All Amos had to decide against was all of the options he didn't have. Ava had to decide if she wanted to pursue an attraction to a man she knew as a teenager and now, only by reputation. In a lot of ways, it wasn't fair to her, but she wasn't offering up a lot of information for him either. Thinking about it made Amos tired.

Ava climbed over the bed toward him. "Maybe we should talk about this in the morning." She pressed her fingers against the tense muscles in his shoulder and kissed the side of his face. Her nose wrinkled. "You smell like cigarettes." She kissed him again, pushing a small bit of her tongue into his mouth then withdrew. "You taste like cigarettes. I didn't think you smoked."

"It's only on rare occasions."

"How rare?" She applied more weight to his shoulders and his neck became stiff.

"About once every two weeks."

She tilted her head to the right looking at him through one eye. "Go brush your teeth. If I wanted to taste ass, I'd lick a toilet seat."

Amos took a shower. When he came out of the bathroom and wiped the toothpaste from the corners of his mouth with a kitchen rag, Ava was curled into a ball on the couch fingering her toes and flicking through the channels.

"So what kind of trouble were you getting into this late at

night?" She didn't stop channel surfing to look at him when she asked.

"Caleb and I went down to the beach."

"What were you doing at the beach this late?" She turned the TV off and rotated on the couch placing her chin on the back.

"Building sandcastles."

She rolled her eyes.

"Do all women do that or just you and my sister?"

"What?"

"Roll your eyes."

"All of us do. None as well as me. I'm a pro."

"No shit."

She pulled on a loose string on the back of the couch. Ariel sat behind it looking up at her.

"Is something wrong?" Amos expected her to want him to retract his bullshit and tell her what he had really done.

"It's really none of my business, but I don't want to be here right now if you were out fucking someone."

Amos almost laughed. "You don't have to worry about that. I'm not sticking my dick in anything but you."

"No?" She took a breath and turned around for a moment then turned again. "I need a kiss."

"Then take me to bed."

FORTY
Kenny

His footsteps thumped over the kitchen floor as he paced. Roberts held his chin over a steaming cup of coffee, his lips quivering with attempted explanation. Kavanagh would stop momentarily in his shamble around the room, sigh deeply, pick up a random object—cookbook, rolling pin, sauté pan, chef's knife—and give his cousin a compassionate but disappointed look. Roberts made a few attempts to say something, but when the slightest bit of sound escaped his mouth, Kavanagh would clear his throat and Roberts would remain silent.

When the cup of coffee in front of Roberts had cooled, Kavanagh finally spoke. "Did my name come up at all?"

"God, no. That deputy was messed up pretty bad, but all he wanted to do was get the fuck out of there. I thought he was going to bleed to death, not to mention the girl."

"Well, I doubt he's going to say anything. How much did they get?"

"Thirty, maybe forty."

Kenny leaned close to his face, baring his teeth.

"Kenny, I'm sorry. I didn't—"

"Don't be fucking sorry. Fix it. Find out who the fuck stole my money."

Roberts lifted his cup to sip his coffee. Kenny backhanded it from his grip. Coffee arced through the room, spraying on the ceiling and the carpet in the living room. The mug fell to the floor. The handle broke off and scattered over the floor and slid beneath the humming radiator.

"How are you going to fix it?"

"I don't know."

"I don't know isn't a good enough fucking answer. *I don't know* is what you said when Bobby Sisk didn't show for a pickup. *I don't know* is what you said when Bobby got plastered all over the fucking papers for trying to what, rob a fucking bar at ten in the morning?"

"What's this deputy's name?"

"I don't—I'll find out."

Roberts had allowed his focus to drift beyond Kenny. Kenny snatched his face and gripped his bottom jaw. "I want this handled quick, understand?"

His focus returned and Roberts nodded.

FORTY-ONE
Amos

Ava slipped into one of his white collared shirts and curled up on the couch with the puppy. The shirt was buttoned up halfway, exposing the slope of her breasts. She'd pulled her knees to her stomach where her elbows rested while she palmed a cup of coffee and blew the steam away before sipping. The window shades let in small teeming rays that spread bands of light across her face and illuminated her eyes to a lighter brown. Ariel rested behind her ass and thighs out of sight except for the occasional twitch of her tail.

It was difficult to get out of bed when she was in it, harder to stay in when she wasn't. The slight whistle in her breath as she slept, the softness of her fingertips against his, the sweeping feathery touch of her eyelashes against his cheek, and all the other affectionate things felt forbidden.

Ariel stirred at Amos's motion and rested her chin on Ava's knee. Her tail shook chaotically, thumping against the leather of the couch. Ava looked up at Amos and smiled. He leaned in for a kiss.

"Ugh. You don't want a kiss. I have bad morning slash coffee breath."

"I don't care."

She tilted her head and puckered her lips. He took the kiss

and started walking back to the bedroom.

"Aren't you forgetting something?"

He turned, bewildered. "I don't know. Am I forgetting something?"

She raised her eyebrows and looked at Ariel. She hadn't moved her chin from Ava's leg. Ava looked back at Amos. "Ariel wants a kiss too."

"Oh she does?"

"Yes."

"I don't kiss bitches."

Ava gasped. "How could you say that? If you don't kiss your puppy, you're not getting laid again."

Amos shrugged. "Meh."

Ava dropped her chin and raised her eyebrows. He leaned over and kissed Ariel on the top of her snout. The dog lashed her tongue at his face.

"Aw. That was sweet."

"Can we go make out now?"

She rolled her eyes and stood to bring her coffee cup to the counter. "Go wash off your hoo-hoo."

"My what?" He asked from the bedroom door.

"Your hoo-hoo."

"What the fuck is a hoo-hoo?"

"Your cock, Amos." She shook her head and took another sip of coffee.

"Why? Did you get it dirty?"

"I'm about to change my mind."

Amos went to the bathroom and washed. She was on the bed when he came out, lying on her side with her eyes closed. His shirt was back on its hanger. There were two moles on her back—one in the middle, a little to the right of her spine, and the other very tiny and high on her right ass cheek. He didn't remember them from their youth. She arched her back from his fingers when he palmed her ribs and she rolled to him.

"Your hands are cold."

A shiver came over him and he crawled under the sheets next to her. For almost an hour he lay there, breathing through his nose against the base of her neck where it met her shoulder, smelling the remnants of her perfume. He wrapped his arm around her, held her bicep, and pushed his erection into her hamstring. She rolled toward him and looked under the sheet then back at him.

"What's he doing?" she asked.

"Waiting for a kiss."

Ruth called for Amos from the living room.

"Who is that?" Ava asked.

"My mother."

"Shit. Really?" Ava asked.

"Ma, what do you need?"

"Are you dressed?"

"Barely."

Ava giggled and slapped lightly at Amos's stomach.

"I need you to watch Seneca for a little while."

"Amos, I'm heeeeeeeeeere," Seneca called.

The puppy tilted its head at her voice.

Ava whispered, "You have a sister?"

Amos slipped into a pair of jeans and went out. Ava put her own clothes back on.

"Where's my puppy?" Seneca puttered, slinging her doll by the arm.

"In the bedroom."

She darted by, smacking the doll's head on the doorframe of his bedroom as she passed through it.

"Is this a bad time?" Ruth glared at Ava.

"Would it matter?"

"I'm Ruth. Amos's mother. And you are?"

Ava had been smiling. She snapped her bangs out of her face and looked at Amos.

"Ava, Mother."

"Oh, how have you been?"

169

"Good, how about—"

"Seneca has a movie. I'll be back to pick her up later." She turned and walked down the hallway.

"Guess she's in a hurry."

"Yeah." Ava shook her head. "Did I do something to piss her off?"

"No. I did."

"What?"

"I kept breathing." He kissed Ava's cheek. "Seneca, come here. I want you to meet somebody."

Seneca marched from the bedroom with her doll and the puppy, each cradled under an arm.

"Seneca, this is my friend Ava."

Seneca flashed a glossy, wide-eyed look. "What kind of a friend? A giiiiiiiiiirrrrrrrrlllllll friend?"

"Cute, Seneca. Be nice."

"You're pretty."

Ava leaned forward and pressed her palms against her knees. "You are very sweet. You're quite pretty yourself."

"Do you want to watch a movie?"

"Sure. What movie?"

"*The Little Mermaid.*"

"That's one of my favorites."

"Me too. Amos said we are going in his boat to find one this summer."

"You are? That sounds exciting."

"Are you gonna come?"

Ava looked at him and winked. "We'll see. I'll be right back." She mouthed *she's adorable* on her way to the bedroom. Amos followed her and slumped down on the bed.

Caleb came into the apartment. "Oh, look. It's the little shit monster."

"I am not."

"The puppy, Seneca."

"Uncle Caleb, do you want to watch a movie with us?"

"I'll have to rain check on this one, kiddo."

"Amos is in the bedroom with his girlfriend. She has big boobies."

"Why do you think your brother likes her so much?"

Ava shook her head in the bathroom. "She has to be the sweetest thing ever."

"She definitely didn't get it from my mother."

She raised her eyebrows and made a noise in her throat as she came out of the bathroom. "Do you ever think about kids?"

"Fuck-trophies? What, like having them?"

"God, Amos."

"What?"

She straddled him. "Do you take anything seriously?"

"Always."

"Be serious. Do you ever think about kids?"

"Can we talk about this later? I'm going back to bed."

"No. You're going to come out there and watch the movie with your sister."

"Do you have any idea how many times I've seen that movie? I swear, if I hear that little fucking lobster sing 'Under the Sea,' one—"

"Crab. It's not a lobster. It's a crab. And you're coming."

"Obviously not in the way I want to."

"Be sweet, and I'll be sweet to you later."

She gripped his hand and tried to pull him from the bed.

"I'll be out in a second."

Ava turned to Amos from the fridge when he came out. "Is Moxie the only thing you drink?"

"Coffee, beer, and Turkey," Amos answered.

Caleb said, "No shit."

Seneca was on the couch with Caleb. The puppy and doll were still under her arms. Ava cracked a can open and took a sip. She pushed her lips together and squinted, holding the can away from her. She fanned her bottom three fingers away from it as if touching the can was as bad as the taste. "Gross. This stuff is awful."

"No shit," Seneca said.

"Hey."

"Good job, Caleb," Ava scolded.

"You know what else Uncle Caleb says?" Seneca released the puppy and turned on the couch to face Ava.

"Yes. And you're not going to repeat it," Amos interrupted.

She huffed and turned back around. Caleb caught Amos's attention with a nod.

"You got a few minutes?"

"Yeah," he answered. "Come in the bedroom."

Ava eyed Amos from the counter. Caleb followed him into the bedroom and shut the door.

Caleb scratched his chin. "It's not good, man."

"What is it?"

"There's a rumor that Bobby was Kavanagh's dealer, but I'm not sure how true that is."

"I heard that, too."

"Where the fuck did you hear that?"

"I have ears, Caleb."

"This is fucked up, man. What if Kavanagh finds out it was us who took out the church?"

"Then he'll come read us a bedtime story. What the fuck? I've never seen you like this. Are you scared?"

"I'm not scared. I just don't think we're ready for a battle like this."

"How the fuck is Kavanagh going to find out it was us? When and if the battle starts, then we'll deal with it. Maybe that vacation will be more like forced retirement."

"Is that a nice way of saying, dead?"

"No, but that's another way to look at it."

Caleb shook his head. "I have to go."

"You got another date?"

"Yeah, I guess you could say that."

As he followed Caleb into the living room, the scene there

stunned him. In the few seconds that Caleb made his way to the door, Amos realized that it was the first time he had so many people he cared for in one room. He took that moment and made it as crisp as he possibly could in his memory. A feeling struck him that there would probably never be another one like it.

Ava started the movie after Caleb left. She sat with Seneca and kept the puppy between them. Seneca moved to one side of the couch and used Ava's thigh as a pillow where she narrated the movie and sang the songs until her voice became a slow whisper and the two of them, after adjusting several times, were cuddled together asleep.

FORTY-TWO
Caleb

As he waited for Richard and Avery, Caleb tugged on the sleeve of his shirt beneath his jacket. A cufflink shook loose and fell into the snow—a tragic fatality for accessories and car keys in Maine during the winter. He began to patter at the soft white until their car pulled to the curb.

Caleb tried to sleep on the way there. He rode in the back seat with Richard's nephew. He'd been introduced and forgot the boy's name purposely. He'd had a set of black eyes that were almost healed, but Caleb could see the fading, yellowing look of them. The boy looked at Caleb with contempt when he climbed into the back seat.

"Did you lose something?" the kid asked.

"Seems that way," Caleb answered.

"Something important?"

"It wasn't my fucking virginity. I'll get over it."

"You seem preoccupied."

"Maybe I am."

"Don't you think you should focus on the job at hand?"

"Maybe you should focus on not worrying about me. I'm not one of three guys who can't handle a woman."

The boy squinted, and Caleb realized where the black eyes had come from.

"Shit. Is she the one who gave you those shiners?"

The boy dropped his glare and looked out his window. Richard and Avery shared glances and Richard cleared his throat.

"Our situation is quite sensitive," he spoke. "We won't really need you for any of the physical stuff, but we will need you to be our lookout."

"Your lookout?"

"Yes. The lookout."

"Jesus Christ. You guys have no fucking clue what you're doing, do you?"

Richard's face flushed with embarrassment. "You'll be our backup in case anything goes wrong."

"Everything is going to go wrong."

"What do you mean by that?"

"You'll see."

"No, I want to know what you mean by that."

"You guys are paying me ten grand to be your lookout, and that's fine with me, but I want my money up front."

"Well, we were hoping you'd reconsider your price now that we've decided we don't need you for the physical stuff."

"I get paid what was agreed upon, nothing less. The only invoices I issue are what you would consider physical stuff. Broken fingers, crushed windpipes, shattered kneecaps, demolished orbital sockets, compound femur fractures—"

"Okay, okay. Jesum crow, I get the picture."

Avery slipped an envelope over the seat, and Caleb took it. He sat back and flipped through the bills.

Richard spoke. "Seth here wants to handle the problem. I didn't mean to insult you. I'm a businessman. I negotiate to a fault."

"Is that what got his face broken?" Caleb jutted a thumb toward Seth without looking up from his count.

Richard squeezed the wheel. "Maybe you're right. I don't have experience with this aspect of the business, which is why you're here. Precautions. A safety net, so to speak."

"For when you guys fuck this up."

"What do you suggest we do to keep that from happening?"

"Keep your goddamn mouths shut. Action. Commit to what you're set out to do, and you're not going there to talk."

"What would you do?"

"What I was paid to. Nothing more. Nothing less."

Silence took over the car. The boy brooded and kept his glare against the glass. Richard and Avery shared a cigarette. Eventually, because he'd already been engaged and his curiosity overpowered his distaste for his company, Caleb spoke.

"Who is this bitch anyway?"

The boy finally broke his gaze from the world passing outside the window. The men in the front seat, too, exchanged glances.

"You'll forgive me, I hope," Richard said. "But I'd rather not say her name. Call it paranoia."

"Probably better you don't," Caleb muttered. "It makes things easier when you don't name your victims."

When they finally arrived, Caleb had just begun to find sleep. He took a moment to look out the back window, peering for any sign of Jones or Stevens, but he knew he'd dumped anyone following him long before he'd met Richard, Avery, and Seth. As he looked through the window, he noticed the neighborhood, the plum-straight historical houses that bore the gleam of paint less than a year old on the wood siding. In a couple months, the dead, abandoned feel of the neighborhood would shift and come alive with the movement and sound of lawn crews whose company trucks with their equipment trailers would turn the already narrow streets into barely passable one-way avenues.

The three of them climbed from the car and Caleb sank a little lower in his seat. They were already drawing attention. He wished they'd given him an address and a photo, like all the other wrench work jobs he and Moss had done. Richard reiterated the plan to Caleb, and Caleb nodded with acknowledgment until they left and walked toward a blue cape, the smallest house in the neighborhood, but by no means a small house. He peered at the windows, trying his best to spot people watching from their homes or through the windows of passing cars, but the neighborhood was practically dead. Footprints packed in the snow and a few of the paved driveways gave the only indication of life there. He gave them three minutes, then climbed from the car to get a better look at the neighborhood, sure he'd have to flee on foot. He took a long study of the street and when he went to light his cigarette, he saw it.

Ruth's car.

Caleb moved slowly toward the house, casing each window, listening for any vehicles coming down the road behind him. Ruth spotting him in the neighborhood only created another witness, one that would make him a sure-as-shit fall guy if his sweet friends decided to corroborate a story and pin it on him. He stood by her vehicle and did his best to pretend to relight his cigarette. The photo of Seneca on her console verified the car was hers. He looked up the street again, then to the house, and at the real estate sign in front, the back side covered in snow where the wind shifted it, but there was no mistaking Ruth's face on the sign. Caleb dropped his head and moved quickly past the house as a Mercedes rounded the corner and pulled into the driveway across the street.

When he rounded the corner he ran, hopped the fence, and trudged through the snow to the back of the empty house. Snow packed into his shoes as he made his way to the back door. He did his best to catch his breath and tapped on the glass.

Richard moved quickly toward the door and let Caleb inside.

"What the hell are you doing? You're supposed to be watching out for us."

"What am I watching for exactly? You guys are taking too long. You should have been back out to the car by now."

Caleb moved past him, past Ruth to see that she was still breathing, swelling rising in her cheekbone, and went to the front door. He parted the curtain near the door slightly and looked out at the neighbor who was outside kicking the freezing slush from his wheel wells. Caleb turned and looked at Seth.

"Probably not a smart idea to bust a round right now. The neighbors will hear the gunshot. Besides, that makes it a murder. Cops get involved. You fuck up a drug dealer, they're not likely to go to the cops, so maybe you should just stick with the beatdown."

Seth squinted. "You're probably right." He looked down at Ruth and slipped the gun into his back pocket. "This bitch deserves a more painful experience."

Seth moved through the room toward the fireplace and perused through the pile of wood. Caleb checked the window again and the neighbor was still at his car. He pulled his hand away from his pistol. Seth moved toward Ruth with a log that his small hands barely fit around.

"First," Seth said, tapping her cheek with the log. "I'm going to make you not so pretty." He slipped the log down her sternum, over her stomach and tapped her crotch. "Then you're going to get what every good cunt should get—some good, hard wood." Caleb moved back toward him as he straddled Ruth's torso and tapped the log in his palm. Ruth's eyelids fluttered.

In the few steps he took to get to him, Caleb forgot about Amos or the threat of prison. Seth's face furled with sinister anger. He drew back the log. Caleb shed his pistol, grabbed Seth's head, and pushed the barrel into the soft part of the boy's throat just above his collarbone. Seth's lungs absorbed the gunshot and he crumbled like a stack of wooden toy blocks. The log dribbled against the floor.

Richard and Avery quivered with an epileptic-like spasm and Caleb pushed the barrel into Richard's gut before he had a chance to move. Two more muffled shots. Avery tripped over the boy as he scrambled for the back door and fell. Caleb mounted him, stripped his belt, and stretched it around the man's throat. He pulled it tight until the man's kicking became soft patters and then there was nothing but Caleb's heaving breaths.

FORTY-THREE
Amos

The credits of the movie had long passed, and the recurring whine of the movie's menu music continued to resonate through the apartment. Ava and Seneca remained asleep on the couch, Seneca shifting every so often to feel for the puppy. Amos couldn't remember the last time he'd slept like that—slept without the abrupt awakening from his dreams of dead men or past violence.

It was as good a time as any to replace the shotgun and pull his cash from the hollow stair in the hallway. Amos slipped the shotgun into a pillowcase in his bedroom and checked on the girls before making his way toward the hallway. Their breathing was in cadence, deep and slow. He trotted down the stairs, checking the railing down to the other floors for hands or movement. At the step, he waited, briefly, for the sounds of anything that shouldn't be there. Amos switched the items and ran back up to the apartment. Ava was sitting in his chair and easily moved her stare from his face to the bag.

"What's in the bag?"

"Leftovers," he answered and checked on Seneca.

Seneca had pushed herself toward the armrest of the couch and pulled her knees into her chest. Ava had turned off the movie, and Amos wondered how she could wake so easily after seeming to be sound asleep. He went to the fridge and tossed the bag inside among the sparse items there—a few cans of Moxie and a bottle of ketchup. Ava went into the bedroom with her phone and whispered.

She came out. "Moss, can I talk to you?"

He went into the bedroom and shut the door. "Who were you talking to?"

She pinched her lip. "Job prospect."

"What's up?"

"I really need to talk to you about where this relationship is going."

"What do you mean?"

"I mean, I can't sit around waiting. I enjoy this. I love being with you, but it's not high school, and I need more than holding hands and dinner."

"What are you trying to say?"

"You need to live a different life."

"What do you want me to do, find a real job? Kill myself for food money? Abandon my friends to sit at home every night and cut coupons?"

"I'd like to know that you're moving toward something stable. If it takes cutting coupons, so be it. I can live with that. I can't live with you continuing to live this kind of life that's continually mired in violence."

"Are you giving me a deadline?"

"I'd like to know that it will happen before you go to prison again. It's not like you have to put in a two-week notice. You just have to stop being a thug."

"That makes sense. How has your luck been with finding a job? I suppose I could go pound nails for pennies a week and see how far I get that way. I'll end up just like my father."

"Your father? How would he feel about what you do?"

Amos bit his lip. "Ava, I can't do this right now."

He left the bedroom and went back to the chair he'd sat in for the movie. Ava came out and went to the fridge. She pulled the bag from the shelf and dropped it on the counter. It was a mistake to let her open it, but at the time, Amos thought her preaching about his lifestyle would change when she saw what was inside. She waited for a minute, staring at him over the crumpled roll of the bag. When he made no effort to move, she opened it. She looked at Amos with disgust after seeing the contents and moved toward the bedroom. Finally, he moved and met her at the door.

"Why are you doing this while my sister is here?"

"Oh, I'm sorry. Should I wait for a more convenient time to talk about being woken up to a gun barrel in my face one night and a bag full of money the next?"

Amos hadn't felt that level of frustration since his mother's *pathetic* comment. He stepped closer to her and spoke through his teeth. "A time appropriate for us to actually talk about what the fuck I do without my sister in the room would be nice, but then again, I don't need to be reminded of how you handle communication with the people you care about."

"Back to that, are we?"

His face flushed with heat and he felt a sweat break against his chest.

She turned and shut herself in the bedroom. Inside, there were sounds of running water, doorknobs turning, heels tapping, more running water, and light switches flicking. She came out dressed in the pajamas she wore the night before. She walked up to him and whispered, "I had a good time." Her jaw clenched until her teeth ground. She walked into the hallway. Amos followed.

"I'm sorry," he whispered, which made him feel more weak and pathetic.

She grabbed his shirt and jerked him in for a kiss. Her tongue slid around his mouth—a fleeting wave goodbye. When she pushed him away she was crying. "My problem is that I...I want an opportunity to give this a chance."

"I don't have a choice."

"Bullshit. You have a choice."

"And one of them is wrong."

She tried to pull away.

Amos held her wrist. "Ava, I didn't mean—"

"Let me go." She looked away.

"I can't."

"Let me fucking go," she yelled.

She moved down the stairs looking up through the balusters— a terse, hateful look that pinned him to the wall. The only thing that pulled him from his position in the hallway was Seneca's sleep-jarred voice calling out for him.

FORTY-FOUR
Caleb

Ruth's silence in the car irritated Caleb to the point that he had a hard time keeping the car on the road. His betrayal with the fed seemed arbitrary then that he'd nearly been present for Ruth's beating and rape and he projected his anger on her.

"You want to fucking explain why a couple of faggots were about to fuck you up over drugs?"

"No, Caleb, I don't."

"Well, considering the fact that your son is going to go ape-shit when he finds out, and that I just killed three men, what you want doesn't really mean shit to me. Start fucking talking or I'll drive this pretty luxury vehicle of yours right to Moss's and I'll leave it to him to get an explanation."

"Why don't you explain why you were there? Is that what you and Amos have reduced yourselves to—hurting women?"

"I freelanced the job, which is another problem I'm going to have with your son. That's a completely different issue altogether. Are you fucking slinging?"

"Slinging?"

"Dealing."

Ruth gently tapped her fingers against the swelling on her face. She pulled the visor down to inspect her injury in the mirror. Dusk dropped away like a fleeting pass of a slow parade and

Caleb drove her car down Route 1 and through the coastal towns that began their nightly slumber early because of the dwindling daylight. The house would be ablaze by then and while Caleb tried to understand how Ruth was involved, he thought about how he would handle Vassar before Amos found out that he'd been a participant in Ruth's assault. Briefly, he tried to salvage the notion that he'd saved her from something worse, but that would do little to preserve Amos's trust.

"Ruth, I need an answer."

"Yes, Caleb. I'm a dealer."

"Holy fucking shit." Caleb pushed himself back in the seat. "How? Why?"

"We have the same boss."

Caleb's eyes widened. "Tommy? No fucking way."

"Yes, Caleb, Tommy. Tommy worked for my husband, Amos's father. When he died, Tommy took over. The real estate market went to shit and I stepped in to stay afloat."

"And all of the shit you've said to your son over the years? What the fuck gives you the right to make him feel like that?"

"Nothing. I'm a hypocrite, maybe worse. I never wanted to hurt him, and I thought that if he knew, I'd just be advocating what he, what you two do."

"What we do? We do what we do because of people like you. And Tommy? Jesus Christ."

"You can't tell Tommy that I told you."

"It's a little late for that. I already called him, but now I know why he wanted us to meet him out of town."

It was the only time Caleb could remember when Tommy didn't have a smoke in his hand or hanging from his lip. They met in a parking lot for car poolers near the entrance of 95 in Wells. Tommy's hands shook as he climbed into the back seat of Ruth's car.

"Jesus, Ruth. Are you okay?"

"I'm fine."

Tommy sat back in the seat and adjusted his belt. "Caleb, why were you there?"

"I freelanced a job. I didn't know it was Ruth."

"When did you start freelancing work?"

"How long have you been a fucking dealer?"

"Since before you were born. Let's not get fucking cute. How many times have you freelanced work?"

"This was a first."

"Who gave you the job?"

"Vassar."

"For fuck's sake. I told you guys to watch out for that guy. Fucking junkie."

"Don't you think junkies are a good thing for your business?"

"We can talk about that later."

"Should we invite Amos in for that conversation?"

"We both know how Amos would react if he found out about this."

"You guys sound like a couple of scared little girls," Ruth injected. "What if Moss finds out? Big fucking deal."

"Ruth," Tommy whispered, leaning forward. "You don't know half of what Caleb and I know Moss is capable of. This goes no further than this car. And Ruth, you're done. We'll talk later about what you need to tell the cops if they start questioning you about the fire."

"Fire?"

"You were still pretty dazed when I walked you out of the house. I torched the place."

"You torched the house?"

"Yeah. What else was I supposed to do?"

"Shit."

"Ruth, you need to get home. Where is Seneca?"

"With Moss," Caleb answered.

"Goddammit. You'd better think of something good to tell him if he sees that black eye. Caleb, you ride with me. We need to figure out what to do about Vassar."

Ruth erupted in tears. Caleb and Tommy sat silent, the two of them unable to comfort her. Caleb felt guilty about the way he'd spoken to her. Tommy finally lit a cigarillo. Before Caleb knew exactly what he was doing, he'd placed a hand against Ruth's shoulder.

"It'll be okay," he told her.

Ruth's shoulders fell forward and she turned and latched around Caleb's neck whimpering apologies that Caleb knew weren't for him or Tommy. Caleb felt the discomfort of his own secrets as Ruth wept against his neck, and the weight of it settled so much against his bones they felt brittle. The more he thought about Stevens and the three of them in the car discussing the necessity to keep it all a secret, and how his secret trumped the severity of theirs, his consoling of Ruth's anguish drifted away. He stripped her hands gently from his shoulders and pushed himself from the car. Tommy followed and Ruth composed herself as she exited the car to take her seat behind the wheel.

She headed north on 109. Tommy flicked his cigarillo and it bounced from the taillight of a parked car. He lit another and leaned his head from side to side to work out a kink in his neck.

"Do you think you can get a handle on this?" he asked Caleb.

"I don't know. Vassar's bound to find out. He sure as shit won't keep his mouth shut then. I don't even understand how Moss didn't know. Vassar offered the fucking job to him first."

"Fortunately for Ruth, you picked it up. I'm still curious why you would, though. This is the busiest you two have been in three years. What's going on?"

Caleb spit and tightened his hands into fists inside his jacket pockets. "I don't know how much longer I can do this. Seemed like a good way to stack some paper."

"We'd better get down to the bar in case Moss shows up and starts wondering why neither of us are down there."

"What if it comes down to that? What if Moss finds out? What are we supposed to do if Moss loses his shit?"

"God help us if he does."

FORTY-FIVE
Vassar

Vassar turned the music up, the bass hurled through the speakers with distorted tweaks. Farrah tried to yell for him to turn it down, her voice falling short amidst the rattle of sound. Vassar could no longer put lines through his nostril, so he tongued them from the cutting board. The coke had made him quiver until the movement in his limbs was labored and cumbersome. His heart rattled. Sweat slipped over his brow. He took in quick breaths over a dried tongue. The thoughts in his mind snapped from tiny threads of coherence.

Farrah yanked the stereo cord from the outlet. The sound dropped from the room and Vassar, his glazed look hovering over her movement, could only produce grunts of displeasure. His mind had gone cold, his brain ceased to make real, interpretive connections and reasoning. Farrah's speech came at him like the garbled sounds of water in a drain. As he approached her, his breaths felt like frost forming against the back of his throat. His vision pulsed and dimmed. He gripped the handle of the framing hammer resting on the table as he approached and the look of fright on Farrah's face was subdued in the first swing.

Vassar woke against the cabinets beneath his sink. A subtle

cramp had set along his right forearm and triceps. He looked down at it and saw the dark, blackish streaks twined around his wrist. The blood flaked off as Vassar tried to massage the ache from his arm. Farrah's feet protruded from behind the loveseat in the other room. She was facedown on the floor. When he called for her, she didn't move. Vassar reached for the counter to pull himself up. His legs were weary, and he stumbled toward the table stomping life back into them. He cut a line, sucked it down and cut another. The lethargy wore off, synapses fired, the blood pulsed into his limbs. He cut another and looked over toward Farrah.

"Farrah, get the fuck off the goddamn floor."

He cut two lines—a pick-me-up for his unconscious partner—and stepped toward her. The small carpet had soaked up most of the blood. The hammer lay next to her right shoulder. Her hair had fanned out over the floor and Vassar sneered at the mess he'd made, her skull so broken and smashed it had settled into two distinct piles. Vassar took a long hard suck of air through his nose and went back to the table. He tapped the straw and finished both lines.

Vassar knuckled the power button on the stereo. An electric snap came through the speakers a split second before the bass and sound shook the house. Paper buzzed against the surfaces it rested on, counters, the coffee table and the floor. Rigor had set in and Farrah's body was the only thing that remained stiff in the vibration. Windows rattled, sawdust from the clothing hung on various screws and nails wafted from the fabric into the air. Vassar pulled the .357 from the drawer he'd once kept his silver-ware. He aimed it at the knots in the stained pine he'd used for the interior walls of his house. Each time he shot he missed, the gunshots drowned out by the noise and the bullets splintering wood on impact. Vassar reloaded and left the gun on the table to cut a few more lines, which he did with a quick ease.

Vassar stood over Farrah's body, studying the transparent, bluish color her skin had taken. He lit a cigarette and smoked it down trying to decide what he should do with her. He needed time to think, he told himself. Vassar grabbed Farrah's corpse by the ankles and dragged her toward the back room where he kept the freezer. The wooden floor slipped splinters into her cold skin. He pulled out the few packages of moose meat that had been in there for more than a year and hoisted Farrah's body into the appliance. He replaced the packages of meat over what remained of her skull and went back to the living room. A chunk of Farrah's skull, her bloodied blond hair still attached, was stuck to the floor. Vassar kicked it loose with the heel of his boot, used a soiled rag he took from the table and picked it up. He tossed it into the woodstove and lit another cigarette. The pooling of her blood had soaked into the wood and didn't look like blood anymore. Vassar shrugged off the sight of it and went back to the table for another line.

FORTY-SIX
Amos

His mother's footsteps knocked through the hallway as she walked to the door of the apartment. Amos waited for her to come in, but she stood in the doorway, a scarf wrapped around her head and sunglasses perched on her face.

"Little dark for shades, isn't it?"

"My pupils are dilated. Seneca, honey. Come on. Time to go."

"Can I bring the puppy?" She asked hopping off the couch.

"Seneca, no. I told you about the puppy."

"Oh, all right." She went to his chair and hugged him. "Bye, Amos."

Amos took a step toward Ruth, noticing the purple hue. He reached for the sunglasses and she slapped his hand away.

"Mind your own business, Amos."

"What the hell happened to your eye?"

"Some idiot contractor left a two-by-four leaning against a doorframe."

She grabbed Seneca's wrist and pulled her toward the door. Seneca dragged her doll, mimicking her mother as she was pulled from the apartment. She looked back for the puppy that stood on the armrest watching her leave.

Amos stared at the doorway listening to the fading sounds of their voices. He felt cold, alone, like all the reaching he was doing allowed him to grasp nothing but the clutch of wet, cold air. He grabbed the church money from the counter. Amos gave Tommy all the money he took from jobs. Regular people had investments and bank accounts and life insurance. Amos had Tommy.

His phone rang as he walked into Logan's. He answered quickly, hoping it was Ava before he could see that it was Vassar. His voice came through in a throat-torn growl.

"I need to talk to you and Caleb. Get your ass up here." He hung up.

"Yeah, I'll get right on that, dickbag," he said aloud.

Justin stood behind the bar talking on the phone when Amos walked through the door. When he got to the bar, Justin turned his back on him to continue his conversation. Caleb came from the back, his step slowing when Amos made eye contact with him. He took the stool to Amos's right.

"Everything okay?" Caleb asked.

"Fucking peachy."

"Want to talk about it?"

"I don't really have much to say. Need a goddamn drink, though."

"Me too."

Caleb knocked on the bar. "Bartender. Two double Turkeys."

Justin ignored him.

Caleb extended his arm over the bar to point. "This dipshit is beginning to piss me off."

Justin turned his head to the side and cut his eyes at Caleb then turned back away.

"Are you kidding me?" Caleb slammed his palms on the bar. "His name is Justin."

"Hey, *Justine*. Get me a fucking drink."

"Man, fuck you," Justin answered.

Caleb sighed. He stood and moved around the bar, stripping his hoodie and draping it over a stool.

Amos pulled a cigarette from Caleb's pack and lit it with a pack of bar matches.

Caleb grabbed two rocks glasses and poured shots of Turkey for them. Justin had turned and put the phone against his chest.

"You can't be back here," he said.

The bottle was almost empty. Caleb twirled a bar towel around his palm and fingers and drank what remained of the Turkey. He held the bottle up with the rag-wrapped hand, smacking his lips. "Do you like Turkey?" Caleb asked Justin as he walked over to him.

"No."

"That's too bad." Caleb shook his head and held the bottle by his waist, reading the label. "Nothing like some good ol' one-oh-one."

"Look, I'm not—"

Caleb smashed the bottle against the side of Justin's face.

"Gobble, gobble, motherfucker."

Justin fell the ground holding his face and moaned.

Tommy came from his office. "What the hell is going on?"

Amos pointed over the bar at Justin. Smoke from the cigarette coiled around his index finger. Caleb took his shot of Turkey, glaring at Tommy. He slammed the glass on the bar.

"He asked for it, Tommy," Caleb said.

"Moss?"

Amos gave a half shrug—half nod.

Tommy shook his head and moved around the bar to help Justin to his feet. The gash went clear through the boy's cheek. There were a few other small cuts beneath his eye, scratches. The phone let out an annoying pulse and Tommy hung it up. "Go in the back and clean up," he told Justin. "Amos, let's talk in the office. Caleb, keep an eye on the front."

Tommy's office smelled like burned coffee and wet cigarettes. An overflowing ashtray sat on a stack of papers on his desk—ashes scattered like dead bugs beneath a light. Empty packs of cigarillos piled atop filing cabinets with mangled hot rod magazines. Tommy sat in his leather chair and crossed his feet on the corner of his desk. There was a newly hung poster on the wall.

It was a centerfold from *Playboy* ten years before. Amos wasn't impressed with her beauty.

"So what was that all about?"

"Attitude adjustment." Amos sat in the metal folding chair next to Tommy's desk.

Tommy scratched the side of his chin. A scrawling sound from his facial hair filled the small room. "I knew this would happen sooner or later."

"Aren't you going to send him to the hospital?"

"Nah. Toughen him up. I need to know he can take a little punishment before I send him out on the street."

"Here's this month's rent." Amos pushed the paper sack across the desk to Tommy.

"Good?"

Amos tongued something from between his teeth in the back of his mouth. "Unh-hunh."

"There's already some buzz about it."

"Oh, yeah?"

"Yep. Roberts, by the way, is Kavanagh's cousin."

"That explains some things." Amos grinned.

"Yeah. Quite the scam they have going."

"No shit."

"Is this it for you for a while?"

"I don't know."

"I'll make the arrangements for the boat. You'll have a pretty decent chunk left. You can always invest in the bar. That option will always be on the table, if you want to stick around or have something to do in the winter."

"Thanks, Tommy. I'll consider it."

"Good. What are you two doing tonight?"

"I don't know. Vassar called me. He wants to talk about something. Probably another bullshit job."

"Maybe you should blow that fucking guy off. You don't need that nickel-and-dime shit anymore."

Amos shrugged. "It's easy nickel-and-dime shit."

"Yeah, well, your new score should give you a reason for a vacation."

"Shit, Tommy. The fuck am I going to do with a vacation?"

"I meant lay low, Swain. Why don't you two hang out here for the night? Call down that little spinner you've been courting. I'll put her on your tab."

"That little spinner spun out of my apartment earlier. I don't think I'll be seeing her for a while."

"Wow." Tommy shook his head. "Fucking women."

"Tell me about it."

"Moss, c'mon. Stay here. I'll probably need you tonight."

"I'll be back soon, I'm sure."

Amos left Tommy's office despite Tommy's grumbling. Justin sat in a far corner with a bloody rag against his face. Caleb leaned against the bar staring at Justin through his smoke rings.

"Everything cool?" he asked.

"Yeah. Let's go."

"Where are we going?"

"Vassar's."

"Vassar's? Why?"

"Said he needed to talk to us."

"Fuck that, man. Let's just hang out here and get shitfaced."

"Jesus, you and Tommy both. Let's go see what he has to say and come back. It's still early enough to get shitfaced."

Tommy called Justin into his office as they were leaving. The kid was still uneasy on his feet and bumped into a pool table on the way there. As soon as Amos opened the doors the wind blew against their chests. It was getting colder.

FORTY-SEVEN
Amos

Vassar handed Caleb a bottle of Mescal when they walked in. He spoke, but the roar of music kept Amos from hearing his mumbled words. Instead, his attention was drawn to the graying of Vassar's teeth. His breath cast the stench of rotten meat. Vassar had put his mouth on the bottle, which did more for Amos's refusal than his detest for the liquor. He handed the bottle to Caleb who wasted no time ignoring what disgusted Amos and swallowed two large gulps. He handed the bottle back to Vassar and lit a cigarette. Vassar made his way to the stereo, stood before the speakers, and took a swig. He killed the sound and ringing in Amos's ears made its faint presence.

A cloud of smoke mushroomed inside Caleb's open mouth while he tilted his head back and made eye contact with Amos.

Amos looked down at his phone to see if Ava had called.

Caleb backhanded him on the shoulder. "Give it up, dude. She'll call when she's ready."

Caleb pulled his flask of Turkey from his pocket and passed it to Amos.

"What? Are you too fucking good for my liquor?" Vassar asked, stumbling back to the table.

Amos lifted the flask to his lips and took a short pull. "I don't like it."

Vassar slumped down in front of an egg-sized pile of white on a cutting board. He plopped the bottle on the table, spilling the booze on the floor and his cutting board. Small drops sank into the pile of white. He drank again. Bubbles rose and thumped against the bottom of the bottle. Amos took his own long pull from the flask and his body coasted into a subtle buzz. The heaviness in his limbs drifted away.

Amos thought about Ava leaving his apartment earlier and a new feeling of pressure and tightness came over him until his fist clenched tight around the flask, hoping it would crumple in his hand. Vassar transferred his drugs to a phone book and rubbed the remaining dust on the cutting board with his finger. He smeared the dirty digit over his teeth and gums. Caleb lit another cigarette. Vassar picked up the business card that was beneath the cutting board and his shaky hands moved wavy lines from the pile. Amos thought of Ava's cheek against his chest—the vibration of her voice and soft stroke of her fingers against his ribs. Tightness in his throat behind his collarbone squeezed for a minute until he felt as empty and hollow as an overturned canoe.

"Did you guys take care of those sites?" Vassar broke the small pile of white into thin lines.

Amos spoke without moving his eyes from the phone book. "The sites were fucked."

Vassar stopped cutting lines and looked over to Amos. "What do you mean they were fucked?" He leaned against the table.

"I mean the sites were fucked, V. There were people living in those houses. How are we supposed to move materials from a site when there are people living there?"

"I gave you good sites." Vassar jawed off a gag and flicked the business card across the table. "If there are people living there that's your fucking problem. If you don't like the sites I give you then find your own fucking scores."

Caleb took a pull off his cigarette. He turned his head toward each of them as they spoke. Vassar tapped his thumbs on the edge of the phone book. His chest flexed beneath his gray under-shirt.

"Look, Vassar. I don't give a fuck if you give me scores or not. If you're not going to give me shit I can take down it's no sweat off my back. I don't get paid and neither do you. All I'm saying is don't give me bullshit sites and waste my time."

Vassar leaned forward, put his elbows on the table, and extended his index finger from his fist, pointing at Amos. "You're in my motherfucking house, asshole. Don't come in here and start bitching at me. I just gave you a motherfucking job that you turned down, like some fucking yuppie snob."

Vassar looked at Caleb and squinted.

Amos tilted his head at the familiar text of the business card. He pulled it from the table. It was his mother's card. Amos flipped the card over to the scrawl that he'd seen before, RICHARD. Before any of the thoughts of why his mother would be wrench work, he had focused on the shit-sneering leer that Vassar was giving him. Flashes of Bailey Mitchell went through his mind. The sound of unraveling blue tarps and the quiet, shocked breaths of the people around him when he'd finished. The light dimmed in his vision. He thought of Ruth's black eye. He felt the brisk sensation of smelling ice in his nose as his hand dropped below the table and he gripped the handle of his pistol.

"Not everyone's a fucking snob, Moss. That cunt would have been easy money for you."

Vassar let out a quick chuckle through his marred teeth and backhanded Caleb's shoulder. Amos pulled his pistol from beneath the table and put three rounds in the center of Vassar's chest. Caleb jumped back. Vassar toppled backwards in his chair. On the floor, Vassar's mouth flexed. His eyes roved over the room as Amos stepped toward him. Vassar pointed a finger toward Caleb, who'd drawn his own gun. Then Caleb put two more rounds into Vassar's skull. The striations of muscle flexed in Vassar's forearm and the twitch of cocaine-induced movement writhed through his feet.

Caleb pulled a hand towel from the handle of the oven. He wiped down the table and door, the handle and anything else they may have touched. He pulled the ashtray from the table and emptied it into the woodstove, tilting his head at the bloody rag inside. He piled in kindling and started the fire. Amos slipped his mother's business card into his pocket and looked over as Caleb pulled his hand from beneath a couch cushion.

"You looking for spare change?"

"He's gotta have some cash kicking around."

"Go check for Farrah."

Amos slowed his mind and scanned the room. He considered everything that could tie him to Vassar's while Caleb searched the house. Vassar's phone. Caleb called out to him, and Amos stuffed Vassar's phone into his pocket before he walked into the back room. Caleb stood over the chest freezer, staring inside. He stepped over and looked in.

"Jesus Christ," Caleb whispered.

"Be a lie if you thought that would never happen."

"She doesn't even look real. Her fucking head's…"

"Let's get the fuck out of here."

They slipped from the house and Caleb drove them out of there. Silence lingered in the car like a bad smell.

"What the fuck was he doing with my mother's fucking business card?"

"Construction, man. It's probably just coincidence or something."

"If it was just fucking coincidence, I wouldn't have wasted that piece of shit. That card was the wrench work he offered me. He even said it."

"Maybe Vassar wrote on the wrong fucking card. He's a junkie, man. He's sure to fuck something like that up."

"It doesn't make any sense."

"Well, you handled it. You don't have to worry about it now."

"Unless he gave the job to someone else."

"He doesn't know anyone else."

Amos rubbed the pressure from his eyes.

Caleb remained silent for the rest of the drive. Before they pulled into Logan's, he cleared his throat.

"Do you believe in Heaven and Hell?"

"I don't think about it much. Why?"

"Sometimes I wonder what it's like to die."

"Jesus Christ, Caleb. Now?"

"A lot of shit has happened. I don't know. Forget it. It's just, you know, with everything that's gone down, I don't know what I'd do without you. You're the only friend I have."

"Remember that when you need a best man at your wedding. Right now, let's go get fucked up. I'm over this fucking day."

FORTY-EIGHT
Caleb

Caleb breathed heavily as he sat up. Another night on the cot in Tommy's office. The throat-lurking stench of smoked cigarillos and the dirty-water, next-day taste of bourbon made him feel grimy. He could feel the stickiness against his clothes, and he desperately wanted a shower and something cold to drink. Bits of his dialogue came back to him, and he felt a slight embarrassment for being so sentimental with Moss the night before. Gurgling in his stomach forced a burp and it tasted like he'd shit through his nose.

"Rise and shine, cupcake," Tommy said from his desk.

"I need to find a better habit than drinking. Fuck, Tommy, when did hangovers start to get so bad?"

"You drank a fucking bottle. Coffee's on at the bar."

"What time did I crash?"

"You were sitting at the bar for a couple hours after Moss left. He barely drank last night." Tommy pushed the desk drawer closed and leaned back in his seat. "How did things go at Vassar's?"

"Moss put him down."

"Fuck. That's convenient."

"Yeah. Vassar had Ruth's business card."

"Jesus, fuck. Did anything come up?"

"No. I wiped the place down and dropped the piece I used on those fags in the couch."

"Sounds like a major problem solved."

"I don't know. Moss wants to know why."

"Shit."

"He won't get anywhere, unless Ruth confesses, but I doubt she'll do that. Anyway, we have this Lynn job and then I think we'll go underground for a while to let things simmer down."

Tommy rubbed his temples with his thumbs. "We're all going to tighten up around here."

"Even you?"

"Yeah, even me. I'll step out of the game for a bit, let some new crews move in. In a year you and Moss will have plenty of work again."

"Did you say something about coffee?"

FORTY-NINE
Amos

Caleb and Amos waited for Crow outside the Fox Run Mall in Newington. Caleb had picked up a different car the night before, a slick little import that felt crushing to ride in compared to the GTO. Most of the snow had melted and patches of muddy ground spread in cloud-shaped spaces. It was warmer until the wind picked up and blew plastic bags through the air and sent other litter skidding along the ground. Packs of kids cutting school came out to their cars to dump the merchandise they had stolen and went back for more.

Crow's arrival came with bass thumping through the parking lot. Polished chrome rims sent off beams of reflected light. The Impala had tinted windows and a purple chameleon paint job, a savage waste of money and a car. Crow approached with his crew who were clad in Patriots apparel and black bandanas tied around their left boots.

"It's about time, Crow. Shit," Caleb said.

"Sorry, guys. I got caught up in Boston."

He hugged Amos, something he'd never done, and rubbed his hand down Amos's spine. He met Caleb with the same greeting, patting his hands over Caleb's ribs.

Crow's new recruits were fresh out of the crowbar club, the razor irritation that cheap, jail commissary blades left was probably still burning on their throats. They wore white plastic framed sunglasses and stood behind Crow scanning the parking lot. One of them was marked with paler patches of skin on his cheeks and neck. There were more patches on the backs of his hands and Amos dubbed him Skin Dysfunction.

"Next Wednesday the delivery comes in. A driver brings in the goods. There are four guys inside with the loot. The passenger stays in the car, but they leave it running. Total time of the exchange is no more than two minutes. Enough time to check the product and the payment."

Crow stopped speaking to light a Newport. While he spoke, he kept scratching the side of his face and looking down at the ground to the left of Amos. He adjusted his zipper numerous times. His boys glared at Caleb and Amos. Something wasn't right with Crow, so Amos was reluctant to do anything but nod.

Crow sawed his lips together. "The other part, Moss," he said. "We need you in and out fast with whoever's in the house left secure. I have something special for them after."

"Sounds like a party," Amos said.

"So we straight?"

"Yeah. We're straight," Amos answered.

Crow went back to his car with his crew. The bass returned as the car rolled past Amos and Caleb. Caleb shivered again and they climbed into the car already rank with the smell of stale cigarette smoke. Half a mile from Amos's house, Caleb pulled to the side of the road, shifted to neutral, and cranked the e-brake.

"You were pretty quiet back there."

"I don't trust Crow."

"Neither do I, but we should have established what our take would be."

"We're taking all the cash and the product."

"Why are we taking the product?"

"I might need it to find out more about why Vassar had my mother's business card. I'm thinking it probably has something to do with her real estate. Maybe some fucking cocksuckers were pushing to use one of her properties and she wouldn't budge."

"How are you going to move product? We don't do that."

"I didn't say I was going to move it. I just think it'll be good to have on hand if I need it. If I don't, I'll push it to Tommy. I'm sure he can get rid of it."

"What makes you think Tommy will know what to do with it?"

"I'm sure Tommy will figure something out."

"But Tommy's not a drug dealer."

"Caleb, I'm aware of that. Tommy knows more people than I do when it comes to that. It's not going to hurt to try. If he can't unload it there's always the dumpster."

"Is there something you want to talk about?"

"I just did. What the fuck? Why do you insist on trivializing the fact that Vassar was commissioning wrench work on my fucking mother?"

"I'm not. I'm sorry. You're right. It'll probably be a good thing to have on the side, just in case."

"I have to go make a couple phone calls."

"To who?"

"Some old friends who might be able to help us out."

FIFTY
Amos

Caleb's celebration effort, and hope to cheer Amos up because of Ava, came in the form of platinum blond and sixty-four ounces of saline. Amos was standing at his counter wearing only a pair of jeans, pouring a shot of Turkey when they walked in. Dawn and Starr with two Rs were Portland's finest. That's what Starr with two Rs told Amos after she'd spelled her name. She even offered to show him the newspaper advertisement that proved it. Dawn, who Caleb had his arm around, went over to him.

"He doesn't want to hear that shit, Starr. Take care of Caleb, honey. This boy's mine."

Starr with two Rs giggled, curtsied, and shuffled over to Caleb. She pulled him by his wrist to the couch and sat him down. Dawn put her hand on the back of Amos's neck, kissed his cheekbone, and slid her fingertips over his ribs. It tickled, and he wanted to rip her throat out.

"It's going to be a good night for you." She pulled Amos into the bedroom.

Caleb didn't pay for all that she gave Amos and he didn't ask, but she gave it to him anyway. Later in the night, after they'd slept off the exertion, Amos watched her dress. He reached out and touched her again. She massaged the teeth-marks on her upper breast that he'd left while her legs squeezed around his ribs. She woke her friend and the two of them giggled as they stole the booze Caleb had brought and left.

Sunlight came over Caleb's shoulder through the bathroom window as he bobbed up and down in front of the toilet and looked up at the ceiling. He whispered curses and worked his hands in front of him like he was opening a small package.

"Nice ass, Caleb." Amos lifted his head from the pillow.

"It feels like I have to piss but nothing's coming out."

"You would have been a peach in the can."

"Fuck you." He looked over his shoulder.

"Does it burn?"

"A little. Is that bad?"

"You're probably dehydrated."

"Maybe. It itches inside my pisshole."

"Sounds like VD."

"I'll fucking kill that bitch."

"It's only a shot in the ass. Just make sure there are no bumps or blisters."

"Goddammit. Fucking-skank-stripper-bitch."

"I don't think the symptoms arrive that quickly. Have you slept with anyone else recently?"

"Just that bartender." He shot a glance back up at the ceiling. "Fuck."

"You ever heard of condoms?"

He was still jostling himself at the toilet as Amos made his way to the kitchen. Cold linoleum stung his feet when he walked out there. After three glasses of water, thirst kept him at the sink for two more. He thought about Dawn most of the morning—his hand around her throat, her hair wound around his other hand, how she made his chest bleed when she bit into his tattoo. Violence and fucking were the same. Both required the same amount of passion, both satisfied an immediate need, and they both became meaningless after. Amos thought of Ava, and how she'd controlled everything the first time in his apartment. Caleb spent twenty minutes in the bathroom trying to convince himself that he didn't have VD. They got cleaned up and headed out.

There were two Dunkin' Donuts in town. Caleb and Amos drove to the one on the south end, the one that wasn't across the street from the police station. It was smaller and generally less busy. They ordered coffee and bagels and waited.

"Who's coming?" Caleb asked with salmon-flavored cream cheese clinging to the corner of his mouth.

"Levi."

"Levi? Who else? Tell me Lucky's not with him, too. That guy is off the fucking chain."

"He's good."

"He's a degenerate, twisted, fucking pit bull." He reached under the table and rubbed his crotch. "I feel like stuff is leaking out. If I have it, does that happen?"

"I guess. I've never had it."

"I better get checked out."

"You might want to do that."

Levi and Lucky pushed through the doors. Caleb and Amos stood to greet them and sat back down at the table. Levi was Amos's first cellmate in Warren. He'd been in for two years when Amos got there, but he never told him what for, and Amos never asked. They'd talked about jobs, their kind of jobs—how they would set up when they got out, if they'd go straight or strap and make some real grip.

His brother Lucky was a maniac. Lucky's aggressive, neck-snapping attitude always made him ready for some kind of violence or vandalism. When Lucky was old enough to squeeze a trigger, he put four rounds in his stepfather's back while he was passed out on their kitchen floor. The old man used to beat them and their mother with a piece of PVC that had holes drilled in it so he could swing it faster. Lucky still went to juvie until he was twenty-one. His stepfather overdosed in a wheelchair.

"God, it's good to see you boys again," Levi said.

"Coom-bye-ya," Lucky responded. "You know it's pretty fucking hysterical there's a Dunkin' Donuts across the street from the police station. Why couldn't we meet there?"

"I heard you got clipped on your birthday," Levi said to Moss.

"It was the day after. And the dumb shit missed. I got hit with the ricochet."

"That's fucking genius," Lucky said.

Amos had considered that fortunate when it happened. But Ava had been in his bed.

"You boys ready to roll? There's a hotel bed with my name on it." Amos rubbed his temples.

Caleb swatted at his crotch.

"Jesus Christ, Caleb. You got crabs or some shit?" Lucky asked.

"VD," Amos told them.

"What did I tell you about fucking your sister without a condom?" Lucky said.

"Fuck you."

"I hope that's not what you mean by pay the penalty."

As they drove out of town, Amos saw the sadness—the lines of women at the human resources office, the people shaking their heads at auto dealerships, the going-out-of-business signs posted along Main Street, and the dark reflective windows of businesses that already had. He would have been content if he had been leaving for good. By the time they reached New Hampshire, Ava had called twice. That torment alone, her moral struggle, had only perpetuated the desire he had for destruction whether it were for the men he was about to face or his own.

The four of them shacked up in Danvers at a Motel 6 with stained sheets and the unpleasant nostril tease of industrial cleaners. They fine-tuned plans for the raid the next night. Caleb continually went to the bathroom to piss with no success.

Lucky and Levi took turns verbally bashing him. They split up the supplies: zip ties, police raid jackets, and badges, cleaned the throwaway burners, changed the batteries in the stun gun, and checked the material in the bulletproof vests.

Lucky sat with his legs folded on one of the beds, playing solitaire. Levi and Amos sat at the table, amused by Caleb's pacing. Ashes fell from Lucky's cigarette onto the cards. He shot a quick breath downward and scattered ashes into the bed sheets. Caleb went back into the bathroom, kicking the door as he entered.

"Hey, Cal. I remember the first time I got the clap," Lucky paused. "In first grade."

"This sucks." Caleb kicked the toilet seat up.

"Was it worth it?" Levi asked.

"No. Christ."

Lucky put his cigarette out in a pool of spit inside his palm. He threw the butt toward the wastebasket and wiped his ashy palm on the comforter. "I remember this stripper. She could get high as gas but could never handle her booze. Anyway, one night we got hammered and I took her home to smash it. I'm balls deep for like a half hour totally crushing it 'til she stops me. I'm like, *what the fuck?* She says she thinks she's gonna be sick." Lucky lit another cigarette. "So I open the window next to the bed and she puts her head out. Well, she's on her hands and knees so I start smashing it from the back. She starts slapping at me." He stood to make pelvic thrusts. Mattress springs chorused his movements. "Then she starts puking out the window. I keep fucking her and she's like, *blat, blat, stop, blat, blat.* I am destroying this piece of ass. This bitch has her face against the windowsill, drooling down the vinyl siding as I'm blowing my load." He sat down.

Caleb stared from the bathroom aiming his irritated member toward the toilet. Lucky started flipping cards for another game of solitaire.

"Did you get the clap?" Caleb asked.

"Who, me?" Lucky looked up from his cards.

"Yeah, you," Caleb called.

"No."

"Then what was the fucking point of that story?"

Lucky put his cigarette out. "I just figured you'd want to know what my mother did after work."

Laughter erupted and stuck somewhere high in the corners of the room. A muddled *fuck you* came from the bathroom.

Amos stayed awake most of the night rummaging through his thoughts. He couldn't convince himself, no matter how hard he tried, to feel anything for Ava other than anger and regret. More than her, he thought about the job. There was no point to it. He didn't need the money any longer. But then he realized it wasn't about the money. What he felt then was indifference. All that he had done meant nothing. His feelings for Ava took away the satisfaction that he had anticipated, and he wanted everything around him to fade away.

FIFTY-ONE
Kenny

Kavanagh slid his fingers over the newspaper article about Amos Swain's arrest. The photocopy paper felt heavy in his thick fingers. The other photos and information that Roberts had collected rested on the table beneath his forearms and were of little interest to him. His doubts and wonder of who had taken his money disappeared as he looked at the young face of a boy being shuffled from the courtroom to begin a prison sentence for burglary. Slowly, Kavanagh crumpled the paper and let it rest on the scattered pile on the table. He looked over at the table to Roberts, who had twined his fingers together in nervous anticipation.

"And this guy just happens to be one of the bouncers at Logan's?"

Roberts nodded.

"So we've solved the mystery. Part of it anyway."

"How do you want to handle it?" Roberts asked.

"I want my money back, and I want to know where the fuck Bobby is."

"Do you still think Bobby is involved?"

"How else would this Swain son of a bitch have known where to find the safe?"

"But Bobby tried to kill him."

213

"And Bobby probably gave him the information to avoid retaliation. Either way, we'll find out when we talk to him. Let's take a ride."

"You're going to go find him now?"

"Do you think we should wait for a more convenient time to get our money back from him? Yes, I'm going to go talk to him now. Get your fucking shit together and let's go."

"But what about Hammer? Shouldn't he be the one to go with you?"

"This is your fucking mess. You're going."

Roberts moved slowly from the table and pulled his coat from the rack by the door. "Do you want me to drive?"

Kavanagh shook his head and guided Roberts from his house. They made the drive in silence and drove slowly through the streets of Amos's town. Kavanagh focused on his decision of what to do. He'd grown less patient over the years, but making an example of the people who made moves against him had tired him. Things were messy when that happened and he'd resolved his decision to do as little as possible to get the most done. He also took into consideration that Amos had given back the money he'd stolen in the job that got him sent to prison. The threat of death was a much more formidable persuasive technique than prison, and the threat of prison wasn't really an option for him. Roberts parked the car a few buildings down from Amos's. Kavanagh motioned him to follow and the two of them crossed the street and entered the building.

Roberts led the way up the stairs, apprehensive, followed closely by Kavanagh who had pulled his .357 snub-nosed from the ankle holster and slipped it into his jacket pocket during their ascent. When they got to the third-floor apartment, Roberts stepped away from the door and gave his attention to Kavanagh. Kavanagh knocked and leaned in to listen for movement. He waited for a while and tried the knob. The door opened and he stepped into the apartment casually. Roberts looked over the railing down the flight of stairs then followed.

Kenny patrolled the apartment. He went through the kitchen opening drawers and cabinets. He moved along the walls. When he found a stashed pistol in the oven, he noted it and moved on. In the bedroom he patted the fabric of Amos's suits checking for things in the pockets. He tapped on floorboards and places in the sheetrock that looked weak. There was the slight temptation to pocket the small stashes of cash he found, but he opted not to. He noted the meticulous nature of the man and the intentional setting of everything in there. Amos Swain left his door unlocked, which meant he wasn't scared. He had a weapon stashed within arm's reach in every point of the apartment. A man with that type of vigilance who didn't lock his door wouldn't allow someone who attempted to kill him get away.

"Are we going to wait for him?" Roberts asked.

"I want you to find out everything there is to know about Amos Swain. Where he eats, the women he fucks, what hours he works down at Logan's, where his family lives, everything. We're not going to wait for him here, but we're going to come down on this motherfucker hard."

"Don't you think he'll just give us the money? What about Bobby?"

"Bobby's dead."

"How do you know?"

"Look around. We've underestimated Amos Swain. He's not just a bouncer. This guy knows what the fuck he's doing. If Bobby were still alive and on the lam from Swain, he'd have come to us. Swain is our guy, and we're going to put him down."

FIFTY-TWO
Amos

Amos wanted Crow to have as little information on him as possible, so they left Lucky and Levi in the car when they met Crow's crew on the train platform in Salem. A large apartment complex sat towering on the other side of a rusted chain-link fence. The gravel around the tracks edged against mud with sprouts of sea grass to the channel of water. Across the channel, cranes moved chunks of metal in a steel yard. Two of Crow's crew were waiting for them.

"Where is Crow?" Amos asked as they approached.

The two of them stood.

"He ain't here," Skin Dysfunction said.

"You must win awards for stating the fucking obvious. Where the fuck is he?"

"He had to make a run up to Revere. Business. You can call him if you want."

"Really? Business? What is this then, a fucking support group? We're ready to roll and he's what, fencing laptops?"

Skin Dysfunction pulled the gnarled tip of a Black & Mild from his lips and blew smoke toward Amos's face. "This is your crew?"

Amos glared at him. "What is Crow doing in Revere?"

Skin Dysfunction shrugged. "That's his business. He didn't

tell us. He just told us to meet you here and make sure you guys were going through with this."

The cranes moaned from across the canal. Gulls fluttered to the mud and picked through bits of trash. Amos bit a sliver of dead skin from his lip.

"What's the layout?" Amos asked.

"Twenty-foot walkway to the front door. Three steps. Eight up the back to the porch."

"Any neighbors?"

"Old couple in the house on the right. House on the left is empty and for rent. Apartment complex across the street. Two-way street. Not a lot of traffic."

"Stellar." Amos pulled a two-way radio from his back pocket and gave it to Skin Dysfunction. "Keep it on channel six. Park at the end of the road and let us know when the product is coming our way. We'll take care of the rest."

He took the radio. "We'll see you tonight."

Amos and Caleb walked back to the car passing a woman and her small waddling child who was bundled in too many layers of clothing.

Caleb stared at him from the driver's seat when they got in the car. Amos shrugged and turned in the front seat to face Lucky and Levi. "Something's not right."

"What do you mean?" Lucky asked.

"Crow's not here. It's up to you guys. You want to bail on this?"

"Let's go take them out now and do the roll anyway," Lucky said.

"That wouldn't be a bad idea except for the two witnesses we just passed. Fuck that. Not with a kid around."

Amos called Crow—the monotonous ring and then his voice came through.

"What the fuck, asshole? Where are you?"

"Ah, man. I'm sorry. I had to get up here and take care of some shit."

"Something more important than this?" Engine belts squealed in the background.

"I had a drop-off. You ain't the only guys I got runnin'."

"I thought this would take precedence over everything else, considering how big this party is. And I don't fucking run for you."

"Look, man. Everything is straight. You the only dog I know that can pull this off."

"Yeah, whatever. I'll call you when it's ready."

Amos and his crew crammed into a booth at the back of a roadside breakfast joint. The vinyl on the seats was cracked and mended with duct tape curling up at the corners. Amos took the inside next to the window. A draft seeped through and coiled around his neck as he scraped at the crystals forming at the top of the syrup container with a fork. The waitress, haggard and overweight, her apron smudged with grease and ketchup stains, took their order. A man with two small children in the booth across from them bowed their heads over their food to pray before eating. His children had ordered some eggs and orange juice. The man sipped his water and coated his toast with jelly, which was all he'd ordered after checking his wallet. Amos looked around their table after the food came, coffee, eggs, toast, corned beef hash, home-fries, sausage, bacon, blueberry pancakes, and melting butter. The children at the other table thanked their father repeatedly, their voices shaky with excitement. Amos took another look at the food in front of them, at his crew shoveling food from their plates to their mouths, and he pushed his plate away. He let his hunger claw and howl from a depth he hadn't felt since he was a child.

FIFTY-THREE
Ruth

Ruth folded towels into thirds and piled them on the kitchen table. She took a glance out the window between each folding to check on Seneca who fell dramatically in the snow, playing with her imaginary puppy, a puppy that she should have let her keep. The ache in her face had diminished quicker than she'd expected, and she realized, with Seneca's delightful playing, how thankful she was for Caleb. Three men were dead, but that did little to her conscience. With her thoughts of Caleb, she thought about Amos, and the muffled laughter of Seneca outside made her think of him when he was a boy—the nights his father would be gone late with Tommy Logan, doing things she never asked about so he could give her the life she'd wanted. Amos was an affectionate child, not a mama's boy, but compassionate. Helpful. Always bearing a cheerful demeanor that helped her find solace in her times of worry for her husband. During the course of her thoughts, Ruth finished folding her laundry. She brought the towels to the bathroom and put them on the shelf in the small closet. When she reentered the kitchen, two men in suits were at the edge of her driveway speaking to Seneca.

Her heart raced. She dropped the wicker laundry basket. The potential danger didn't occur to her until she was outside approaching the men quickly and with a ferocity she never had

the chance to acknowledge. Both men were streamline rigid. Their
suits were cheap but crisp. Square jaws and short barber-cut hair.
Blue suit, gray suit. One of the men turned to face her and
nudged his associate's arm.

"Ruth Archer?" the man in the blue suit asked.

"Can I help you?"

Simultaneously, they pulled wallets from their inside jacket
pockets and flashed their badges. "We'd like to speak with you
about one of the properties you represent."

Ruth's chance for relief vanished between the moment she
realized they were cops and the moment they mentioned the
property. She shivered in the cold. "Is there something wrong?"

"Ma'am, you look cold. Would you like to talk about this
inside?"

Ruth led the men into the house. Before she turned, she noticed
the look of contempt on Seneca's face. She loved her brother, and
already she had taken sides against the police.

Ruth made coffee and the men didn't wait for an invitation
to sit at her table. She eased the trembling in her hands. They
pulled small leather folds from their pockets and clicked the
pens they'd taken out along with the notebooks. Ruth stood at
the counter waiting for the coffee to brew.

"Ma'am, I'm Detective Brown and this is Detective Carpenter.
I'm not sure if you're aware yet, but the property we mentioned
was destroyed in a fire."

Ruth covered her mouth. "Dear, God. That's...Oh my god,
which one? How?"

"Well, the fire was set intentionally to the property at 19
Madison Drive."

"Intentionally? What do you mean?"

"Somebody burned the house down."

"But that's such a nice neighborhood. Why would that
happen?"

The gray suit detective pulled a small stack of photographs
from his jacket pocket. "Ma'am, we believe whatever happened

is drug related. Do you recognize any of these men?"

The detective's thin fingers spread the pictures out and Ruth went to the table to look at them. She wanted to lie, but decided it was best to be a little honest. They didn't suspect her, she knew, otherwise they wouldn't have said anything about drugs.

"I showed that property to them a couple of weeks ago. Are they responsible for the fire?"

The detective pushed his lips together. "No, Ms. Archer. These men were found inside. They were murdered and we think the fire was set to destroy any evidence."

"Murder? Jesus."

"Yes. We're trying to fit the pieces together. Any information you can give us would be a big help."

"Detectives, I'm sorry. I don't know how much help I could be. I showed the property to them and they didn't really say much. I don't really know anything about them except that they seemed like a nice couple. They turned the property down because they said it was out of their price range. I did my best to sell the place, but the market is so horrible it's tough to be persuasive."

"I'm sorry to hear that. Any detail would help."

Ruth pretended to think for a moment. "I can't really think of anything. I'm sorry."

"Did they ask you any questions about the property that seemed a little peculiar?"

"No, just the normal things. Wait. Actually, they did ask how often the neighborhood was patrolled by the police. I thought that was a little strange, but I just thought maybe they wanted to feel safe."

The detectives made notes.

"Does that help at all?"

"We'll look into it," the blue suit said. He pulled a business card from a pocket and handed it to Ruth. "Thank you for your time. If you remember anything, even the smallest detail, give me a call."

The coffee finished brewing and she stood.

"Would you gentlemen like a coffee before you go?"

"Thank you, Ms. Archer, but we need to follow up on a few more leads."

The detectives gathered their photos and stood at the table. Ruth followed them to the door. They both waved at Seneca as they passed, who, in turn, crossed her arms over her chest and scowled at them. After the detectives had pulled out of the driveway, Ruth felt her knees weaken and exhaled loudly. She whispered, *shit,* and went to the trash can where she ripped the detective's card in half and dropped it into the bin.

FIFTY-FOUR
Amos

Low lamp light inside the house gave the shades an orange glow. They fluttered every few minutes from someone inside peeking out. The house was angled on the lot so the windows were visible from where Amos sat on the sidewalk against a large maple tree. Music shot through the air from the apartment complex across the street when someone opened their patio door. Three cars passed as they waited. Garbage cans and claw-torn trash bags littered the curb.

Amos's stomach was already swelling and painful from the two liters of water he had chugged. Cramps punched the insides of his ribs. Crow's crew parked at the corner waiting to signal them for the delivery car. Caleb and Levi were behind the aluminum shed in the backyard of the house. Lucky crouched in some shrubs across the street next to a dumpster. Different patterns of breathing broke through the earpieces of their radios. Malt liquor bubbled in Amos's stomach after tipping the forty. The earpiece crackled and Crow's driver whispered that the car was approaching.

Amos stood and made sure the stun gun was on. The fluids in his stomach made him ache to vomit. After taking another sip of the forty, he leaned against the maple pretending to piss. Headlights hit the bark on the tree and the lights grew bigger.

After a deep breath, Amos turned and began stumbling toward them. High beams flashed on as the car stopped. A silhouette of the passenger stood on the sidewalk behind the light shooting toward him, duffel bag hanging, and then it moved toward the house. Amos stumbled to both sides of the sidewalk tipping up the bottle and sliding his feet over the cracked and bulging concrete where tree roots had broken sections of cement. He timed himself to reach the front of the car when the passenger entered the house. The door shut. Amos dropped the bottle—a hushed sound of a glass pop. Headlights shot into his eyes when he bent over. Instead of reaching for the bottle, he gagged himself with two fingers and hurled on the hood of the car.

The distraction.

"Oh, what the fuck? You drunk bastard," the driver said as he got out of the car.

Amos smacked his lips as he wiped the two fingers on his hoodie, slowly inching his other hand toward his back pocket to grasp the stun gun. "Slorry." He faked a hiccup. "My bad."

"What's up," a voice said on the driver's speaker phone.

"Motherfucker just puked on the car."

"Get him out of here."

His hand grasped the hood of Amos's jacket. Before his grip locked, Amos had the back of his head with one hand and jammed the stun gun into his neck under his chin. It sparked tiny blue flashes against the man's throat.

Lucky charged by him as Amos brought the driver's body to the ground and zip-tied his twitching hands and feet. He stuffed a rag in his mouth. The man's body shook, his forehead bumping off the curb. Amos stripped the hoodie off to reveal the yellow letters of the police raid jacket, pulled a ski mask over his face, and ran toward the door. Lucky kicked the door in. The door guard toppled, and Lucky grabbed his shotgun and drove the butt of it into his stomach, thrusting him backwards over a coffee table where he took another person off their feet and the two of them landed on a plastic-covered lily-print couch. The back door flew open. Caleb and Levi came in yelling *police* and pushed two more bodies toward the couch.

Amos walked through the door and grabbed a two-foot bong from the coffee table. The bottom had heft from water in the base and moved quickly when he swung it against the head of the man closest to him. It shattered spraying black oily liquid over the others. An odor crept into the air like the smell inside an old bicycle tire. The injured man grasped his face with both hands and fell to the brown carpet at the feet of the others. Lucky flipped the glass coffee table over and held his pistols inches from scared, wide-eyed faces.

Aggressive gain of control.

Five people were on their knees in front of them huddled together with their hands in the air. Glances of anger and fear worked over the blue nylon jackets and ski masks Amos's crew wore. Caleb and Levi swept the back rooms. Lucky and Amos zip-tied the five people and pushed them into a cluster at the center of the room facing away from them. Top halves of the bedroom doors were cut off. Cardboard had been taped to the back windows. Holes were scattered over the walls and ceilings. A patch of green carpet sunk over an open space in the floor.

"Man, this ain't right," one of them said over his shoulder.

Lucky clapped his burners against both of his ears. "Shut the fuck up, mouth."

He pressed his ears toward each shoulder trying to kill the pain. "Fuck you. I want to see the warrant. I'm suing you motherfuckers." Mouth pivoted on his knees.

Lucky holstered a pistol and grabbed Mouth's throat. "Stupid fuck. Shut the fuck up."

Mouth's eyes squinted in anger when Lucky released him. "Do you motherfuckers know who you're fucking with? I'm gangsta up in this motherfucker." His head bobbed to the right when he spoke.

Amos kicked the man in the side of the face. He mumbled over the blood that oozed from his mouth as his chin slumped against his chest.

"What's up now, *gangsta?*" Amos asked.

The others in the room inched away from the men in raid jackets, closer to the wall.

Caleb and Levi checked the bags. "Cargo's good," Caleb handed one of the bags to Levi. They went through the kitchen. Their exit was through the back door where they would cut across the neighboring yards to the car. Skin Dysfunction was in the doorway when Amos turned with the muzzle of his pistol pointed at his chest.

He thought about Ava, his father, prison, an assortment of things that made him not care, made him want to get bullets punched into his chest. When Amos saw how dark the night was in the doorway behind Skin Dysfunction, he expected it to expand through the room and there would never be those thoughts again.

A sudden force slammed into Amos from the side as a gunshot ripped through the house. Lucky teetered back from where Amos had been standing and dropped to his knees. Caleb shot from the back door, hitting Skin Dysfunction in the shoulder. Amos sprung from the floor to his knees, raised his arm, and shot twice. A large bloody crater hollowed Skin Dysfunction's left eye socket and cheekbone. His head bashed into the doorjamb as he fell.

Lucky shot from his knees through the doorway reaching for his other burner. He pulled it and shot. The other barked, then the other—two dogs barking at each other on opposite sides of a chain-link fence. Amos sprawled to his feet as Lucky's pistols emptied and the slides locked back. He stood. Caleb and Levi made their way to the car. Amos looked at the dark spot on Lucky's raid jacket left by the bullet he took. Caleb's car peeled around the corner and skidded to a stop in front of the house. The passenger door flew open.

Lucky and Amos stepped over the other two members of Crow's crew. Small pirouettes of smoke rose from their chests.

They had fallen to the bottom of the porch steps, arms and legs tangled like dolls in a toy box. Lucky shoved another clip in his burner and put an insurance round into each of their heads while Amos grabbed the hooded sweatshirt he'd left on the lawn. Lucky dove into the back seat with Levi then pulled the front seat back for Amos to get in. Caleb pulled the car forward, where the guy he'd hit with the stun gun made an attempt to roll himself on the sidewalk. Lucky extended his arm through the window and shot him. Caleb gassed it to the end of the road, made a right, and drove the speed limit to the interstate, piercing the rearview with stares.

"What the fuck just happened?" Caleb asked. He yanked his earpiece away and slammed it into the windshield. The wire whipped against the dashboard.

Amos stripped the ski mask off and pulled a garbage bag from the glove box and put the ski masks and raid jackets inside.

Lucky massaged his chest.

"I feel like I got hit with a fucking cannonball."

Amos turned in his seat to look Lucky in the eyes, thanking him with a glance.

"Any time," Lucky responded.

"What the fuck?" Caleb yelled. "That fucking piece of shit, backstabbing fuck."

"It's over Cal." Amos sunk into the seat.

"No, fuck that. I want to smoke that motherfucker." His lips quivered.

Bands of darkness and light between highway streetlights scanned over the car.

"Cal, it's okay."

"No. It's not okay. It's not fucking okay." Caleb punched spider webs into the windshield between words. "He tried to kill you."

Crow trying to hijack him left Amos wondering, why? Why would he make a move like that with a diluted crew? Two of his boys had been pinched and they'd just dropped the rest of them. Amos looked over at Caleb, and he couldn't force himself to imagine what it would be like without him.

"So what do we do?" Lucky asked.

"We go to his house," Caleb said.

Caleb drove to the parking lot at the train station in Salem where they'd left Levi's car. They transferred the guns, cash, and product. They doused the GT with white gas and torched it with everything else.

Caleb gave Levi directions to Crow's place from the seat behind him. When they arrived, Caleb had Levi park across the street a few car lengths from the light of the only working streetlight. There was a chain-link fence around Crow's house. The gate to the walkway hung from one hinge and overlapped part of the fence. Patches of dead grass showed through the thin layer of snow.

"He's mine, Caleb," Amos said when Levi turned off the ignition.

He waited a moment to answer. "I know."

By the time Crow arrived, which was almost two hours later, the warmth of the car had been gone for a while and shivers began to infect them all. Amos's toes ached in his boots. When Crow pulled up to the curb across the street, Amos didn't think about either of those things. Crow got out, looking at his phone, and slammed the door.

Some men are killers because they have to be. Some are because they choose to be. There was always the fear of prison or death or a punishment equally terrible. They could suffer that way, but paying the penalty was not losing life or freedom. It was something deeper that started inside them and pushed its way out—made their eyes blink less and kept their hands from shaking. It made them ignore the fear of losing their own life and the guilt of taking one. The sheer fragility of life is never fully understood unless you take it from someone.

Amos hit the safety on the .45 and stepped into the street. Crow looked at him, dropped his phone, and reached for his waistband. Amos brought the gun up, and it broke through the darkness. He pulled on the trigger. Before Amos could fire a round, Caleb had stepped into the middle of the street and kicked two rounds into Crow's legs. Crow crumpled against the door of his car. Caleb walked through the light. Crow tried to push him away as Caleb jerked on the shoulder of his jacket to sit him upright. He pressed his gun into Crow's temple and shot him. Crow rolled facedown on the driveway. Caleb turned and walked back.

"I couldn't let you do it," he told Amos as they got back into the car.

In the car, Lucky broke the guns down and cut the barrels with a pair of bolt cutters. Levi slowed at the Piscataqua River Bridge, and Amos tossed the pieces of the guns over. Caleb rested his head against the window and bit the end of his thumb the entire ride home.

The boys split the money while Amos stood by the window in Caleb's living room, peering into the darkness outside. Caleb slammed whiskey with more urgency than he'd ever drank and continued to curse Crow. Amos wondered why he'd prevented him from killing Crow. Amos's phone vibrated again, and again, it was Ava. She'd called more than a dozen times.

Levi stepped away from the couch where they were sitting with a stack of money and handed it to Amos. Amos looked down at it, then back out the window.

"I don't want it."

Levi chuckled. "Right. Here man, take it."

"You guys split it." Amos turned from the window, pushed Levi's hand and the money from his path, and left.

FIFTY-FIVE
Caleb

Caleb moved his hand to his pistol when he saw Stevens's car pull into the rest stop and hurtle around the bend in the parking lot. Caleb thought about ignoring his request to meet, but he thought it would be better than having Stevens show up at Logan's or his home. Stevens slammed on the brakes and the car slid several feet before stopping at an angle near the edge of the sidewalk where Caleb waited. Stevens yanked on the door handle and kicked the door open. It swung out quickly and bounced back, shutting and silencing the cursing that emitted from the car. Caleb flicked his cigarette away and opened the door slowly. Stevens pulled away before Caleb was entirely in the seat, forcing him to clutch at the dashboard. Again, at the end of the parking lot, Stevens skidded the car to a halt and pulled into a parking spot.

"You have to be out of your fucking mind," Stevens stated and drove the shifter into park.

"What are you talking about?"

"You fucking killed him."

"Who?"

"Don't play fucking dumb with me, motherfucker. I'm done with your shit. I hope you enjoyed your freedom."

"Go fuck yourself. You're not going to do shit."

"I'm not?"

"No. You can try to do whatever you want. I've already accepted the fact that I'm going down. The fall is going to be a lot longer for you."

"Caleb, what the fuck makes you think you can compete with me on any level in this game?"

"I'm not competing. I'm just done."

"Done? You actually think you can fucking quit this?"

"What makes you think I can't? What are you going to do? Go ahead and arrest me. I fucking dare you. I know you fucking played me. There's no way you didn't know that Crow was going to try to take us out. You probably set it up."

"You're right, Caleb. I did set it up. But your friend is going to get a nice little surprise now."

"What the fuck are you talking about?"

"I know something about you and Amos that you weren't quite honest with me about."

"You don't know shit, cocksucker. Go fuck yourself."

Caleb climbed from the car and took a breath of soft, cool air. He looked back in at Stevens. "You're a fucking piece of shit." He sucked the phlegm from his throat and spit onto the shoulder of Stevens's suit. Stevens tore from the car and shed his Glock. He stood in Caleb's path and Caleb shrugged.

"Do it. I'm sure that these security cameras will conflict with whatever story you're going to make up. I don't care what Moss finds out. I don't care about what you have on me. I especially don't give a fuck about dying."

Stevens holstered his gun. "Maybe you don't. But, now, you're speaking for Amos Swain. It's on you now, whatever happens to him." Stevens turned and got back into his car.

The heaviness of Caleb's guilt sat close to him on the drive home. He drove until he couldn't breathe and pulled to the side of the interstate. His inability to find a way to solve his problem bore into him worse than what he imagined Moss would do or say when he found out. When he finally got a breath substantial enough to shake off the dizziness that was setting in, he exhaled and brought with it a shedding of tears so profuse, he created a new threat to his breathing. As he sobbed, he imagined the look of betrayal that Amos would bear, the words he would use to express his anger and pain. He cared little about what Amos would do to him, but the value of his friendship destroyed by his betrayal left him little hope for anything redeeming. Caleb, as he gained control of his inner turmoil, drew his pistol and put the barrel in his mouth.

Gun oil nauseated him. The trigger felt like it was pushing back against his finger. His tears had stopped, and his thoughts had wandered to darker places. Kavanagh was sure to find out, and the retribution that he would seek against Amos was a far more painful thought than Caleb's betrayal. Amos didn't deserve that. Because of Stevens, Caleb had convinced him to do the job. And if he checked out, leaving Amos without the help he needed to protect himself, that was a far worse betrayal than anything. Caleb pulled the gun from his mouth, smeared the moisture from his eyes, and got back on the road.

FIFTY-SIX
Amos

Several days after the Lynn job, Caleb called from the parking lot outside his apartment and refused to tell him why he needed him to come out. Amos had spent several days organizing his thoughts and trying his best to eliminate the sting that Ava had left. His curiosity about Vassar and his mother did the most to help him forget, but even then, Ava and his longing for her voice would subdue his other thoughts and he would be reminded of how much more helpless she had made him feel.

"Fucking chlamydia," Caleb said, when Amos climbed into the front seat.

"Seriously? This is about your dick?"

"No. Tommy wants to meet us at the river."

They'd never met outside the bar for anything Tommy wanted to talk to them about, and the last time they'd met at the river, it was only a couple days after Amos had killed Bailey Mitchell. Amos wondered if Tommy had found some information about his mother or who had wanted her tuned-up. Tommy and another man stood on the bridge fifty yards from the spring. The Mousam River ran below it, and the icy branches of the trees tilted in the snowy banks on either side. When they got to the bridge, Lucas, Tommy's former bouncer who became a state trooper, extended his hand.

"What's going on?" Amos asked.

"A whole lot of fucking heat is what's going on. The state's initiating an investigation into drug trafficking, specifically targeting known nefarious elements right here in our little town." Tommy muffled a cough into his sleeve.

"And?" Caleb asked. "The fuck do we care? They started an investigation? We're not dealing, and if they had shit on any of us, we'd have already been pulled in."

Lucas spoke up. "It's not that simple. Moss's name came up. It's the only name that came up."

"What? How?" Caleb asked.

Amos took a step and held the railing of the bridge.

"I've been banging this low-level legal aid. She works with the state prosecutor or in the office or I don't fucking know. Anyway, we're talking and she mentions Logan's, because she read some files and knew it was a bar in my hometown. I shrug it off, not trying to make her nervous, but I want her to keep talking. She does. And she tells me that some fed from out of Boston claims that he has an informant here, in this town, giving him information on Amos Swain."

"That's fucking bullshit. What the fuck could they possibly have on Moss?"

"Murder," Amos said. He stared down the river. The water flowed by, a steady pace toward the ocean. He wanted to fall into the water and let it carry him into darkness, but for reasons other than the answer to Caleb's question.

"Moss, he just fucking said drug investigation. How the—"

Lucas held his hand up to Caleb. "I'm not done. Another name came up: Vassar Twombly. They found his body yesterday afternoon. And apparently he had some chick in his freezer with her head bashed in."

"Oh shit," Caleb muttered. He shook his head. "But how?"

"That, I don't know. Shit gets even more weird and there's some connection to another fucking murder down in Kennebunk, but that's all I could get for the time being. If I can get anything

ALL THE GOOD IN EVIL

else, I'll let you know. My best guess is that Amos has maybe an eight-to-twenty-four-hour window before you start catching a tail, or even worse, they find something to bring you in."

Tommy blew threw his nose as he talked. "You two have to dump everything. No more jobs out here on the street. Do some spring cleaning and take everything up to the playground." He flicked the cigarillo into the water. "I'll try to find out who this rat fucking piece of shit informant is."

Tommy and Lucas left the opposite direction that they had come. The sound of the river and the word *informant* drowned out anything that Lucas had said after. Amos's mouth dried out until his tongue felt bony. To him, it should have been obvious, why she'd come back into his life, the notes in her journal, her constant ebbing from him as soon as they got closer to establishing something, and her dramatic departures. She'd done what she had to do to keep him just close enough. It made more sense, all of it. It made sense enough for Amos to believe that Ava was the informant.

PART III

FIFTY-SEVEN
Amos

Caleb and Amos moved back to the car. They stood in silence staring at each other over the frosted hood. Their breath fanned against the sparkling crystals.

"Looks like it's going to be a long night," Caleb said.

"I don't think it will be the longest."

"Man, relax. We've been through shit like this before. How long have you been duping Jones? You'll think of something. You always do."

"That's not what's bothering me."

"What then?"

"Whoever the fuck tipped them off."

Caleb smoked while the car warmed up.

Snow began to fall. Light from the streetlamps sparkled off falling flakes for a moment until they hit the windshield, became water, and the wipers cleared them away. Caleb drove down the thin gray lines car tires left behind on the road. They circled the block around Amos's apartment, checking for cars and anyone watching. Nothing.

The snow picked up as Amos entered the building. He started in the bathroom, pulling the .38 from beneath the towels, and tossed it in a duffel bag. After that, he went for the roll of hundreds in a metal Band-Aid container from the medicine cabinet. Before he could move on to the five grand he kept in the nightstand, Amos noticed the bills faced the opposite direction he'd placed them. The .45 and the double barrel sawed-off beneath the mattress had been moved. Movement on or off the bed could have adjusted the guns, but the money in the nightstand was not a mistake. Ava must have found it at some point, he thought. He swept the rest of the apartment, putting the .357 from the oven and the other .45 beneath the couch cushions, the cash in the dryer hose, and more cash from a hollowed-out square in the knife block into the duffel bag. It hung awkward from his hand because of the proportion of weight at one end. When Amos was on probation he'd never felt secure because he couldn't have anything in the apartment.

Amos had been so distracted by the dilemma of protecting himself in his home that he didn't notice that the puppy was missing. He dropped the bag on the counter and walked around the apartment calling for her, expecting to hear her claws digging into the floor from some hiding place unknown to him. He thought for a moment that maybe the puppy got out, but the door was shut. Amos called his mother.

"Yes, Amos?" she answered.

"Did you come by my apartment today?"

"Yes."

"Did you take the puppy?"

"Yes."

"Were you going to, I don't know, tell me you came into my home while I wasn't here to take her?"

She sighed. "Amos, you tantalized her with the puppy. I figured you would know I came and got it. I grew tired of Seneca's whining."

Amos hung up, took a deep breath, and kicked the trash can across the kitchen into the fridge. Cans fell out and clinked on the floor and the trash can thudded on its side. "Bitch."

"Tell me how you really feel."

Amos half pulled the .45 from his waistband and turned to

face Jones in the doorway.

"What are you so shaken up about?"

"I think you know, Detective."

"I've come by several times already. I guess you've been busy. Are you going to invite me in?"

"Since when have you needed an invitation?" Amos walked to the counter.

Jones shook snowflakes from his hair as he moved through the room.

"You have a big fucking problem, Swain."

"I know. Thanks for the fucking heads up."

"Don't get pissed at me. I'm still here to help."

"I don't see how much good you can do. I'm pretty fucked here."

"Moss, they don't have anything. All they have is some fed's anonymous source that you might be involved in drug trafficking with some week-old corpse with bullets in it."

"And where the fuck did that come from?"

"Did you have anything to do with it?"

Amos scowled at him. "Really?"

"You know I gotta ask."

"Fuck, man. How could she know anything about that piece of shit?"

"She?"

"Ava Metzger."

"The girl you were with the other day?"

"Yeah."

Jones pulled out his notepad. "What's her name again? Ava?"

"Metzger."

"Let me see what I can dig up."

"How the fuck is that going to help me now?"

"It may help me. I don't like this fed. There's something sketchy about him, more so than the feds already are."

"How much do they have to work with?"

"Nothing, really. You're just the only potential suspect and they haven't even listed you as one, yet."

"Yet..."

"Maybe you should give them a reason to move and dilute the investigation."

"Like what?"

"They might get hasty if they think you're going to skip town."

Amos scratched his head. "What about Curry? What's he doing about all of this?"

"Curry's been reassigned, per my recommendation. He's no longer a worry for you. I have to get going. Keep your shit together, Swain. This will pass."

When his footsteps faded down the stairs, Amos wiped his prints from the .45, grabbed the duffel bag, and ran to the bathroom window. He strained his eyes staring through the falling snow for cars, people at the corners of buildings or rooftops. The wind pushed falling snow back and forth in vertical waves. After prison, Amos hadn't been without a gun. It was like being forced to cut off a finger. He dropped the duffel bag into the dumpster below. It hit garbage bags and dinged against the inside of the container. Snowflakes cut through his breath as he figured out what he had to do to dump the cops. He ducked back inside and called Caleb to tell him he was ready.

Amos stared at the open space beyond the door where Jones had passed and took a breath deep enough to choke on. He stared until Caleb's car rumbled down the road. Caleb gassed it a few times as Amos made his way to the street. He pulled his duffel bag from the dumpster and Caleb met him at his truck.

"She played me." Amos held the back of his neck to warm his hands and fingers.

"What?"

"Ava. She's the informant."

"No, she's not."

"You really want to challenge me on this one, Caleb?"

"I just don't see how," he mumbled.

"How could I have not seen it?"

"Are you sure? Why would she do that to you?"

"I don't know. Jesus, it's almost like she's been trying to warn me the whole time."

Amos started the truck.

"Maybe you're just paranoid."

"I'm not paranoid. Tonight, after we do this, get us two one-way tickets out of here. I don't care where as long as it's as far away from here as possible."

"That doesn't make any sense. We can't fly. The cops will be monitoring that shit. They'll show up at the door tomorrow."

"That's the point."

Caleb grinned. "What time for the tickets?"

"Evening."

Plow trucks growled past them clearing the road and spiraling snow into small tornadoes behind them. Amos creeped the truck through the falling snow, watching for headlights behind him until they arrived at the junkyard.

They got out and kicked through the snow. White Mohawk plumes surged ahead of their boots as they walked to the gate and climbed over it. In the wide flat space of the junkyard, rusted hunks of metal lay in rows. Leaning forward, they pushed into the wind to the back corner of the yard. The snow wet their gloves as they cleared the trunk of an old Ford Fairlane and popped it open. They dropped the bags inside and shut it.

It was quiet, so quiet the snowflakes hitting the ground emitted a hiss. Caleb and Amos stood in the gray light of the junkyard casting their turbid breaths toward the sky. The urgency of the situation was clear then, a lifestyle that Amos had chosen to pursue the dreams he wanted had transformed to some ugly retreating break for survival. The snow fell faster and felt heavier, too heavy. Amos wanted to sink into a snowbank and melt away when spring came. He wanted to cry and laugh. He scooped snow from the ground in front of him, packed a tight snowball, and pegged Caleb in the chest.

"Are you fucking serious?" Caleb asked with his eyes closed.

Amos made another and hit him again. That time in the neck. Snow found its way beneath the collar of his jacket and shirt to his skin. "This is the playground," Amos answered. "Good thing you're not wearing your nine-hundred-dollar suit."

Caleb pulled the collar away with a finger. He made his own ball from snow on top of the Fairlane and threw it hitting Amos in the shoulder. He returned fire. They dodged each other's snowballs through the cars laughing and swearing at each other until they were breathing so hard that their breath was a constant stream of fog.

"Holy shit. We haven't had a snowball fight since senior year," Caleb said as they leaned into the trunk of a car trying to catch their breath.

"I always remember you making snow angels."

"I never made a fucking snow angel."

FIFTY-EIGHT
Amos

Snow fell through the night. A foot and a half layer of delicate white padded the ground. By noon though, the sun had come out and much of the snow melted. Small streams of water ran down the roads. Cars passed with the gray, scabby patterns drying snow and ice left on them. The sound of tires smashing slush crawled up the building and came into the apartment.

Amos stood and waited until the Crown Vics sped up the road and stopped in front of the building. Men in blue raid jackets like the ones Amos and his crew had worn for the Lynn job scrambled from their cruisers. A few of them stood outside their vehicles with shotguns and AR-15s. Overkill. The cops couldn't wait to grab a rifle or shotgun, put on their pristine raid gear and their toughest scowl just in case a reporter snapped a photo. Amos's eyes watered and he felt something similar to anger only with anger came power. He felt nothing but fatigue.

Amos pulled a couple beers from the fridge as the doorway of his apartment flooded with nylon jackets, bad ties, and even worse cologne. A tall, blue-suit detective with a flat-top and horn-rimmed glasses introduced himself and entered. A group of other cops followed with their hands on their guns. Some of them were staties. The others were local.

"Can I help you, Detective?"

He handed the warrant to Amos. Amos flung the warrant onto the counter.

"You need to put that beer down," one of the uniformed cops said.

"Going to be awfully hard to drink it if I do that," Amos replied.

"Look, I'll ask you nicely to put the beer down."

"Okay. Go ahead."

The cop looked confused. "Could you please put the beer down?"

"Go fuck yourself."

The tall detective squeezed his eyelids shut and shrugged.

The men moved through Amos's apartment—mattress, stove, freezer, knife block, medicine cabinet, dresser, the dryer. The detective stood near the window with his hands on his hips. He stared at the duffel bag beneath the end table and looked up at Amos.

"Are you even curious as to what this concerns, Mr. Swain?" the detective asked.

Amos took a slug of beer. "Not at all."

"Spoken like a guilty man."

"Usually up to a jury to decide guilt, isn't it, Detective?"

"Touché."

The detective walked over and pulled the duffel bag from the floor and placed it on the couch. Cops emerged from the bedroom and began to search the kitchen. The detective unzipped the duffel bag and pulled a stuffed pig from inside of it. He clenched his jaw.

"Clever," the detective said.

A vein in his temple throbbed and he moved to stand in front of Amos.

"You got tipped off, Mr. Swain. That's very interesting to me."

Amos shrugged.

Amos finished his beer and put the bottle on the counter. He coughed into his hands and put them in his pockets.

"Do you want us to keep going?" one of the staties asked.

The detective parted his lips and paused for a moment. "Tear it apart."

They sliced couch cushions, the mattress, even some of the suits in his closet. They pulled every book from his bookshelf and left them scattered in a heap in the living room like a collection of banned material waiting to be burned. Everything in a drawer or cabinet was pulled and strewn across the floor. They dumped the trash and contents of what few things he had in the refrigerator. Clothes flew through the air in his bedroom. When everything had been littered through the apartment, the detective told them to search it again. At the precise time that their flight to Vegas was departing, the detective called the search and they left.

FIFTY-NINE
Amos

The next day Amos sat at a study table in the back of the public library waiting for Jones. The snow had turned to rain. The drops fell against wood, cement, and plastic forcing a gloomy symphonic rhythm outside. Tall shelves of books stood like rows of narrow buildings sheltering whispers and the flutter of pages. Jones strolled down the aisle running his fingers over the spines of books and sat down across from Amos.

"Nice move, kid."

"I feel like shit. How could I let this happen?"

"You're probably in the clear. They'll put a tail on you, maybe. Probably bug Logan's. Or, they might just let it all fly. Either way, it's probably time you find yourself a less edgy line of work."

"Yeah. Feels like I have a few too many loose ends to step out now."

"Speaking of which, that's something else I wanted to talk to you about."

"What?"

"The girl."

"And?"

"She was a teacher. Community college in Seattle. About two years ago, she dropped off the grid. Still has a Washington driver's license."

"So that's it?"

Jones rolled his fingers over his chin and tapped his cheek with his index finger. "No. When she was teaching, the subject she taught was criminal justice."

Amos couldn't hold it in. He began to laugh. Quietly, at first, and then he rolled into a full-on bellow for a moment until he could gain his composure. He pointed over the table at Jones then grabbed a pencil at the edge of the table.

"You ever..." Amos snapped the pencil in half. "You ever wonder how things might have been different if...

"Every day, kid. Every. Single. Day."

For an hour Amos moved up and down the rows of the library trying to answer his own questions. He thought about Bowdoin, and when everything had seemed to be opening up and his chances to build a life before everything else that had become his past happened—the rolls, the cops, the violence, the killing. Then, he thought about his father, his funeral, wondering why he couldn't cry. The glossy, sheltered world around him had collapsed and withered down like a slow leak in a tire. Amos thought of Ava and despite everything, he wanted her close to him.

Tommy and Caleb were whispering when Amos walked into the bar. They stopped as he made his way past the pool tables. He moved past the hicks he and Caleb had seen the night his mother told him he was pathetic. "What's up, Moss?" One of them said. Amos answered cordially. Tommy grabbed the bottle of Turkey and a glass. Caleb and Tommy looked at Amos with flat expressions.

"What's going on?"

Tommy set the bottle and the shot glass in front of him. "You want a shot, kid?"

"Why don't you tell me what the hell is going on first?"

Tommy looked down and wiped the corners of his lips. "It's bad news."

"Oh, what the fuck now?" Amos snatched the bottle of Turkey. The cork squeaked when he pulled it out.

"There was a fire last night."

Amos stopped pouring his shot. His mother was always gone. Seneca was constantly at the house by herself.

"Down at the boatyard."

A brief sense of relief. A new panic.

"Three boats were destroyed. Your father's was one of them."

Caleb hunched against the bar when Amos threw the bottle. It spun counterclockwise into the cement wall to his left and shattered. Even Tommy squinted. The hicks and the ten other people in the bar went silent. Justin came from the back. Amos could feel his face burning and he tried to think how he should feel. Lines of cold seeped beneath his cheeks. Caleb pulled out the stool next to him.

"Tommy, can I get a beer?" Justin asked.

"Go clean that glass up first."

"Are you serious?"

Tommy slammed his fist on the bar. "What the fuck did I just say?"

Amos could see the boat in his mind—flames burning black holes through the white cover and forming wrinkled faces in the bubbling paint. He could see his father holding Seneca as a baby while he held the helm and bent over to kiss her forehead, an image of him Amos always held, which had never happened.

Justin walked by Amos mumbling.

Amos didn't see Tommy move from behind the bar and he surprised him as he passed. When Amos turned to see where he was going, he had Justin by the back of his neck. He said nothing as Justin yelled and reached for Tommy's wrists. Tommy walked him to the front doors, motioned one of the hicks to open it for him and pushed Justin into the pavement. He walked back to the bar.

"You all right?" Tommy asked.

"Did they find who did it?"

"I don't think this was random."

Amos shook his head, ignoring what Tommy was hinting at.

"Moss, this is a message. Moss. Moss."

Amos looked up at him.

"I'll get what I can off the street," Tommy said.

"Do you mind giving me a bottle?"

"Kid, I really don't think you should."

"I'm going to drink this one."

It didn't seem right that something burned so close to the water. If ships could die, would they prefer to sink, to drown in what they were made to conquer? What had all that he had done brought him, he wondered. The boat forced him to ignore what he wanted to know about Caleb. He walked home, found a bottle of Turkey, and tried to drown himself while darkness slipped over his windows.

SIXTY
Amos

Amos couldn't sleep. Closing his eyes only made him more awake. Each creak and pipe rattle sent him through the apartment with his gun looking for an intruder he was sure was inevitably coming for him. A box of strike-anywhere matches had been dumped on the counter when his apartment was raided. Amos spent the night lighting them off the side of the box and drinking. When morning finally came, he slept. There was something about the daylight that made him feel safe. The hangover crept in and he lost the destructive ambition he'd had for himself. He needed to be around something pleasant, to forget, if only for a while, what was coming for him, so he went to see Seneca.

She was in the backyard, bundled in her down winter coat standing over the puppy, scolding it. She chopped her mitten through the air a few times then leaned over to push on Ariel's hind quarter forcing her to sit.

"Good puppy." She pushed a small treat into its mouth. She waved at Amos then jerked the puppy from the ground and draped it over her shoulder. The treat fell from its mouth and the puppy perked its ears and stared at it.

"Hey, kiddo. How's Ariel?"

"She won't sit."

"Maybe she's retarded."

"Nuh-unh." She tilted her head.

She switched the puppy to her other shoulder. "I saw a show on TV about a gangster named *Al Pacone*. They said he hurt nice people. Are you going to Hell because you're a gangster 'cause Sister Margaret says that gangsters are murderers and thieves and I said you were not a murderer or a thief you were just tough and she said that I was too young to know anything about that—and I said she was too old and she had crinkly skin and everyone to her is young and she said I need to be quiet and I did, but I wanted to call her an old crap bag 'cause she's old and she smells like shit."

Amos laughed and lifted her off the ground to hold her close to him. She pressed her nose into his cheek and kissed him. Her wool mittens tickled his ears.

"Don't squish the puppy." She giggled.

"Seneca, come in and get ready for dinner," Ruth called from the door.

Amos carried Seneca into the house where she loosed the puppy and stripped her jacket and mittens. She ran to the bathroom and washed her hands. Ruth set the table and sighed at the sight of Seneca's jacket on the floor.

"Seneca, come pick up your jacket. I've told you not to leave it lying on the floor."

"I know, Ma. I'm washing my filthy fingers."

Ruth moved by Amos and put the plates on the table.

"Are you staying for dinner?"

Amos hadn't eaten dinner with his mother since before his father died. His absence at the table reminded Amos of when they were still poor and the only things his mother could cook were hot dogs and macaroni and cheese. That was a life all of them had tried to forget—a life Ruth had said she would never go back to.

"Yeah. Sure."

"Get yourself a plate."

Seneca scrambled from the bathroom and rushed her clothes

up to her room. Ruth brought a platter of pork tenderloin to the table. Amos made himself a setting and waited for Seneca to come down and Ruth to bring the fiddleheads and carrots. Seneca immediately cut a piece of pork for the puppy but waited for Ruth to look down at her plate to give it to Ariel.

"Seneca," Ruth said, "don't feed the dog at the table."

"Can I go in the living room?"

"Don't be a smart mouth."

Seneca looked at Amos and rolled her eyes.

"And don't roll your eyes. Did you get your homework done?"

"Yep." She stuffed a carrot into her mouth with her fingers.

"Use your fork."

She picked up the fork, stabbed a carrot hard, and lifted it to her face. She pointed at the carrot and crossed her eyes.

Ruth dropped her fork. "Seneca."

Amos laughed.

"It's not funny, Amos. I wonder where she gets it from. Seneca, you're at the table. Act like a young lady and eat properly."

"Mommy, can Amos read me a bedtime story?"

"If you behave, maybe."

She straightened up in her chair, pulled the napkin over her lap, and rested her left hand on it.

"Amos has a pretty girlfriend."

"I know." Ruth looked at Amos. "I see you've rekindled an old flame."

Ruth had always loved Ava. Amos didn't understand why she had been such a bitch to her. He couldn't expect any normalcy from his mother. Those days had faded out long before. He thought of what she was like when he was in high school, when his father sat where he was sitting. His mother was happy then. She always smiled, always winked at him and made jokes about girls at school—how he'd be drowning in them when he got to college. She used to kiss him good night, even through high school. His mother, at one time, could look him in the eyes without the look of shame abruptly dropping across her face.

"It's nothing serious."

"Really? I couldn't imagine why. Does she know you're a—" She glanced at Seneca, cleared her throat, and plucked a cube of tenderloin from her plate. "Does she know what you do?"

"Yes."

"He's a gangster." Seneca kicked her feet under the table.

"Your brother's not a gangster. He just pretends to be." She cut a piece of pork. "I never thought that girl was very bright." She bit the meat off her fork.

"She has big boobs, Mommy."

"I'm sure."

"Am I going to have boobs like that when I get older?"

"Let's not talk about boobs at the table."

"Can me and Amos talk about boobs?"

"Do you want him to read you a bedtime story?"

Ruth took small, elegant bites cutting each piece of her food into the same nickel-size piece. Seneca pushed her fiddleheads to the side of her plate.

"Do I have to eat the fiddleheads? Blah. They taste like crap."

"Eat all of your carrots."

"Noooooooo problem."

Seneca held her fork like a dagger again and went after her carrots. Ruth labored through her dinner. He could feel her eyes on him as he ate, but she looked away when he tried to make eye contact. The one time he did she gave him a smile that more resembled a toe-stubbing wince.

The rest of dinner was quiet. Ruth asked him to lock up when he left and went to her bedroom. Amos hoped that hadn't been the routine every night and she didn't leave Seneca to be lonely around the house. Seneca tossed the puppy a few more chunks of tenderloin and began clearing the table. She pushed herself up on her toes at the sink and dropped the plates in.

"So what story am I reading you tonight?"

"*The Poky Little Puppy*," she said, snatching Ariel from the floor. "Come on, Amos."

Seneca led the way up the stairs holding the railing. Everything in her room was soft except the sharp corners of the picture frame beside her bed displaying a picture of Amos holding her right after she was born. She tossed the puppy onto the down comforter and climbed into bed. He broke his concentration from the picture and sat down beside her.

"Here you go," she said, handing him the book. She pulled Ariel onto her lap.

Amos read. Seneca pointed to pictures and explained them to the puppy. When he finished, Seneca pressed her cheek into the sleeve of his sweatshirt.

"That was a good story," she said. "Amos, why does your sweatshirt smell like matches?"

"Is it smelly?"

"No. I like it."

She closed her eyes and took a deep breath.

"Amos?"

"Yeah."

"Why does Mommy cry?"

"What do you mean?"

"Sometimes she looks at pictures and cries."

"What kind of pictures?"

"Pictures of you and Dad. She doesn't let me look but I sneaked once and found them. She keeps them in a book in her nightstand. There's even one of you and Mommy and Dad and your pretty girlfriend. I took it though. It's right here."

She pulled the picture from under her pillow. It was wrinkled and the corner was chewed off.

"Ariel tried to eat it. Sorry."

Amos thought about the absurdity of his mother crying over pictures. She hadn't spoken his father's name since he died. Amos couldn't understand it. If she had cared so much about him, why didn't she let him know? What right did she have to cry over pictures when there was plenty of crying she could have done before?

The picture returned Amos to what he'd missed. It reminded him of how much his life had changed—how everyone in the picture was gone from his life one way or another. Even his own image was detached in his memory. It was a group of people who he had only a vague familiarity of their connection in the past. He wished he'd never seen it. Amos handed the picture back to Seneca.

"No. You can keep it."

He took it only to please her, because he didn't have the heart to refuse.

"Amos, can I have your sweatshirt?"

"Why?"

"Because it smells like Fourth of July."

He stripped the hoodie and handed it to her. She balled it up, stuffed it beneath her head, and took a deep whiff of sulfur.

"Get some sleep, little angel."

Amos kissed her cheek and moved to the door. He stopped to listen at his mother's room. He wanted to hear if she was crying. Nothing. For a moment he thought about talking to her—hammering her with all of the *why* questions he had. Handing her the business card he found at Vassar's just to see her expression, to see if she knew what he had tried to keep her from. He didn't, and it didn't matter. All they would ever feed him would be more lies. Amos left the house and sat in his apartment with a bottle of Turkey instead.

After that night his life became a schedule of sleeping until two or three in the afternoon and waking up to drink whatever Turkey he'd left in the glass from the night before. Amos didn't own anything that he cared about enough to clean up, so he left the mess and kicked his way through it when he passed. He felt like the quivering glow of a dying light bulb. He spent hours in the dark releasing the clip from the forty-five. It was simple, click—slam—squeeze. He dry-fired it over and over warming to the music it made like the cranks that hoisted the sails of his father's boat.

SIXTY-ONE
Amos

Amos dreamed that he was drunk on the roof of his building. He was out of Turkey, leaning on the edge and tapping the bottom of the bottle against the brick. He stood on the edge of the building, let the bottle go and counted to four before it smashed against the pavement, shattering with a few shards strung together by the label. He closed his eyes and leaned forward—a rush of air against him and the inability to catch his breath. He woke, but not before the windows of the car he landed on exploded and the alarm went off. He jerked from sleep to his phone ringing. The empty bottle of Turkey spun against the floor.

"This Amos Swain?"

His palms were clammy from holding the gun all night—like he'd slept with a handful of pennies.

"Who is this?" Amos wiped crust from the corners of his eyes with his middle finger.

"I'm the motherfucker on Ezekiel Avenue waiting for you to bring me my money."

The handle of the dresser broke off when he yanked it open. He thrashed a pair of jeans over his legs and stomped his bare feet into his boots. The hook of a white plastic coat hanger snapped when he ripped a shirt from the closet.

Amos grabbed the burner from the cushions and rushed through the open door. His laces tripped him at the second step. The side of his left foot rolled under his ankle—the sound of dogs chewing bones. His unbuttoned shirt flapped as he flailed down the last six steps. His right boot fell off and he didn't stop to pick it up. He gimped out of the building.

Amos squealed the truck to a stop behind the Caprice in his mother's driveway. Two men climbed from the vehicle. The man from the passenger seat was short and small, possibly still in high school, if he'd even gone, and wearing a jacket several sizes too large. He had a tattoo on his neck, an illegible word in cursive, and he held the handle of a small frame pistol tucked into his belt behind an oval, gold belt buckle. Amos held the door of the truck for support.

"Snicker said I gotta pat you down."

Amos handed him his gun. He patted Amos down anyway while he shivered.

"Man, where's your fucking boot?"

"Hiding your welfare check."

"Funny guy, hunh. Now go inside and deal with this shit."

His teeth ached he clenched his jaw so tight. Amos went into the house. The floor brought a tingling warmth back into his bare foot and his knee tried to give out on him from the pain in his ankle.

Seneca and Ruth sat at the kitchen table across from Snicker who was shrouded in more baggy clothing. The man was enormous, hovering over the table like something daunting that wanted to fall and crush it. Seneca stared at him with a curious anger, her nose scrunching. Ruth quickly adopted the same look toward Amos. Ariel sat on the floor beside Seneca staring up at her and pawing the leg of her chair. Seneca squirmed from the chair to Amos. Snicker's eyes followed her like a current. Amos squatted to hug her, and her tiny fingers dug into the back of his neck and pulled on his hair.

"I'm scared," she whispered.

"I'm here now." Amos moved his eyes from Snicker's to hers. "I want you to go to your room and watch TV. Take Ariel. I'll come get you in a minute."

"Nah, man," Snicker said. He flashed a piece near the edge of his chair then tucked it into his pants at the small of his back. "Living room TV."

"Okay, Sen. Hop up on the couch. I'll be right in."

"I don't like him," she whimpered over a puckered lower lip.

"Me neither. I'll be right in."

The dog groaned when she scooped it up and ran out of the room. Amos stood, his eyes fixing back on Snicker. Ruth said nothing, just glared at Amos as she passed and followed Seneca.

"Cute kid," Snicker said when Amos sat down.

"Fuck you."

"That's not the kind of language I'd expect from a church-going man." He pulled a razor blade from his mouth and flipped it back and forth over his fingers. "Maybe you haven't been to church in a few weeks."

"Yeah, I don't go to church anymore."

"I bet you don't. Not the church I go to anyway. It's up on 202, toward Waterboro. Nice little church, actually. But then someone came along and took something out of that church that didn't belong to them. And now I have to get it back."

"Was this a Catholic church? If it was, I don't think you're going to get back what they took from you. You seem like you might have been an altar boy."

"You got jokes. They might seem funny now, but that won't be the case for long."

He was putting the razor blade back into his mouth when Amos hit him. A back hand to his chin left his fingers and knuckles coated in blood. Amos grabbed the back of his head and slammed his face into the table. Grapefruit jumped from the wooden bowl and he grabbed that. He two-handed the bowl and brought it down on the bridge of Snicker's nose, and again against the side of his face. The razor blade was lodged between his front teeth and had split his upper lip all the way to his nostrils. Citrus thumped as they dropped to the floor. Snicker reached for the pistol tucked into the back of his pants, but Amos grabbed his wrist and pushed his knuckles up his spine toward his shoulder blades. He moved behind him, grabbed his collar, and pushed Snicker to the floor. Blood spread over the linoleum. Ruth jumped past the doorway toward Seneca. Amos slipped the gun from Snicker's waistband. Ruth's footsteps pounded up the stairs.

"*Uggin gill ooh.*" Snicker sputtered globs of blood from his mouth.

Amos checked the window. Snicker's boys were still in the car. Amos passed by the door and hit the deadbolt. Snicker swung his fist back at him and connected with his ankle. Amos dropped and the pistol flew from Amos's hand. Snicker was on top of him before he could pick his head off the floor. His wide hands pushed against Amos's mouth and the other formed a fist high above his head. Blood slobbered off his chin onto Amos's face. Snicker brought his fist down and smashed Amos's nose. Sparkles surrounded his vision. He saw the blur of Snicker's fist come up and down again, but he only felt pressure. A week of whiskey hangovers. Drenched with wet tissue weakness. The back of his hands flat against the floor. Amos was going out. Snicker pulled his palm away from Amos's mouth and reached for the pistol. Ruth's crystal, single-rose vase rose over Snicker's shoulder. His head jerked. The vase came down again and Snicker collapsed on top of him, forcing an exhale that felt like M-80s went off in his eye sockets.

Ruth held the vase with both hands. Her neatly trimmed nails dug into the glass—fingers forming deranged claws around the end. Her stomach heaved out as she breathed. An arc of blood draped across her nose. The daze slithered away, and Amos squeezed himself from under Snicker. He rolled to his knees and grabbed the gun.

Snicker began to moan and reached for the gash on the back of his head. Ruth stepped toward him bringing the vase up again, but Amos stopped her. He turned to a sitting position and pushed himself against the wall. He pulled his phone from his pocket and held it out to his mother. "Call Caleb. Tell him to get over here."

She knelt beside Amos, placing the vase on the floor. "The cops. Why not the cops?"

"How the fuck do you think these guys probably got the address? Don't call the cops. Call Caleb and get him over here. Don't say what happened."

Amos dropped the phone into her trembling hands and waited for her to make the call. She did what he told her. Amos got up and hobbled over to check the windows for Snicker's boys who were slapping at each other in the car. He limped through the kitchen, opening the freezer and refrigerator doors into the path of entry into the house. Ruth gazed at him, curious, angry, wondering.

"Amos."

"You have to do this. You have to listen to me so I can get us out of this."

"What if—"

"There's no, *what if.*"

He'd never expected his mother to do what she did next. It startled him. She stepped toward Amos and held the base of his chin. Looking into her eyes was difficult because he realized someone he thought had hated him for so long looked back at him with worry and love. Snicker slid one hand in a circular motion in his own blood, massaging his pain into the floor as Amos pulled his boots off.

"Go stay with Seneca. Make sure she doesn't see this. When you get upstairs, open the window and toss these boots on top of the car. Got that?"

Ruth pursed her lips and moved away. An overwhelming

urge to kill tensed Amos's hands and forearms as she made her way upstairs. When he told her, she dropped the boots and the thumps were followed by their doors opening. Amos slipped behind the doorway of the kitchen bathroom behind Snicker. Snicker's boys entered the house like the proficiently dumb fucks that they were. Amos shot twice. Each bullet jerked their heads and pierced the door of the freezer. Seneca wailed upstairs and Ruth's voice tried to hush her.

Caleb's car rumbled into the yard and he came through the doorway with his gun drawn. Amos's nose fizzled like there was mouthwash burning through it.

"What the—?"

"Grab your bat."

SIXTY-TWO
Amos

The phone that Snicker had on him had three text messages. All from the same number. Ruth's, Amos's, and Logan's addresses. Ruth attempted to come into the kitchen, but Caleb stopped her. She moved around the house like it was foreign to her, and she was trying to find a way out. Caleb wrestled Snicker into the basement and propped him up against a wall on top of a blue tarp.

Amos's pain dissipated with his focus on revenge, the core of him cold enough to emerge and frost the walls of the house. Caleb cringed and turned away when Amos yanked out the razor blade lodged in Snicker's teeth with a pair of vice-grips. When he took Caleb's bat and went to work on him, Amos felt only as if he were taking deep gulping breaths too close to a bonfire. He swung until a cramp stitched itself inside his ribs. Snicker confessed to everything he knew—Kavanagh and the bar in Limerick where Kavanagh waited for a phone call. Snicker begged Amos to stop, but when Amos had the information he wanted, he took one final swing leaving only the sound in the room of the bat connecting—a bag of ice being slammed against the pavement.

* * *

Tommy arrived shortly after Caleb's call with two guys in a furniture truck who didn't say anything, and Amos didn't want them to—cleaners. They wore suits under their coveralls, and each carried a five-gallon bucket. They looked the car over and followed Tommy into the house. Caleb pulled a half gallon of ice cream from the freezer to make Seneca an ice cream sundae. There was a bullet in it. He worked around it and brought the ice cream upstairs. The cleaners backed their truck up to the back door and hauled two twin box springs into the kitchen, the insides of them lined with plastic. They unzipped the furniture and rolled the bodies inside.

One of them stopped at the counter and began cleaning the kitchen. He had perfect teeth and professionally groomed eyebrows—a man Amos knew he'd seen before but couldn't remember where.

Caleb came back downstairs and sat at the kitchen table with them.

Tommy spoke. "You two have to get Kavanagh out of that bar. It's the only way you're going to be able to take care of him. Call Lucas. See what he can do for you. I'll stay here and help take care of this mess."

SIXTY-THREE
Amos

Amos had spent years believing his mother hated him. It spun a new perspective on everything, even if it was only for her self-preservation, she still saved his life. Knowing that he was closer to death with every breath he took sat in Amos's stomach like drying cement. He tried not to breathe too much. They only had a couple hours of daylight when they arrived at Junior's, the bar in Limerick where Snicker said Kavanagh was waiting. Amos chambered a round into the barrel of the Glock and tucked it into his belt.

Caleb grabbed his arm. "We didn't come this far for you to do something stupid and end up back in a cage for life."

Amos glared at Caleb. His mouth drew open. His breaths tickled the clotting blood in the back of his throat. "Caleb, you have no idea how much I want to ice this motherfucker right now. I'm not going to do anything stupid. Call Lucas and make sure he's set."

Amos got out of the car and climbed the steps of the porch leading to the bar. He went through the side door and moved past the coat rack and old arcade games. His guts dropped and he had to shit. Dryness curled through his mouth like a dead leaf. He gimped through the bar, moving slowly, post to post over to the booth where Kavanagh sat. Kavanagh twirled a matchbox on the table. Amos's ankle was numb and the pressure there from walking felt like stepping on a water balloon. He kept one hand through his sweatshirt pocket on the handle of the gun. Kavanagh's eyes were fixed to some spot directly in front of him. He lifted his drink and took a sip without moving his eyes.

"Have a seat, Amos Swain."

Air wheezed through a crack in the green bench seat as Amos sat across from his stare.

He strummed his fingers on the table, index to pinky—L-I-V-E. "How about a shot?"

"Turkey."

His fingers stopped. His eyes dropped and fixed on his chest. Amos adjusted his grip on the pistol. Kavanagh's thin tongue came out of his mouth to lick the foam from his lips after a sip of his drink. He checked the time on his phone and looked toward the door.

"You waiting for someone? Because that candy bar motherfucker isn't calling. Neither are those other two milk duds."

Kavanagh pushed himself back and held the edge of the table with both hands. "Yeah, I'd have to say that's pretty obvious if you're here." Kavanagh snapped his fingers at the bartender. "Hey, Brenda, will you bring us a couple shots of Turkey?"

Brenda wore stonewashed jeans that snapped at her belly button. Her perm and blue eye makeup had either been bought at a thrift store or she couldn't let go of the glory of her high school days, which had obviously spanned some of the 80s. She brought the shots over. "Who's your friend, Kenny?"

"Amos Swain," he answered. "The dreamer."

"He's pretty cute." She glared over Amos's swollen nose and pushed her jaw to the side.

"He sure is." He lifted the shot glass and drank with Amos. "Keep 'em coming, babe."

"Sure thing, Kenny." She collected the glasses and brought two more.

Amos tossed the money across the table, five grand. "I have the rest of your money. I can even get you some product. All I want is for this to end."

Two more shots. A warm dull feeling coated Amos's body just under the skin.

Kenny licked his teeth and leaned closer to him. "I'm going to get my money. But you're all done."

"No, Kenny. You're all done. I'm offering you your money back as a courtesy, so you'll leave my family alone when I blow town. I already have an indictment coming down. So, you take the money. You take the product. Or I start talking about churches embezzling drug money and a sheriff's deputy getting his dick sucked in a church parking lot."

"That's kind of a bitch move, kid."

"What the fuck do you call sending men to my mother's house?"

Three shots came and another guy approached the table. He sat beside Amos. His head was shaved and he wore a leather jacket, gold bracelet, and pinky ring. A scar ran from his left eyebrow over his cheekbone to his jaw. It was red and jagged, less than a year old and stitched poorly. Amos teased the trigger. His buzz kept him from being scared.

"Now it's a party." Kenny lifted his glass and took the shot. The other guy took his. "Amos, meet Hammer."

Amos pushed his shot across the table toward Kenny.

"Fucking lightweight," Kenny said.

"I see what it's done for you."

"Oh. Easy there, killer. Running your mouth like that might get you hurt." Hammer growled. The scar on his face folded in toward his eye as he spoke.

"He's already gonna get hurt." Kenny said.

Three more shots came.

"Better drink up, kid. It'll be a lot less painful." Kenny chuckled.

Caleb came in and sat at the bar. Amos took the shot. "Party's over guys."

"No," Hammer said, grabbing the shoulder of Amos's sweatshirt and slamming him against the wall. "The party hasn't started yet. Believe me. It's gonna get fucking loud. You ever hear a sledgehammer hit someone in the knees?"

His strength was incredible. More effort and Amos was sure he could have put him through the pine boards. His knuckles pushed into Amos's neck. He almost pulled the trigger. Caleb had his burner out, tucked close to his leg. Amos turned his head to look at him. He moved the gun from beneath the table and pushed it into Hammer's ribs. His smile disappeared. Kenny's nostrils flared.

"Do something and my boy over there will put one in both of you."

They both looked at Caleb. Then back to Amos.

"Like I said, party's over." Amos twisted the gun in Hammer's ribs. "Now, back the fuck off, teapot."

He looked at Kenny, who bit his lip and closed his eyes. Then he glared at Amos. "You're fucking up big time, Swain."

Hammer let him go and stood.

"If you want the rest of your money, Kenny, come and get it. It's a thirty-minute drive to New Hampshire from here. Poor People's Pub. It's public and plenty busy. If you're not there in forty minutes, I call the DA."

Amos pushed himself from the booth, pulling the burner back under the hoodie and backed out of the bar. Caleb opened the doors for Amos and helped him into the car. Kenny came out and flicked a cigarette over the railing of the porch. Hammer followed.

Caleb studied the rearview. Amos stared at the barrel of the shotgun bouncing slightly on the back seat. Kenny stayed close behind them as Caleb picked up speed until they were going ten over. The roads wound deeper into thicker stretches of forest, and when they passed Lucas coming in the opposite direction, relief came over Amos. Not enough, however, to get his hands to stop shaking.

A mile farther and the blue lights of Lucas's cruiser crested the hill and sped toward them.

Kenny didn't slow down at first but put his bumper inches from Caleb's and pointed over the steering wheel at them. He slowed and followed Caleb onto the shoulder. Lucas pulled in behind them, and Caleb slowly crept back onto the tar and down the road. When they passed a corner and could no longer see Kenny or Lucas, Caleb dropped down a gear and spun the car around. The speed of the car turning pushed Amos toward Caleb. Smoke from the tires came into the car and Amos was reminded of Vassar's the day he took the puppy. He reached over the seat for the shotgun—a sawed-off Benelli loaded with three-and-a-half-inch shells.

"I'm going to need a drink after this," Caleb said.

"We can still make happy hour."

He laughed and let his foot off the clutch. The car sped back toward Kavanagh.

Lucas was supposed to be the distraction—making it look like a routine traffic stop for speeding. When Caleb and Amos pulled up he was going to drop out of the way and Amos was going to baste the inside of Kenny's car with triple aught. But that's not the way it happened, and their plan went to shit in the time it took Caleb to change gears.

Lucas was at the window when they rounded the corner and Kenny had just slid his pistol up and dumped one in Lucas's chest. Lucas wobbled like a coin and crawled across the tar on his hands and knees toward the dirt shoulder. Kenny stepped out of his car, and Caleb gave the GTO all the pedal he could. The speed squeezed around Amos's throat. Lucas kicked himself backwards in the dirt and Kenny moved toward him raising his arm. Hammer was already out of the car with a shotgun of his own thrown over the hood, aimed for Caleb's car. Caleb bent his elbows slightly and hugged the wheel. The barrel of Hammer's shotgun flinched. The rear passenger and back windows of Caleb's car shattered, and shards of glass trailed behind them like laughing pixies.

The front bumper took Kenny out at the knees and his body collapsed the windshield before it rolled over the roof and dropped into the street a broken heap of bones. Then Caleb clipped the front end of Lucas's cruiser. Metal gnarled against metal and a sensation of weightless spinning tightened the seatbelt around Amos's stomach. The sky, trees, dirt, tar all spun around the imploded windshield in an earth-tone kaleidoscope. The car landed hard on the passenger side. Muscles in his neck pulled and tore as Amos's forehead bashed against the door. The car rolled over onto its roof. The moaning and denting of metal shook through the car along with a metallic grind as the car slid forward. It kept rolling and lobbed upright again and the tireless rims scooped through the sand on the shoulder and stopped.

Amos hunched against the dashboard, his nose bleeding again but almost painless. The trigger guard of the shotgun had snapped his finger and his left shoulder was dislocated. The sun pierced the cracks in the windshield and sent erratic rays of light throughout the vehicle. Caleb was hunched against the wheel facing Amos. His arms were woven through it and draped over the dashboard, broken. Amos turned his wrist to free his finger from the trigger guard. Caleb opened his eyes and moaned.

"My arms." He tried push himself from the steering wheel but couldn't and whimpered. "I don't think we're going to make happy hour. How's my car, Moss? Is she still as pretty as me?"

A glint of sunlight rose into Amos's eyes and the shadow of Hammer spread across the windshield. He pushed a stainless-steel revolver against the back of Caleb's head and pulled the trigger. Pieces of the stereo splintered and littered the air and Caleb's face exploded and rocked against the wheel. Amos shook for a moment. The sudden noise against the calm locked up every fiber in his body while it waited for his heart to beat again and break him from the shock. Hammer tried to reach the pistol over Caleb's back to aim at Amos. The caved roof and Caleb's body hindered his shot.

Amos couldn't move his left arm. Hammer tried to pull Caleb from the wheel with one hand but only jerked his body slightly. Amos slipped his middle finger into the trigger guard, but he couldn't lift the end of the gun. The revolver tapped against the hood and Hammer slipped both hands in on Caleb. Amos worked the foot of his injured ankle under the shotgun so it rested on the laces of his boot. Hammer tugged on Caleb and slung him back against the seat then looked in at Amos. Amos set his good foot against the floor and flexed his leg. Hammer reached for the revolver and Amos pushed himself back on the seat and lifted the gun with his foot and set his heel against the dash. Hammer stepped back and Amos pounded a round into his solar plexus that sent Hammer streaming across the street. Amos's leg fell from the dash and bounced against the floorboard and he screamed until the pain screamed back.

SIXTY-FOUR
Amos

The state police wanted statements. Amos wanted Caleb to be alive. Maine Medical Center wanted to put him back together. The hospital went first. They set Amos's nose and finger, nursed his sprained ankle, and popped his shoulder back into place. His anger came with their efforts to put him back together. He didn't want to be fixed. He wanted to be left shattered—a victim of a failing lighthouse dashed against the rocks and sinking hopelessly. They gave him drugs to kill the pain and refused to listen to him when he told them he didn't want any. They put him in a room by himself and posted two Portland cops outside the door.

Ruth arrived. Seneca's voice furling softly behind his mother's brought Amos to a panic with the realization that he would have to explain to her that Caleb was dead. They came through the door so fast Ruth nearly fell when she got to his bed. Her hands were cold on his face. Seneca pulled on the blanket and diverted her looks when he made eye contact. Amos reached for her hand. Ruth's face lilted naturally into a crying expression, but she held back.

"When will this end, Amos?"

"It's over." He said it so plainly, like it had been something regulated by a time clock and referees.

"Caleb?"

Amos shook his head.

She let out a sob and covered her mouth. Then she quickly reached for Seneca and pulled her into her hip, stepping back.

"Mommy, don't cry. He's okay." Seneca squirmed from Ruth and pushed toward Amos.

Seeing his mother weep made her even more of a stranger to him. She had always prided herself in her ability to control her emotions. Instead, she slumped into the chair in the corner of the room and pushed her knees and toes together. The skin around her eyes wrinkled and grew red as she tried to quiet herself. Seneca searched her, confused. Her experience of sadness was limited to the whimpers she'd heard Ruth release. Seneca had none of her own, until then.

"Where's Uncle Caleb?" she asked tapping her lips with her fingers.

"Seneca, Caleb died."

Ruth heaved in the chair across the room and let out a muffled shudder. Seneca looked at Amos in an effort to understand. Death had never made a presence in her life in any way but an abstract concept. Her face wilted like cellophane in a flame and the realization came to her—dead meant gone forever. She threw her face into Amos's chest. He pulled her close to him, so her face was against his. Then he became choked to the point that the muscles in his neck cramped. Amos held her, twisting her thin blonde hair between his unbroken fingers while she soaked his neck in tears.

State police detectives were outside the door waiting for his mother to leave. They came in with clashing blazers and slacks, black and khaki, pastel-colored shirts. The drugs kicked in and Amos's vision blurred. They introduced themselves, Detective Paquette and Detective Brewer.

"Mr. Swain, we're here to ask you a few questions about the events today," Brewer said. He was the older of the two or at least looked that way, portly with a jovial look on his face. Amos guessed he'd dressed up as Santa Claus for more than one police benefit.

"I don't remember anything."

"Bullshit." Paquette flicked his pen against his notebook. Moustache, thick connected black eyebrows, and the general tenseness that he carried pissed off Amos.

Amos shrugged his uninjured shoulder.

Brewer played good cop. "Swain, we know that's not true. We really need to put some pieces together and we need you to help us."

"Why don't you start by telling me what you know, and I'll fill in the rest."

"Because that's what we do."

"Look, drop the good cop bad cop thing all right. This isn't amateur hour. I've been through this before. You want someone to blame and I'm the only one alive."

"Yeah, but you put a shotgun round in one of the guys who did." Brewer closed his notebook and put his pen back in his pocket.

"He was going to kill me."

"You're claiming self-defense?"

"Is there any other way to see it?"

"We want to know how Trooper Fraley came into the situation."

"He pulled over those other guys."

"You don't know those other guys' names?" He folded his arms over his chest. "Don't give me that shit."

"Hey," Brewer said, "go grab us a coffee. Swain you want something to drink?"

Amos shook his head. When Paquette left, Brewer pulled his chair closer to Amos's bed.

"I know there was something going on that involved Fraley."

"I don't think so."

"He didn't call into dispatch like he should have before pulling someone over. Not to mention that Limerick isn't even close to where Fraley patrols. Seems pretty suspicious to me."

"Aren't you trained to think everything is suspicious?"

"What was he doing there? Come on. You can tell me."

"Like I said. He was pulling that other guy over."

"Let's think of it this way. Let's say that you were facing a lot of jail time. Cooperating would probably reduce that a little. Hell, there might not even be any jail time for you."

"So we're speaking hypothetically? What would these hypothetical charges be for this hypothetical jail time?"

"Murder, conspiracy to commit murder, gun possession, aiding and abetting. Should I go on?"

"Conspiracy? Aiding and abetting? These are some bullshit charges."

"Oh, they'd stick."

"I guess when you have real charges and not hypothetical charges, you should come back and talk to me. Right now, you've got jack shit, Detective. We both know it, and I'm done talking to you."

Amos had learned that if he ever needed to get out of something, the worst thing he could do was talk to the cops. They don't give a shit who goes down for what as long as they get the collar and the points. If they pushed charges, get a good lawyer. Go to court. Charges always get dismissed or reduced. Juries are suckers for wayward souls who try to do well, like preventing a state trooper from being executed. Caleb was killed inches from Amos. He was sure that the jury would understand if he felt his life had been in danger. As far as what happened, he was the only one alive besides Lucas who knew the whole story. And Lucas wasn't going to say a fucking thing.

Paquette returned with the coffee and the two of them left. Amos was sure they'd have him shackled to the bed within the hour, but they never came back. They'd wait until he did something stupid.

277

SIXTY-FIVE
Amos

The townspeople ripped newspapers from the racks to read the articles that filled the papers for a week. With Amos's face on the front page every day, his celebrity grew to something obnoxious. In the small grocery store near his apartment, its name spelled phonetically in local accent, Amos stood in line for a pack of smokes, Caleb's brand. Two teenagers whispered behind him until Amos looked back at them. They threaded themselves with baggy jeans and untied boots, oversized shirts and flat-billed baseball caps tipped to the side.

"Yo." One of them threw Amos a nod. "You're that Amos Swain motha fucka, ain't ya?"

Amos reached for a piece that wasn't there, only the callous against his hip from where he'd carried one for so long. He expected them to be the typical town punks who thought they were living in a rap video and wanted some bragging rights for jumping him.

"Yeah." Amos looked away and asked the clerk for a pack of cigarettes.

"I knew it was him." The kid nudged his buddy. "Mutha-fuckin' gangsta."

Amos patted his chest with a closed fist, a polite gesture to mask his annoyance. The clerk took Amos's money and shot a quick, dismayed look toward the two young men.

"Last man standing," the other kid said.

Amos took his change, thanked the clerk, and left before anyone could see his eyes begin to water.

The bar was worse. He listened to the same types of comments from the patrons. They'd tap his shoulder or bring him a shot and offer their condolences over Caleb, and he'd either lose his shit and leave or keep taking the shots until he blacked out and would wake up in Tommy's office.

For all the wishing he did to have died, the pain still came, warped and suffocating like he'd been twisted—his throat ripped out and tied around his neck. He drank Turkey on his fire escape watching the ice slowly melt and expose the lake. He drank more to sleep, but it only kept him awake. He heard car crashes in the night to find the streets completely empty. His ears rang from imagined gunshots in absolute silence.

Tommy made the funeral arrangements for Caleb that they waited for until spring. Spring pulled green from the ground and tips of tree branches, flushing color into the gray landscape. Patches of tan and dark brown were wrestled away by photosynthesis. When Amos arrived the day of Caleb's funeral, the funeral home director offered him nothing but a handshake and the clarity of where Amos remembered him from before he'd dragged bodies out of his mother's kitchen. He was the man who'd buried his father.

Everyone wore their best suit and if they didn't have one, they bought one. With all the black suits and ties and dark colors and gray skies the thing that made most of them look the same was the puffiness sorrow pushed into their eyes. Tommy and Amos sat in the front, accepting the weak handshakes and hugs of agony. They bought Caleb a custom. It was the best suit he ever wore, only the casket was closed and none of them got to see him in it.

Friends came into the doorway and soon Amos grew annoyed with the surprises—Lucky and Levi sat next to him in the first row.

When Seneca came in with his mother, she huddled behind her, scared at the amount of people crammed into the room. Her tiny black dress showed claw marks on her legs. The black head band through her blonde hair pushed her eyes to a deeper shade of blue. They walked to Amos.

"Mommy, can I sit with Amos?"

Ruth left her with him. He lifted Seneca onto his knee. She looked at the casket and then into Amos's eyes.

"Is Uncle Caleb in there?"

"Yeah, Sen."

"But how come I can't see him?"

"Uncle Caleb got hurt really bad. We can't look at him."

She wrapped her arms around his neck. Amos envied how easily she could express her sorrow. Her wailing caused pain in his ear, but he was alive, and Caleb was dead. Her wailing was no great penalty.

Amos looked to where there should have been a picture of Caleb but wasn't. No one had one, not even him. The closest thing Amos had to pictures were the images of Caleb seared into his memory between muzzle flashes.

People stood to speak about Caleb. People who barely knew him. Those who knew Caleb, the few people who were actually close to him, said nothing.

SIXTY-SIX
Amos

The man introduced himself as Special Agent Stevens when Amos walked out of the funeral home. He was the last to leave, trailing behind his mother and Seneca. He noticed Ava moving slowly down the street to her vehicle. Amos paused for a moment with the desire to see her face, but then he realized how much rage she'd induced in him, and how much more that spiked as the fed tucked away his badge. Tommy, Lucky, and Levi, waited for Amos at the end of the walkway. The others went to their cars and waited for the procession to begin. Amos kept moving toward the fed.

"Can this wait?" Amos asked him.

"Let's take a ride."

"I'm going to my best friend's burial. If you're trying to make me miss that you're going to need a lot more than a request."

"It's not a request. I'll take you to the cemetery. Just come with me."

Tommy moved over to them. "What's going on?"

"I don't know, Tommy. I'll meet you guys there."

Tommy clicked his jaw from side to side and walked back to the group. Amos followed Stevens to his car and opened the back door.

"Get in the front," Stevens said.

Amos looked down the street again for Ava, but she was gone. The fed got into the car and hit the door locks when Amos got inside.

"You like these shoes?" Stevens asked.

Amos looked down at the polished leather.

"Yeah. Sure."

"I have expensive taste. These are good shoes."

He handed Amos a large envelope. The procession had started. In some ways it wasn't final yet—the fact that Caleb was dead had not presented itself as anything but a concept. They were going to put Caleb in the ground. They were moving closer to the finale.

"What's this?"

"Take a look."

Amos pulled dozens of snapshots from the envelope—Caleb, Caleb and Crow, Caleb and a girl, Caleb taking money from Crow. The car felt drafty all of a sudden, like it was winter again.

"I don't get it. I thought—you were on *us*?"

"Not *us*, as in you and Caleb. Not entirely anyway. But Marcus Poulin. The guy you know as Crow."

"What do you mean, not entirely?"

"Your best friend was working for me. Unofficially."

Amos could feel waves rolling around the backs of his knees, gripping the tendons and pulling his feet out from under him—water pulling on his ankles and the tide pounding into his chest and holding him just below the surface.

Stevens lit a cigarette, offered Amos one, and he took it.

Stevens took long heavy drags from his. Amos tried to get the cigarette to his mouth without dropping it. His hands felt like they would shake from his wrists.

"You giving me a heads up on everything I'm going down for?"

Stevens blew a stream of smoke into the rearview and pulled behind the line of vehicles.

"If you think I give a shit about you two robbing dealers

then you're wrong. But that's all you two were doing. I ended that construction bullshit with that Vassar fuck after Poulin gave you that Lynn job, which obviously went to shit."

There was a picture of Caleb sitting on the hood of his GTO laughing, holding a finger up to Amos, who stood by the passenger door. Sun glared off the left corner of the windshield. Amos stopped looking through them and stared at that one.

"When did you get him?"

"A little over three months ago on his way down to Mass with a truckload of stolen construction equipment."

"I'd hate to be the one to break it to you, but Caleb is dead. And so is Crow, from what I hear."

"Don't get fucking cute with me."

"What the fuck do you want?"

Stevens flicked ash from his cigarette against the top of the open window. "Caleb and I had a special arrangement."

Amos looked over Stevens's suit, his shoes, the diamond-studded Rolex Caleb had stolen, glinting in the sunlight. Clarity.

"How much?" Amos asked.

"You are a smart motherfucker. Caleb kicked up a third of what you guys took down. He didn't want you to know so he covered your end, and then some, if I felt like you guys weren't claiming enough."

"So how much?"

"Considering the fact that one of you cocksuckers popped Poulin, I'm thinking fifty. It should be more considering the mess you've made that I've had to clean up."

"When and where?"

"I wasn't done. This last bit of trouble you found got me curious, and it seems that the two of you knocked over a high-level player by the name of Kenny Kavanagh. I also learned that Kavanagh had a partner. His cousin, who works as a pastor in the church he was embezzling money through. In short, the cousin needs to go. We can't have him running around with the motivation to settle the score with you."

Amos took a hard drag from the cigarette.

"You are an impressive motherfucker, Amos Swain. I should congratulate you. Having Caleb get those tickets to Vegas forced the cops to move. That was a good play, but it was also the play that got you fucked. See, when you shook the cops, I didn't have any leverage on you like I did with Caleb, but you," Stevens pinched on his cheek, "you gave me everything I needed with that *Limerick Massacre*. Really, though, Caleb should have known better to try to fuck me out of money."

Amos could never stab, shoot, or hit Stevens enough times to ever be satisfied.

"You need help making money, go suck dicks at a truck stop. I'm out of this shit."

"No. It's you who needs help. I have enough shit on you to put you away for five lifetimes. Call my bluff, motherfucker. This shit with Vassar isn't over. Neither is this shit with Kavanagh. If you want me to keep you out of it, you'll do anything, and everything I tell you. Think about your future. Don't end up like Caleb."

Stevens changed hands on the steering wheel. Amos stared at the picture of Caleb. The coldness he felt somewhere along the way had disappeared and he felt warm, the way religious people described the way God touched them when they prayed. Stevens spit out the window as they pulled into the cemetery. Amos wanted him to keep driving and let him fall from the vehicle into the grave.

"So how does this work?"

"Like I said. It's fifty to start. Consider it a fine. Then it's thirty percent on everything you take down. That keeps me from producing everything I got from your so-called partner. You don't have any options here."

"Yeah, there's always a choice."

Stevens put the car in park and turned toward Amos. He looked around the vehicle then pulled his piece and put it to Amos's temple.

"Motherfucker, I will pop you. Whatever pipe dream you

have of living happily ever after, forget about it. Just so you understand, so you are crystal fucking clear about this. It happens tonight. If you and that money aren't ready by midnight, I'll torch something else of yours. That boat was nothing compared to what I'll do to you and the rest of your shitbag friends and family."

Amos envisioned a bullet hole between Stevens eyes.

"Where do I meet you?"

"Out of town. Sal's Diner in Hampton. You know it?"

"I'll find it."

"Be there or I swear I will bring you down so hard you'll be begging to go to prison, so help me God."

Amos got out of the car. "God's not going to help either of us."

Amos focused on the tombstones as he passed them. They were real and solid. They stood over the dead guarding their secrets the way the living had ruined and mangled themselves guarding their own. They would keep secrets because they had no choice not to. Tombstones were the only things that made sense.

Caleb? Amos couldn't begin to understand. Tommy stood a distance from the gathering and watched him approach. He didn't say anything when Amos got to him but looked over his shoulder several times. They walked toward Caleb's grave where it would all be over, and Caleb could pass his secrets on to his tombstone along with the answers to the questions Amos had.

They lowered the casket and the group of them wavered. That was the end—no denying that Caleb was gone. The tension of the straps teasing the hole with the casket seemed to be connected to Amos's back. He felt something pulling him toward the open gash they fed Caleb to. He gripped the rose like a .45 and let the thorns burrow into his hands. He looked across the group of people huddled together almost corralling the casket into the hole.

The ceremony ended, and the crowd dispersed. The people

who couldn't wait to speak about Caleb after the eulogy were the first to go and looked down at their watches as they hurried to their cars. The tombstones marched in rows standing taller as the grass flattened from the approaching rain.

SIXTY-SEVEN
Amos

Tommy took them down to Logan's where they kept the lights off and sat at the bar. The four of them—Levi, Lucky, Tommy, and Amos—poured themselves shots, lifted them, and drank. Tommy kept looking at Amos as if to say something, but Amos didn't care enough to ask what it was. He looked around the bar and saw Caleb everywhere—shooting pool, passing out on the table, tossing quarters at karaoke singers. The background became smudged and faded until Amos could no longer see him. He couldn't be there. He couldn't sit there and listen to the reminiscence.

"I'm taking off," Amos said.

"What? We just got started. Hang out," Lucky requested.

"No. I need to be alone. Tommy, I'll be back in a couple hours for a withdrawal."

"Hey, Moss. Let me talk to you a minute. Out back," Tommy said.

Amos made his way to Tommy's office.

"You two stay out here." Tommy followed Amos.

Amos entered the office and hit the light switch. Tommy's hands grasped the shoulders of his suit and Amos's feet came off the ground. Tommy spun him into the filing cabinet and it toppled over.

"What the fuck," Amos said, getting to one knee.

Tommy kicked him in the kidney, then turned and locked the door. Amos rolled around on the floor for a minute, begging the pain in his back and nuts to go away.

"You piece of shit." He lifted Amos by his throat. The nub of his severed finger dug into Amos's neck. "Is that why there are no indictments?" Tommy got Amos to his knees and slammed an elbow into his forehead.

"You fucking rat piece of shit."

A kick to Amos's stomach sent him into the corner. Tommy's hair was pulled from the ponytail holder and disheveled over his face. Amos spoke when he caught his breath.

"You fucking idiot—"

Tommy kicked again and Amos's head dented the filing cabinet. Tommy took a step toward Amos and lifted his leg to kick again. Amos heel-kicked him in the balls from where he sat. Levi and Lucky pushed on the door. They yelled and pounded against it. Amos got to his feet. Tommy reached for him. He twisted Tommy's wrist and thought about breaking his arm at the elbow. Instead, Amos shoved it away, cupped his hands behind Tommy's head, and broke his nose with his knee. Tommy fell backwards to the floor between a chair and the other filing cabinet. Amos pulled the pictures from beneath his shirt, took them from the envelope, and scattered them over Tommy's stomach and legs. Levi and Lucky kept pounding.

Tommy kept a .44 special in his desk drawer. Amos pulled it out and cocked the hammer. He grabbed a couple of the pictures and pushed them into Tommy's face. Everyone told Amos how sorry they were about Caleb but none of them had to see him die.

"Look, motherfucker."

Amos put the gun to Tommy's head. The door flew open and the handle lodged in the sheetrock.

"Jesus Christ. Moss, put it down," Lucky said.

"Fuck you." Amos turned back toward Tommy.

"Moss, seriously, don't."

"Fuck you. I was there. I saw it. I fucking saw it."

"Moss, we know, man. Just put the gun away. Let's just go do another shot. Everything will be cool. Let's just calm down."

Tommy held the pictures in his palms. Levi pulled the gun from Amos's hand. Moments later they sat with a bottle between them in the aftermath destruction of Tommy's office, but none of them drank while Amos explained what Stevens had told him.

"What are you going to do?" Lucky asked.

"All that's left to do."

Lucky took a pull from the bottle. "We're here, man. We roll with you."

"I appreciate that guys, but I'm doing this one solo."

Tommy reached for the bottle.

SIXTY-EIGHT
Amos

The rain fell like a sleeping breath, slow and almost silent. It rolled down the sleeves of Amos's suit, over the cuffs, and his knuckles. Outside his apartment building, Amos held his hands out and let water pool inside his palms.

He found Ava's letter taped to his door. He thought about a drink but talked himself out of it. His jaw cramped from where Tommy had kicked him. He pulled the letter out, handwritten—her swooping large letters over the page.

Sorry.

Amos dropped the letter and let it drift to the floor with the scattered mess in his apartment. He'd spent so long reaching for the past, and all he had in his life was even less than he had before. Momentarily, he entertained the possible outcomes of different decisions, but that only led to regret. There's no stronger thread to the past than regret.

Ariel stood when he entered Seneca's room. The puppy crawled over her legs to the foot of the bed, and she lapped at Amos's wrist as he rubbed her skull. Seneca opened her eyes and slid a hand beneath her pillow. The window showed the sky's darkness curling behind the clouds.

"You awake, Sen?"

She pulled her hand from beneath the pillow and sat up. "I didn't know it was you."

"Who did you think it was?"

"I don't know."

Amos walked to the side of her bed and lifted the pillow.

"Seneca, what is this for?" he asked, lifting a steak knife from her bed. "Do you know how dangerous it is to sleep like that?"

"I'm sorry. I was scared."

"There's no reason to be scared."

"But the bad men came and they hurt you."

Amos placed the knife in front of her picture and sat next to her. "Seneca, I'm sorry those things happened. I really am. But those men were mad at me, not you. You never have to worry about them ever again, okay?"

Her eyes were wide and unblinking. She pinched at the ankle of her pajamas and kept her focus on Amos's shoulder.

"What did you and Uncle Caleb do to make those people mad?"

"We stole their money."

"So you did a bad thing."

"Yeah. It was a bad thing."

"I have money in my piggy bank. You can have it."

Smiling felt like he'd spent too much time in a dark room and the lights suddenly came on.

"Mommy says we have to move."

"Yeah. I know."

"She said I can't tell people about the bad men because you will get in trouble."

"Mom's right. You need to listen to her, okay?"

"Is Uncle Caleb in Heaven even though he did a bad thing?"

"Yes. Uncle Caleb is in Heaven."

"Are you going to go to Heaven?"

"I hope so. But not for a long time."

"I'm still scared. Will you stay with me tonight?"

"For a while. I have to go in a bit."

Amos dropped his hoodie to the floor and lay on the bed next to her. Seneca gripped the corner of her white down comforter. She arced it up and wrapped it over his shoulders then tapped it around his neck. It was tight. The puppy curled into a ball on the pillow, and Seneca draped her tiny arm over his shoulder. She kissed the back of his head and squirmed closer to him. Her eyelashes tickled the back of his neck.

"Amos?"

"Yes?"

"Are we still going to look for mermaids?"

Amos's ribs tightened and he waited for them to snap like an old, brittle fishing line.

SIXTY-NINE
Amos

Roberts slept on the couch in his pants and a T-shirt. He had one sock on. The television purged pulsing light into the room. Amos could feel the texture on the pistol grip through the glove. Roberts whimpered in his sleep. Amos touched the top of Roberts's ear gently with the barrel, and he swatted at it. He brushed it against Roberts's cheek, and he scratched his face. Amos pulled his lower lip down. Roberts rubbed his mouth. Amos grazed his eyelashes. Roberts squinted. He gave Roberts a stiff tap on the bridge of his nose. His face twitched and Roberts opened his eyes. He shot up on the couch. Amos stomped him in the gut and backhanded him with the pistol. He grasped the hair on the back of Roberts's head, jerked his head back, and smashed the butt into his forehead. Roberts went cross-eyed and slumped forward, unconscious. Amos scooped under his arms and tossed him in the recliner.

In the kitchen, Amos filled a stew pot with ice and water and waited for the ice to stop cracking. He went back into the living room and dumped it on Roberts, who nearly shook himself off the chair.

"Please don't hurt me. I'm a minister."

There was a small lamp on the end table. Amos turned it on and took a seat on the arm of the couch and pulled a Bible from

293

the coffee table.

"You been sleeping alright?" Amos asked.

"Oh, my head. What do you want? I'll give you all the money I have. It's in the safe in my bedroom."

Amos smashed his nose with the trigger guard. Roberts cupped his face and bent forward.

"I already took all the money I want from you."

He pulled his hands away from his broken nose. He sat there with his mouth open turning his head slightly.

"What do you want?"

"A couple things."

"What? I'll give you anything."

"Anything is not what I want."

"Then what?"

"Caleb. I want him back. I want my friend back."

"I don't know where, who?"

"Caleb. My partner. Your boy Hammer killed him."

Roberts shook his head and moaned.

"What are you, fucking retarded? Go get him."

"I-I can't."

"Why not?"

"He's...He's dead."

The light went blurry around Amos as his eyes filled with tears. He slammed the pistol against Roberts's nose again, withdrew and hit him again. Amos's hand cramped with tension. The gum he chewed began to feel like a spitball. Roberts lifted his quivering hands to his face and brushed his fingertips against the mangled cartilage.

"You're a man of God aren't you?"

"Y-yeah."

That time Amos hit him in the teeth.

"Stop fucking stuttering asshole."

Blood dripped off his chin and fell onto his wet shirt. The drops made small orange dots.

"Tell me what happened. How did you find out it was me

and what did you do?"

He stared. Amos raised the gun again and Roberts covered his face with his arms. He peered over his elbow. Amos shrugged. When Roberts lowered his arms Amos rapped his cheekbone. Roberts's face shook and his arms flew out.

"Start fucking talking."

"Okay. I put it together after Bobby Sisk shot up the parking lot at Logan's. I found out you worked there. Then I found out about Bowdoin, and me and Kenny put it together. Then, after we were in your apartment, we—"

"You were in my fucking apartment?"

"That's when Kenny knew for sure that it was you."

"Your people went to my mother's house. My little sister was there."

"I had nothing to do with that. That was all Kenny and Hammer. I-I'll do anything just tell me. What do you want me to do?"

Amos looked down at the Bible in his hand.

"Pray," he said.

"Oh, God. Oh, God."

Amos nodded. "Oh, God. Oh, God. That's a good start. If I didn't know any better I'd think you were a fucking preacher." Amos jabbed Roberts on the end of his chin with the barrel. "Pray, motherfucker."

"Dear God—"

"Oh, it's *Dear God*, now."

"Dear God, please forgive me—"

Amos smashed him hard that time. Roberts drooled blood into his palms.

"Not for you. For Caleb."

Roberts dipped his eyes toward the floor. "God, I wish you to accept the soul of dear Caleb. Take him into your heart and into your kingdom. Bless him Lord with your grace. Please Lord, comfort his pain with your compassion and cradle him in Heaven. In Jesus's name we pray. Amen"

Roberts looked up.

"W-was that okay."

"That was excellent."

"I'm sorry. Really, you have to believe me. I didn't want anyone to get hurt."

"People are definitely going to get hurt." Amos pulled the thin carton of saran wrap from his jacket pocket. "Let's go get that money."

Roberts cowered in front of him as he led the way to his bedroom. The windows of his bedroom faced the side of the church. Amos thought of the deputy who'd found him and squeezed his fingers into the spine of the Bible. Roberts pulled money from a small safe beside the nightstand—cheap particle board material that matched the dresser on the other side of the bed. He made a two-inch stack of money and wrapped it in the saran wrap. He looked at Amos when he finished.

"Get in the tub."

"Please don't do this. I'm begging you, please don't."

"I'm not going to kill you. Just get in the tub so I have enough time to get out of here."

Roberts walked slowly to the bathroom holding his face. He flicked the switch and the lights above the mirror came on.

"Hold that." Amos handed him the Bible and put his hand in his pocket. Roberts white-knuckled the Bible. Through the bathroom door Amos could see the windows in Roberts's bedroom where the lights had come on the night he went into the church. Roberts's chest swelled as he sucked in a breath. He pulled the book to his chest. Amos's hands shook, trembled until he almost dropped the pistol.

"Get on your knees."

Roberts held the side of the tub as he lowered himself. Amos stepped to the side closer to Roberts and beneath the light. A shadow fell around Roberts. Amos thought of all that he had ever wanted to be and pressed the barrel into the bridge of Roberts's nose.

"Don't do this. Please don't do this. This is murder. This is evil."

"I'm sure I can find some good in it."

SEVENTY

Amos

The door of the diner was unlocked despite the closed sign on the door. The shades were drawn and only the lights over the grill were lit. When Amos entered, the cook locked the door behind him. Stevens sat at the back of the diner rotating a spoon in a cup of coffee. Every movement felt sluggish, and Amos wondered if he would feel lighter when he gave Stevens the money. Amos felt like he was tired from treading water, but he wasn't weak enough to let himself drown just yet. He waited for the cook to pat him down, but he went to his seat at the diner. Stevens's arrogance made Amos want to reach for his throat. Amos looked at the watch when he sat across from Stevens.

"Cutting it pretty close, aren't you."

Amos pulled the bundle of Roberts's cash from his sweatshirt pocket, pinching the corner of it with the sleeves of his hoodie. "With what's in that you could have a little patience."

"I'm out of patience. Hands on the table if you don't mind."

Amos pressed his wrists against the edge of the table and clasped his hands together. The cook took a seat at the counter and flipped through the pages of a magazine. His apron was brown with the splatter of grease and sweat. He was overweight and the man's pants flashed the crack of his ass. Strapped around his ankle was a .38. Stevens brought a Jennings 9mm from beneath the table and tucked it into the fold of a newspaper at the edge—a throwaway. They'd wait for Amos to get up to leave and the cook would make his move. Stevens hadn't asked him there to keep him in business. *He* was the loose end, and Stevens didn't respect him enough to think that he didn't know that as soon as he handed him that envelope with photographs of Caleb. Stevens wanted one more payout and then to finish what he wished Kavanagh had done.

"I'm taking a vacation. Don't worry, though. I'll be back in a week to touch base with you. We'll decide then how we're going to approach fixing this situation. I have a couple ideas, but they'll have to wait until I get back."

"Where you headed?"

"Mexico."

"Drink lots of water when you get there."

"You're a funny guy, Swain. I like you."

"Give it time. You're not going to like me for very long."

Death was a better option than prison. Amos felt like the last few years of his life had been a scam, like they had all been a part of a sick joke—Ava, Caleb, Jones, Stevens, all of them. They watched him stumble his way through and sat off to the side and laughed. The pain in his stomach then was worse than anything his prison sentence ever caused.

"You know it could be worse," Stevens said. "Jones could have gotten you on something before all of this and you would be rotting in prison instead of sitting here with me. I'm better company, I'm sure, than whoever would have been your cellmate. Lots of drug dealers in prison. Probably a few who wouldn't like you very much if they found out how you got there."

"I was never worried about Jones. Are you fucking joking? Jones never came close to me. All he ever had was boredom and nothing else to fulfill his title as detective except tracking down stolen bicycles."

"Now, now, now. All this anger. This is not the way to start off our arrangement. You keep making moves, pay some operational fees, and we both make out good. Now, I know you're mad about Caleb, but he did this to himself and you."

"We're not going to talk about Caleb."

The cook flicked his lighter. Stevens took a sip of coffee.

"You're right. We have the future to think about. Let's not tarnish that with thoughts of the past."

Amos pointed down at his sweatshirt. "You mind if I get a smoke?"

"Slow movements Swain."

Amos reached into his hoodie pocket and pinched the pack of cigarettes. His thumb brushed over the hammer of his pistol tucked behind the hole in his sweatshirt pocket. He put the pack on the table and pulled a smoke from it.

"Can I use your lighter?"

Stevens pushed his lighter across the table. Amos looked at the stack of Roberts's money, the saran wrap around it smeared with Roberts's fingerprints. He thought about Tommy's cleaners moving Roberts's body from his house and he picked up the lighter. He made his hands shake as he lifted it and spread his fingers. The lighter dropped in Stevens's coffee.

"What the fuck, Swain?" He pulled the lighter from his cup. "I thought your hands were a little more deft than that."

"I'm sorry." Amos turned in the seat to the cook. "Hey, man. Can you give me a light?"

The cook grabbed his lighter and Amos scooted from the seat and stood. He put the cigarette to his lips and gripped the bottom of his sweatshirt. The cherry lit up and Amos took in a short drag and turned, slipping his right hand to the handle of his pistol. Stevens reached for his coffee and Amos jerked the bottom of his sweatshirt up.

The slide cut into his stomach on the first shot through Stevens's cup and into his stomach—a burst of ceramic and coffee. The second shot went through Stevens's neck and blood whipped against the shades behind him. Stevens slumped in the seat, reaching for the pistol he'd knocked to the floor, squeezing only the edges of the newspaper in his fingers. The cook dropped from the stool to his knees and fumbled for the pistol around his ankle. Amos switched the gun to his left hand and put the barrel against the cook's red earlobe. A white oval formed around the barrel like a ghost.

SEVENTY-ONE
Amos

Now

Amos leaves through the back of the diner. The light from the street in front crawls across the roof and looms against the far wall of the alley. He stays in the dark, stepping through the sludge back to his truck and drives into the night. He lights a cigarette. His past, the images and feelings he'd held, the nostalgia, he blows through the crack of his window with smoke and lets them tumble along the road in the night behind him.

Amos passes few cars on his way back home, back up 109 to the place he'd grown up, the place he'd tangled himself in trying to find a way out. The place he'll never leave. He's happy to be driving at night, so close to midnight, the separating line of past and present, the shift between then and now.

He hovers on that line, like the slow drift of a sheet of paper. His eyes carry the tired weight of his body. Tommy is back behind the bar and he walks straight toward him through the crowd and sits down. Tommy smiles more than Amos has ever seen him do when he steps to the bar. Amos sits and feels the last slip of air entering from the doors directly behind him. Tommy puts a bottle in front of him, holds it with one hand. He reaches over the bar and grips Amos's shoulder and lets the bottle go. Tears strike his eyes, and Amos feels the world behind him shatter, finally.

"I'm not the only one who's been waiting for you." Tommy moves his head to the dark corner of the bar. Ava sits there, swirling a straw around the melting ice in her drink. "She asked about you when I came in. I didn't know what to tell her. She's been here all fucking night."

Amos looks at her place in the dark, and thinks back to the night she walked in. He missed the look of fear in her eyes then. He should have known. He should have been smarter. Because he wasn't, he'd put everyone in danger, even her. He pulls the pourer from the bottle and takes a pull as she makes her way toward him.

"Come here often?" she asks.

"That's quite a line, stranger."

"I save the best for all the good-looking guys."

She pushes her empty glass to the edge of the bar. Tommy moves toward them and extends his fingers toward the glass. "Another drink, miss?"

"Please. And you should tell your bouncer there's someone harassing me."

Tommy frowns and he looks at Amos. He knows they're both thinking about Caleb in that moment. Tommy gets her drink and goes to the far end of the bar to bullshit with one of the regulars.

"I'm sorry about Caleb, Moss. I really am. I know how much you loved him."

They sit in silence for a while and Ava works her thumb over the lip of the glass. The crowd thins and in the small portion of mirror where Tommy took the bottle of Turkey from, Amos spots him when he comes through the door. He pulls the Ford cap low. It's easy for Amos to see him fix his eyes on him, Ava, then back to him. It's easy to know why he's there. Amos pulls out a pack of cigarettes and bites one from the pack. The match snaps and the crisp smell of sulfur is in his nose. Tommy runs tabs at the other end of the bar. Amos is alone, except for Ava. The dimness of the bar makes him want to sleep. Right there, just shut his eyes and wait for dreams or nothing. He moves his hand to his hoody pocket. The drag of the cigarette fills his lungs. Ava's body moves closer to him and she rests her head on Amos's shoulder, like a cold, dying breath. Amos slams back the shot of Turkey and reaches for the bottle with his left hand. Ford hat's focus is on the bottle of Turkey. Amos can call out to Tommy, and he'd have the gauge out and a round of buckshot would sprawl Ford-hat onto the floor. But Amos locks into his own silence. He's tired of pacing in the dark. Ford-hat sheds the gun from his waistband, pulls the brim of his baseball cap lower, looks for anyone noticing then focuses back on Amos. Ava's hand is on his neck. He's tired, so tired. He doesn't understand why people fight so hard to live in this world.

Ava turns her head, puts her lips to his ear. "I'm in love with you, Amos Swain."

Amos draws the pistol from his hoody pocket and holds it as still as he's ever held one.

JOE RICKER is a former bartender for Southern literary legends Barry Hannah and Larry Brown. He has also worked as a cab driver, innkeeper, acquisitions specialist, professor, and in the Maine timber industry. He currently lives in Reno, Nevada, and spends much of his free time walking uphill.

JoeRicker.com

On the following pages are a few
more great titles from the
Down & Out Books publishing family.

For a complete list of books and to
sign up for our newsletter,
go to DownAndOutBooks.com.

Trouble No More
Crime Fiction Inspired by Southern Rock and the Blues
Mark Westmoreland, editor

Down & Out Books
October 2021
978-1-64396-230-6

The authors bring the rough living of the Southern Rock genre to the page, and communicate the ache of the blues.

Edited by Mark Westmoreland with stories by Bill Baber, C.W. Blackwell, Jerry Bloomfield, S.A. Cosby, Nikki Dolson, Michel Lee Garrett, James D.F. Hannah, Curtis Ippolito, Jessica Laine, Brodie Lowe, Bobby Mathews, Brian Panowich, Rob Pierce, Joey R. Poole, Raquel V. Reyes, Michael Farris Smith, J.B. Stevens, Chris Swann, Art Taylor, N.B. Turner and Joseph S. Walker.

Velvet Elvis
Greg F. Gifune

Down & Out Books
October 2021
978-1-64396-231-3

Sonny Cantone is having a really bad day. He's broke. His girl-friend left him. He drinks more than he should and smokes a lot of pot. And now some lunatic stole his car.

So when Sonny's partner in crime and stoner buddy Crash of-fers to bring him in on a caper that promises to yield some quick money, he has to listen. But nothing has prepared Sonny for the vortex of mayhem and madness he's about to fall into.

Sonny Cantone is having a really bad day. Wait until he sees the next twenty-four hours.

Stalker Stalked
Lee Matthew Goldberg

All Due Respect, an imprint of
Down & Out Books
September 2021
978-1-64396-229-0

What happens when the stalker gets stalked?

A fan stalks a reality show personality only to discover that she's being stalked as well, and learns the only way to beat her stalker is to use her own prowess to outsmart them at their own game.

Blood Like Rain
A Big Island Mystery
Albert Tucher

Shotgun Honey, an imprint of
Down & Out Books
August 2021
978-1-64396-192-7

Detective Errol Coutinho of the Hawaii County Police faces the most difficult case of his career, when his wife's best friend is murdered.

Eleanor Swieczak's current boyfriend is a man without a past, but Eleanor's own history turns up other suspects, and someone is trying to put Coutinho among them. And what do a legendary marijuana dealer, a rightwing militia, and the coldest murder case in Hawaii history have to do with the case?

Must blood fall like rain before Coutinho finds out?